THE
SERPENT'S DAUGHTER

CELINA MARQUEZ

This is a work of fiction. Names, characters, places, and incidents either are the product of the author's imagination or are used fictitiously. Any resemblance to actual persons, living or dead, events, or locales is entirely coincidental.

ISBN 979-8-9853641-0-1 (paperback)

ISBN 979-8-9853641-1-8 (hardcover)

ISBN 979-8-9853641-3-2 (ebook)

ISBN 979-8-9853641-2-5 (audiobook)

www.celinamarquez.com

To my mom, who always believed in me.

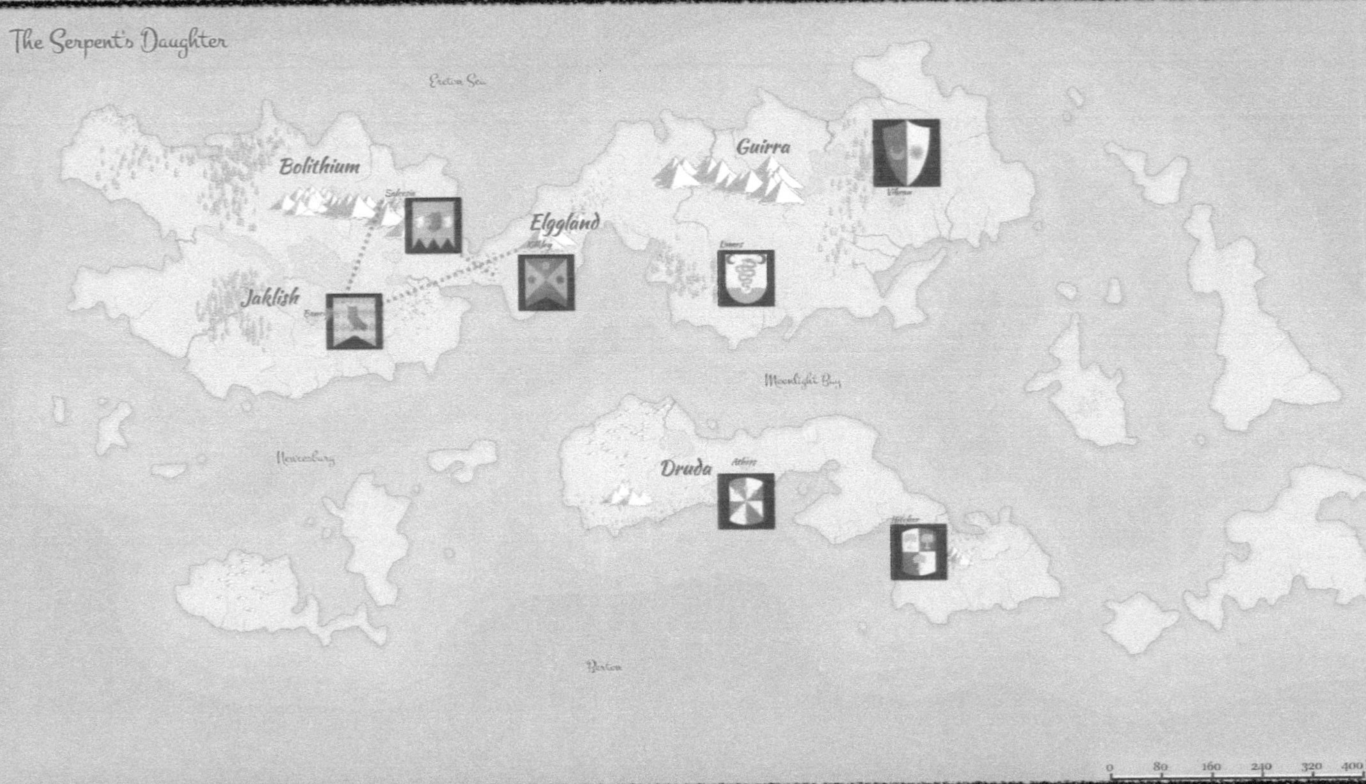

The Serpent's Daughter
Eretix Sea
Bolithium
Jaklish
Elggland
Guirra
Moonlight Bay
Druda
Henixburg
Herton
0   80   160   240   320   400 km

CHAPTER

ONE

There was a ringing in my ears that I couldn't drown out. Flashing lights and cameramen jostling around each other to where I was at the center of the basketball court. The crowd continued to cheer, but all I could do was feel numb in that moment until my teammate brushed their shoulders with mine.

"We did it! We won!" she exclaimed as tears were lining her eyes. All I could do was smile, as I didn't feel her same contentment. Winning the national championship was the dream I'd always had, but there was something missing—or rather *someone* was missing. I wanted to run over to my mom to hug her, but she was nowhere to be found. Looking in the stands of thousands of people, I couldn't find her face anywhere.

The reporter pulled me aside. "Sasi Avias, how does it feel to win the national title for your university?" The words the reporter asked hit me with a sting. "It feels shocking, but if you'll excuse me, I have to go." The

1

reporter stood there astonished as I disappeared into the locker room.

I quickly took off my uniform and went into the shower to wash off the smell of glory. My teammates wanted to celebrate. Their parents and siblings were gathering around, but not mine. I once again felt alone in a crowd full of people. I thought for sure my mom would be here. After all, the title game was in New York City at Madison Square Garden, where my mom was living. She didn't have to travel far. I grabbed my sweats and sweatshirt from the locker room and sat down. I put my head in my hands and rubbed my face to try to peel off the exhaustion I had. Taking a deep breath, I put my clothes on and combed out my hair. My teammates all patted me on the back as I was leaving the building. I felt a cool breeze hit my face as I stepped into the city streets. I hugged myself to get some warmth as I waved my hand in the air to get a taxi to my mom's workplace.

"Hey, where you headed?" the driver asked as I slid into the backseat.

"Can you take me to this hospital?" I pulled out my phone and showed him the address.

"You're not hurt, are you? Because I will charge extra for that." He turned his head to get a better look at me.

"No, I'm visiting my mom. She works there." I smiled slightly so he could turn back around in his seat.

When he did, I let out a breath I didn't realize I was holding. I don't know why but talking to other people drained me. I put on my headphones and heard the connection signal for the BlueTooth. I made my way over to my playlist and pressed shuffle as I sat back and closed my eyes.

I kept thinking of what I would say to my mom. If I should tell her what was really on my mind. I looked out the window and saw the buildings glistening and people in their own worlds. I thought about their life and if they were happy. There was one man who had headphones dangling from his ears, and he wore a tattered hoodie. There was no trace of hair on his head, and he had dirty jeans on as well. He looked over at me, and we briefly made eye contact. It was like I stared into his soul, but when I was about to look away, his eyes glowed a light blue. I quickly tried to look back at him, but I lost him in the crowd of civilian life. A chill ran up my spine. I noticed the taxi stopped. I paid the fare and got out.

I kept my head down as I got out of the car. I felt a drop of water fall from the sky, which multiplied. I hurried into my mom's workplace, and a woman with dark-brown hair greeted me.

"Is Sira still here?" I asked the nurse, who was standing in the hospital's hallway. My mom is a surgeon, so she's hardly ever home and often on call.

"Yeah, she's in the back." I rushed through the hallways of the hospital to make my way back to the break room.

"Hey, kid, I didn't know you would be in town," the security guard, Jennifer, told me. Jennifer was always friendly with me. She would let me skip the lines in the hospital when I was in town from college.

"Hi, Jenn. I had a basketball game, so I'll be back for a few days. Do you know if my mom is ready to leave soon?" I put my hands in my sweatpants so I wouldn't do any nervous fidgeting.

"She should be ready to leave soon, but you can go to the back." Jennifer smiled sweetly and buzzed open the doors that led to the more private area of the hospital. I neared the door to the break room and heard laughter echoing through the wall. I slowly reached my hand up to knock and held my breath.

"Come in!" I heard my mom's voice say through the door. I turned the handle on the door and peeked my head in.

"Hey, mom, it's me." I shuffled into the room and put my hands back into my pocket.

"You didn't tell me you were here?" My mom already pulling out her phone to see if she missed a text from me. She creased her eyebrows together as her eyes moved back and forth. I always felt like I could actively see her mind working through her own thoughts when she did that.

"I told you about my game three weeks ago, but I understand you're busy with surgeries." I went to sit in the chair across from her before I realized there was another person in the room. He was in a leather jacket with slicked back, black hair. He had piercing green eyes and smirked in my direction.

"Well, I'll see you later, Sira." He leaned down a bit and hugged her as he made his way out of the door.

"Who was that?" I asked, looking at my mom. She just smirked and brought her coffee mug up to her lips. I finally got time to notice the bags under her brown eyes. Her brown hair was in a messy bun as well, with pieces of her hair out of place. Every time I saw her, she looked more tired than she would let on.

"He is just a friend from where I grew up. Now tell me about your game. Did you put that ball in that hoop?" It always amazed me how she would never understand the game of basketball. I sighed and pulled out my phone.

"Well okay. If you're not going to talk to me, you can wait outside. We can talk about your game after I get dressed in some regular clothes." My mom got up from her chair and moved to her locker.

I knew I should've answered, but I didn't feel like explaining myself. I got up from my chair and left the room. I made a right down the hallway to find a door that led to the roof of the hospital. I usually came up here when I waited for her to finish getting ready, but I hoped there wasn't any more rain.

Even though I had won the championship, I felt like I had lost the biggest game in my life. My mom and I have never been that close, but for once, I thought she would be proud of me. Thinking to myself, I felt like disappearing. I felt the cold air enter my lungs as I pushed open the door. I heard the noises of cars honking and an ambulance in the distance. I looked over the city and felt lonely.

I took a deep breath and whispered to myself, "Sasi, she will never be close to you. Stop trying."

I let out a whimpering cry as I tried to steady my breathing. I heard something but I couldn't make it out. I brushed it off until I felt a weight on my shoe.

Looking down at my feet, I noticed a snake was going over my shoes. I jolted back in surprise. As I stepped back, the rattler stared at me with a confused look. Slowly, the snake inched closer with a devious look in its eyes, causing me to move back toward the edge. *How did this snake even get up here?*

The snake launched its body at me, its fangs in perfect view. I felt my life flash before my eyes. I saw the hospital getting larger as I fell off the balcony.

I saw a blue light reflecting in the snake's eyes as they met my own. I turned my head, and there was a blue light we were both falling into. I closed my eyes as I let my body go with gravity, hoping for the best.

CHAPTER
TWO

I slowly blinked and noticed it stopped raining. I rubbed my face and felt sore in every area of my body. I searched my surroundings as I felt an icky goo run through my hands. The realization hit me; I wasn't in New York anymore. I was in a red meadow with the goo surrounding me. The sky was a lavender color with no clouds. *Where was I? Did I die? Surely, I died falling like I did. Am I in heaven? Why would heaven have goo?*

I put my hood on my head to shield myself from the gust of hot wind that brushed my face.

"Hello? Is anyone here?" No one responded. *Was I dreaming?* I touched my face to see if I could feel it.

I slapped myself. *Well, that hurt.* I slowly got up and looked around. There was a forest beyond the meadow. Seeing the different insects made me wonder where I was. I saw a bug that looked small, but when I went to touch it, the bug grew larger.

Suddenly, I felt something breathing on my neck, making my hair stand up. I turned around to face an animal that looked like a pig combined with a buffalo. Its breath smelled like someone had put a dozen onions in its mouth and tried to mix it with garlic.

"Honk! Honk!" The animal roared at me, spraying slobber on my face. I closed my eyes and reached up wipe away the saliva. I stared at the animal as it looked me in my eyes. It looked starving and may have just found its prey. I slowly stepped backwards, letting my shoes squish in the red mud.

"I will not hurt you. I'm just trying to find out where I am." I put my hands up as I kept stepping backwards and looking over my shoulder to make sure I wouldn't fall over. The animal stared at me with its yellow eyes and walked over to another area with grass. I took a deep breath and turned around, knowing I wasn't in immediate danger from the enormous beast.

Large boulders were everywhere, and tiny dips were in the ground, which made me stumble, feeling a fresh sting on my legs. I slowly got up to brush off the mud on my sweatpants. I kept walking until I reached some trees where I could lean on.

I glanced around the area I was in, noticing I was near a village. A man was walking, carrying two swords with blood dripping from them. I quickly moved behind a bush to stare at him. He had deep-tanned skin and curly black hair. He was wearing clothing that I had never seen before: metal armor and an owl head piece.

I watched him walk to the village that was nearby. I kept my eye on him until I heard him speak to a woman. When he spoke, it wasn't English. It sounded like gibberish, but the other people seemed to understand him.

The village had a somber feeling from the way the people carried themselves. The people were covered in red mud, and the women were sewing tiny clothing that appeared to be for children. Suddenly, a hand went over my mouth. I heard a deep male voice whisper in my ear, "You need to blend in and try not to get caught."

I turned around and realized it was the brown-skinned man with the owl headpiece. He winked and put a finger to his lips. My breath caught and my heart was racing. He pointed to a clothesline in the village. "Hurry!" he whispered urgently. "It isn't safe here for you. Come back, and I will get you to safety."

I figured he had a point. When no one was looking, I ran over to a nearby cabin and took the clothing from the clothesline. As soon as I changed out of my sweats and sweatshirt, I grabbed the mud sitting there and tried to make the designs the people had on their faces on my own.

I looked around and noticed that no one was around me. I peered my head around the cabin to see more of the small village. The people had a big pot of food boiling over a fire, and others were cutting up an animal that I had never seen before. I felt a hand on my shoulder, and an angry woman met my eyes. She yelled at me in their language, pointing to the clothesline. I couldn't tell what she was inferring. The commotion drew attention over to me. Out of the corner of my eye, I saw a man walking towards me with a sword wearing a gold wolf headpiece. I turned around ready to run, but before my feet could command what my mind told them to do, I was lifted and pinned to the outside of the cabin.

"I'm sorry. You must have mistaken me for someone else. I won't harm anyone!" I told him. He looked at me confused and asked, "What?" in English, so I kept talking. "I live in America and don't live in this place." He threw his neatly trimmed bearded face back, releasing a hearty laugh.

He collected himself after he finished and turned towards me. "We don't have time. We heard of your arrival, and I must take you to the castle. The Semjists are going to attack tonight."

"The what? No, you don't understand. I came from a blue light, and I fell off a building." I scrunched my eyebrows together trying to figure out what he meant by castle and Semjists.

He put his finger to my lips. "There is no time for nonsense. We must go to the palace to get you ready."

Before I could respond, he threw me over his shoulder and started his journey. I felt an immense desire to fall asleep. I heard a voice in the distance calling my name. I let my eyelids fall with the image of his boots and the ground moving.

கூ

I woke up in a pure gold room with pictures of a woman whom I didn't recognize. I looked down and saw I was still in the garments I stole from the village. Right across from the bed was a gold closet halfway opened. I got up from the bed and carefully padded my bare feet across the marble floor to open it.

In the closet, a gold-plated armor suit hung. I opened

the case for the headpiece, and it was a wolf head, gold plated with diamonds. The headpiece was the same headpiece from the man that carried me here. I carefully touched the armor, feeling the different grooves in the metal. There were gold-plated hilts on two swords next to the armor. The swords had an inscription on the side of the sword. To the right there was also a golden bow with four diamond arrows next to it. All I could do was stare in awe at the amount of gold in front of me. *Where am I?* I took in the room before me and noticed the woman on the walls was the only color this room had.

It's hard to believe twenty-four hours ago I was in a world much different from this. This had to be a dream. I closed the closet door and padded back to the luxurious bed in the room's corner. *How can I even get out of here?* There was one window to the side, but I couldn't possibly fit through the tiny slit in the wall. I didn't even know how high up I was. I stared at the wooden door before me and made an executive decision.

Opening the door, I saw guards wearing the same armor from the closet standing there. Their feet shuffled towards me, startling me. They were looking at me expectantly. "We didn't know that you'd be awake so soon. We will take you to the queen right away." I gave them a confused look but continued to follow them, taking in my surroundings.

There were pictures of the woman again, which had to be the queen they spoke of. Cracks in the stone walls were apparent as we kept walking through the corridor. I had the sense I had been here before, but I shook away the thought. The hallway was cold, and the whole place felt hard to breathe in because of the humidity. I noticed the banners in the hallway had a snake emblem on them. *That's different.*

Entering the throne room, a woman was staring out of a large stained-glass window. She was wearing a very elegant white gown with gold embroidery at the bottom. The crown that was shining on her head gave off the impression she was the queen. She turned and smiled at me. Before I knew it, she was walking over to me and touched my face gently as if I was porcelain. I could see that she had glowing blue eyes. It reminded me of the man I saw earlier on the streets of New York. *Blue light and blue eyes?* I had to be dreaming.

She hugged me and kissed my bare forehead, pushing my brunette hair aside.

"Ah, so nice of you to join us. It is lovely to have a guest at the castle." I stared at her with a stoic face. *She couldn't possibly mean me, right?*

"Guest?" I asked with a puzzled face.

"Of course, Sasi, what is the meaning of this?" I stepped back and looked at her glowing blue eyes. *How did she know my name?*

"What is your name?" I asked.

"My name is Aurelia, Queen of Bolithium of course. Are you feeling okay? Also, please don't mind the noise from outside. That's just a minor disagreement we are having with some rebels who don't know how to take no for an answer." She smiled sweetly and turned her attention back to the stained-glass window.

I didn't even know what she was talking about until I peered over the window and saw men lined up and grouped together like they were going on a march or something.

"I am fine, just a little tired." I smiled to conceal my confusion. "I will be right back," I replied. I turned and hurried out of the throne room, looking for an exit. *What did she mean by disagreement?*

I heard footsteps echoing through the hallway and metal clinking together. I peeked my head around the corner, putting my face against the brick wall. All I saw were guards marching in the opposite direction. I felt the deja vu feeling again and turned with them without knowing where I was going.

I blended in with them, marching through the castle. With all the twists and turns, I realized it might be harder to figure out this castle than I thought. We finally ended up in front of a spiked gate. *Well, this wasn't the exit I was looking for.*

I gathered my thoughts and realized I was standing outside. The tattered boots I'd stolen from that village were now sinking into the mud the longer I stood. The soldiers looked at me expectantly, and one by one, they made a path for me to reach the front of the line. The air smelled of anticipation mixed with a tinge of fear and death. Everyone stared at me as if I knew what to do. My thoughts caught up to what was about to happen. Why was I even here? I have never been in war, nor do I plan on it.

Back over my shoulder was the palace. In front of me was the wooden gate, standing tall with soldiers at the top of the wall, looking down at me. I turned around while my boots sloshed in the mud.

"I guess you can open the gate?" I asked with uncertainty. Maybe this would be my chance to escape from this place and to go back to normal. As the gate opened, it creaked, making the clanking of the chains echo off the walls. I glanced around and saw empty cart stands. *Where was everyone?*

Thick forest surrounded the battlefield. Maybe I could escape through the forest and try to retrace my steps to the light. Looking back at the soldiers' faces, I realized they looked as scared as I was. I took a deep breath as my mind kept racing with thoughts. I closed my eyes and looked at the forest and looked back at the crowd of soldiers who might lose their life over something I didn't know. I tried to think of what I would do if I were an actual warrior. I had only played video games like this.

I awkwardly started walking and realized the soldiers were following me. Looking across the battlefield made my stomach churn. Before I knew it, my feet moved before I could even think. I made a quick dart towards the forest. Puddles covered the ground, making me run harder than I expected as I kept slipping. I saw body after body sliced and cut during the battle. Just as I ducked, I met a burly, hairy man coming toward me, but before I could register, one soldier from the castle stepped in front of me to parry. I saw the burly man's soul leave his body as the jeweled sword entered through his being. His eyes were emotionless.

My hands shook at my sides as tears rolled down my cheeks. Another man came for me, but a man in gold armor got him. I kept dodging men left and right, hoping that I could get to the forest. A man approached me with a sword. I ducked as he slipped backwards from the mud. *Well, that's one thing that worked out.* I weaved around him and kept trying to make my escape. The forest was in my sight. I hid behind a boulder and braced myself for anyone to come near.

All I could hear was the leftover clinking metal from men as they walked. I gathered up the strength to get up from my hiding position. I held my hands up and hoped for the best.

"Is this another one of them, sir?" the man in the golden armor asked a larger man.

The larger man removed his helmet and looked at me closer.

"No, this is the one Aurelia wanted to see. Well, come on then. I guess we should take you back to the castle." He walked over to me and jostled me in the castle's direction. All I could see were black spots on the grass that were on the battlefield before, but there were no bodies. *In a war, there would be bodies, right?*

"Um, where are the men from the other people?" I looked around the battlefield as I kept stumbling to the castle.

"They're gone. Keep moving." He pushed me slightly harder.

My feet made a slosh in the mud as I kept walking. The gate looked slightly damaged from the last time I looked at it. I looked back at the forest again and hoped that later I could escape through there, just not today, apparently. Inside the gate, there was no evidence there was even a war at all. The streets looked pristine as we walked back through with our boots hitting the cobble-stone. The people of Bolithium came out of their homes. Claps slowly emerged, which eventually led to cheering. I walked through the crowds, pushing my way through to get into the palace.

Servants started pulling off the armor of the warriors next to me. The castle smelled like mildew. I tried to make my way through the castle, but a servant led me back to where the rest of the guards were sitting.

I sat down at the dinner table and took in all the food that was there in front of me. There was an assortment of fish and meat surrounding the table. I realized I hadn't eaten since yesterday. At least I assume it was yesterday when I fell off the building. I put a piece of meat and some vegetables on my plate and noticed none of the men at the table had silver-ware to eat with. They were eating with their hands and wiping the leftover food on their garments. I awkwardly took the food with my hands and tasted a little of the meat. *College food is nothing compared to this.* As we were eating, they began storytelling. There were so many stories about the kingdom, which made me even more lost than I was before. They told me the history of how they got the kingdom from the supposed beasts.

"How did you kill these so-called 'beasts?" I asked, which caused them to raise their eyebrows, looking at me with confusion.

"What do you mean, child?" Queen Aurelia took a drink of her wine and creased her cracked lips together.

"I mean, how could a 'beast' rule a kingdom?" I

looked at her and shoved another piece of meat into my mouth.

"It was the serpent rulers who had a vile personality, really. They called themselves good when they would walk around with snakes around their necks. I mean, they even had other animals that were deformed in their wars. They had some sort of aura about them, but don't worry, they're all gone now," the queen announced as she creased her smile at me. I got the impression she was lying.

I remembered the snake in the building and the snake emblem in the hallways. "Wait, aren't you the serpent rulers?" I looked around the stone walls and saw the snake emblems still hanging.

"No, sweetheart, our emblem is an animal like a wolf, but much more powerful. Especially since it has three craniums of its own." The two rulers laughed at the comment.

I looked again at the stone wall, but now it was some sort of creature with the similarity of a wolf, and the snake image vanished. I looked down at my dry, cracked, brown hands. "I think I'm going to retire for the evening. This was a lovely dinner." I forced a smile and pulled back from the chair I sat in.

"Of course. Guards, please escort her to her chambers." The queen motioned her hand towards the gold-plated men.

As I walked through the melancholy corridor, I kept seeing the wolf-like emblem on the walls instead of the snake one I'd seen earlier. The guard opened my chamber door for me. I politely nodded as I stepped into the gold room. I shut the door and let out a sigh of relief. I walked towards the tiny window in the corner.

I looked outside of the window, and I could tell that the sky was still clear with no clouds. I stripped out of my garments and saw the golden bathtub already had water in it. I dipped my toes in, feeling the lukewarm water first before I put my whole body underneath the water. I let all the events of the day wash off of me as I scrubbed my cuts and red dirt off my skin. I looked at my arm, and there was a wound there, along with a throbbing sting. *How did I get that?* I got out of the tub and looked at the blades in the closet again.

I couldn't comprehend that I'd be playing basketball one day and the next be in a war. Well, hiding in a war. Looking at the mirror, my eyes had changed to a glowing blue color just like I had seen in the queen earlier. I stepped back and kept looking at myself.

When I looked at my wound again, I noticed I had a tattoo of a snake with blue eyes instead of the cut. The blue light appeared in my room. I gasped as pictures kept appearing on the blue light, and it was pictures of my mom back home looking stressed and a man in a police uniform looking for me, trying to calm her down. It also showed a picture of Aurelia beside a picture of my real mom and a woman I have never seen before. I didn't know what it all meant. *Could my mom actually be looking for me?*

I looked out the window again and noticed that the sky had turned back to purple. The light projecting in my room had disappeared. I took a deep breath and pulled back the golden duvet. As I got into my bed, I closed my eyes and heard the entire kingdom chanting, but differently. Millions of people were crying and pleading for my help. I opened my eyes and heard the buzzing of silence. I closed my eyes again and heard the chants in the background. I put the pillow over my delicate ears, trying to muffle the noise before I finally drifted off.

CHAPTER

THREE

I woke up the next morning, looking around the same golden room. I sighed and got out of bed and saw that they already picked my outfit out for me. It was a white garment and a distinct grey fur coat. I put it on and noticed a pin with a gold owl next to it. I put the pin in the pocket of my coat and strapped on the black boots with the outfit.

I hesitantly looked at the closet again and debated on taking a weapon. On one hand, I didn't even know how to defend myself. I felt uneasy in this castle and needed to get out of here. I shakily held my hand out and took one knife. I didn't really like violence, but I guess I had to be protected. I still didn't fully trust the queen here.

I looked at the mirror and put my brown hair into a single braid that went down the middle of my back. I checked my arm where the wound was and noticed the tattoo wasn't there anymore, and it was back to a scratch. *Maybe I dreamed that part and didn't really see a tattoo.*

Today, I wanted to get out of the castle, but I didn't know how to dodge the guards. I opened my door and saw a guard there as I'd predicted.

"Good morning. How may I be at your service?" the unshaven man asked.

"Is there a garden here by any chance?"

He looked at me puzzled and straightened his stance. "There is, but no one goes there."

"And why is that?"

He stared me down and let out a sigh. "Okay, I'll take you there, but I can't answer your previous question." I stared at him and started walking through the vast castle. I kept glancing in rooms we passed by just to see if I could see the snake emblem again just to give me a clue.

I saw shadows reflecting off the walls in the distance. Walking towards them, they seemed to move with the flames reflecting on the wall. Behind me, I heard whispers about someone or something coming for us. I turned to see where the whispers were coming from but saw nothing. I looked in front of me, only to still find the guard leading me to the supposed garden. I walked further and further until I entered a strange garden that lurked in darkness. I sensed a presence staring at me, whispering the same thing over again in another language.

"Alright, this is the garden. I'll be over there in the corner if you need anything," the unshaved guard said as he wobbled over to his position. I slowly made my way behind a bush so he would lose sight of me. Lifting my head, there was not a single soul around me in the garden. Not even a hint of animal life. An eerie silence took over. Not even a bird sang.

I looked in the distance and noticed a single sparkling rose that shined throughout the gloom that was surrounding me. My gut told me not to walk towards it, but the temptation of another presence pulled me closer to it.

I felt my feet gravitating towards the most beautiful rose ever before, finding myself standing right in front of it. I looked back to see the guard, but he wasn't there. I turned to the majestic rose again. I wanted to lay my delicate hands on the soft petals. Suddenly, I felt someone's hot breath on me. Looking up, I saw a white stag staring at me. I got the sense it was looking inside of me, seeing my fear and my sadness.

"Hello, Sasi. I am Glyden. Do not be scared because I hear your thoughts loud and clear. I will teach you and show you the truth about this realm," the stag said in a low, deep melodious voice. "Come with me."

"How do I know you won't kill me?" I said in a shaky voice.

"Well, how do I know you won't kill me?" Glyden responded. "The thing is, Sasi, we never know what to expect. We must trust and try instead of shooting ourselves down before we fly."

Glyden looked down and bowed his antlered head. I didn't know what to expect from this entire experience. I felt like something else was watching me, and I looked towards the trees. As I studied harder, it was a white owl surrounded in a soft silver glow like a full moon, silently watching my every movement.

"Fine, I will go with you. Should I bring anything? I mean, I only have these clothes and this knife, so it's not much," I said as I opened my fur coat a bit more.

"Oh, well, you could bring something if you would like. I assumed you would want to know more about this place," he said with a smirk.

Something about this stag made me want to trust him, but something also said not to be deceived by him. I glanced up to check if the owl was still there. It was and still looking at me. But now it wasn't just looking at me, it saw the stag as well. I couldn't gather my thoughts on how weird all of this seemed. I felt safe with the owl looking upon me. All my worries went away in an instant. I couldn't remember the last time I had this feeling.

I reached down into my coat and touched the cold metal owl pin. I felt a sense of relief flood through me. Looking up, the owl vanished. I looked at the stag, right in Glyden's eyes. His eyes were the color of honey. I sensed he was powerful, majestic, and mystical. I guess this would be a journey for both of us.

"Well, are you going to get anything or are you ready to go?" Glyden asked with a smirk.

"Yes. Let's go. I don't really have anything in my room, anyway." I looked back to where the guard was posted, and he still wasn't there.

"Oh, don't worry about him. I took care of him to where we can slip out of here without a trace." Glyden already started walking away, his hooves crunching in the hard grass. *What did he mean by taking care of him?*

I picked up my pace to catch up to him and went out

of a gate I didn't even know was there. I was starting a new journey that felt right. I wanted to know more about this kingdom since something summoned me here for a reason.

FOUR

As Glyden and I started our journey, I felt nauseous, which I attributed to the enormous amount of food I'd eaten the night before. I pulled my hood up as we walked through the kingdom and went the opposite way towards the bridge. When we were near people, Glyden would disappear, but I knew he was right next to me. After we passed the guards and crossed the bridge, we were on this stone path that took us into the forest.

"So, Sasi, how has your time been in this realm?" Glyden asked as we went and climbed the steep stone path into the forest.

"I didn't know I was in a whole other realm, but to be honest, I don't really know what is even happening most of the time here." I pulled up my gown slightly so I could get better traction walking on the stone.

"Well, I'm sorry to hear that. We tried to get someone for you when you arrived. But Aurelia had other plans. It was a little tricky to get in the kingdom, but at least you are with me now." Glyden admitted as we kept walking up the hill. *What did he mean by 'we'?*

"Also, Sasi, I know all your thoughts, and I meant 'we' as in Terra and I. I don't think we will see her any time on this adventure. I'm going to take you to someone who can explain everything to you a little better. But first, we still need to get out of Bolithium." I stood there, astonished that he could still read my mind. I shook my head and followed him deeper into the forest. The stone path was turning more into the red dirt with rocks.

We went through winding, red dirt roads and climbed a rocky hill before we took camp under various trees. We kept away from people, hoping no one would recognize me. Although, once or twice, we went by some farmhouses, and I stole some bread and water that the villagers had left out. Which was a good thing, considering I packed nothing for the journey.

"We can camp out here for the night. No one should harm us." Glyden looked around after he walked in a circle to lay down.

"I guess it's a good thing I kept this fur coat. It is pretty warm, and the wind is picking up." I hugged my coat closer to me as I sat down on the dirt.

"I'm glad you can find some comfort in all of this," Glyden smirked before closing his eyes.

"Can I ask you a question?" I peered over to Glyden to see he'd opened one eye to look at me.

"You just did, Sasi. Goodnight." He closed his eyes again and pushed out his legs.

"No, I meant like how can you talk? Or read my

mind? Like your mouth moves but animals aren't supposed to talk." I looked at him expectantly.

Glyden sighed and lifted his head to look at me.

"I am built off magic. I know that isn't a thing back in your realm, but here it is very prominent. At least it was at one point. Aurelia banned magic in Bolithium, but there are some places in this realm that still have magic. My home is Guirra. It is very far from here, and it usually takes days to get there. That's the only place that still has magic, like the kind I use. However, there is a place called Jaklish that has been rebelling against Bolithium. They see magic as a good thing."

It took me a bit to process everything he just said, but I turned to him, still wanting to know more.

"So, this Terra lady, does she have magic too or no? Where I'm from, people often write about magic, or there's this thing called *Harry Potter*, where the character had magic with a wand. So magic isn't that foreign to me. My mom back home also was very superstitious." I smiled, thinking about my mom and how she used to put up certain plants in the windows to keep out negative energy. She would also collect rocks and line them up on the windowsill on a full moon.

"She sounds like a very gifted woman. And this thing you speak of with a wand? That isn't even a thing. Now that is fiction for you, Sasi. Your people try to be us, but it will never happen." Glyden smirked at me and rested his head on the tree branch. "But to answer your question, Terra, I guess, created me. I am very loyal to her, and she was very insistent about keeping you safe. I just am trying to do what I was told."

"Why would she want to save me? I randomly fell off a building, and now I'm stuck here. Also, why wouldn't she get me herself?" I drew lines in the red dirt with a nearby stick.

"You aren't random, Sasi. Not just anyone can come here. Don't worry, in a few days we should make it to the place where I need to take you, and you should understand more. Right now, we just need to keep being safe. Plus, Terra can't exactly leave Guirra." He closed his eyes and took a deep breath.

I sighed and listened to him. At least I felt safer with him than I did with anyone else. I closed my eyes and let sleep take me away.

We ended up traveling for many days and nights. I was glad for my fur coat, as it kept me warm at night. It rained, and the path was slow and muddy. We tried to walk under the cover of the trees to stay dry on those days.

As we journeyed, I imagined my mom when I was little. I was pondering at the idea of feeling like she was safe to be around, but she was hardly around once I turned ten. I remembered for a brief period in my life we'd lived in New Mexico. There had been an older woman who lived with us, but I'd known she wasn't my grandmother or anything. She'd just been there to help me if I needed anything while my mom was out doing something. I'd forgotten about that woman, but sometimes I thought of her mannerisms. I couldn't remember what she'd looked like. She'd been nice and would play with me in the yard, but after we'd left New Mexico to New York, I never saw her again. I zoned back into reality, which was still hard to wrap my head around.

I felt nauseous when we got to a higher-up area. I was carrying my fur coat, and I tried to rip the sleeves off of my white and gold gown. I felt like I was burning up. Before I knew it, I was retching over the side of the trail. I felt like my insides were bursting at the seams. I was so weak. All I had eaten was stale bread that I had pilfered days ago. I needed to stop and rest.

I called up to Glyden, and he came back towards me. "I need to stop. I feel sick. I don't know what's wrong with me." He looked at me, concerned. He glanced towards the path, then back towards me.

"We can only stay near this area for a little while, okay?" He nudged his wet nose towards me, and I put most of my body weight on him as he led me to a darkened area. We sheltered near a stream in a cave. At some point, I must have dozed off. I felt a wet nose nuzzle my cheek. I looked up and Glyden had a root in his mouth he pushed towards me. There were some freshly baked loaves of bread and cheese beside me.

"I think you need to eat this. It will help keep some loaves of bread down. I need you to be healthy for what is about to come tomorrow," Glyden spoke with a worried look on his face.

"What do you mean? I don't think I can rise from this illness so soon. This is taking forever. Why do you think this will all be better within a day?"

"Sasi, this is a very special herb I have given you. Please eat. It will help nourish your body back to full strength."

Elfroot was a magical root that was prized for its many healing properties, I learned later. I gracefully picked up the plant and held it in my delicate hands. It was prickly on the sides but softer in the middle. I could see the pink in the middle that was the primary source to stop all of this madness. I looked at Glyden through his trustworthy eyes and gently ate the plant. It wasn't the best meal that I had hoped for. In fact, the stale bread was better than this plant.

Soon after, I had passed out. My thoughts raced, wondering what I was doing here again. I wanted to see New York. I wanted to see my mom. I wanted to go home. It felt like I had left my old life for months. I felt like I hadn't touched a basketball in months. The itch kept approaching to play one more game, but I knew those days would never come again. I heard my child-hood songs echoing through my head. My mother's singing and her voice quivering with worry, wondering if I'd ever go to sleep.

I began thinking about all the splendid memories I had shared with her. I felt as if a part of my soul had been taken from me. I couldn't go about this for long. Perhaps I felt as if I needed her to be there for me even though we didn't communicate well these days.

Soon enough, I had awoken from my restless slumber. I picked up my knife and walked towards Glyden. I was still weak, so Glyden insisted I ride him. I mounted Glyden to his destination. The trees weren't like the kind in New York. These trees were massive, as if I were in the Redwoods in California. I saw markings on ancient stone that were barriers to the new village we were approaching. There, I witnessed a kind of being that I had only read in stories. These people had faces that were long and had ears that were pointy. They dressed rather fashionably in their armor. They looked fancier than other people I had seen in this realm. They all had a blue lapis rock around their neck.

"Are you noticing their necklace, Sasi?" Glyden said, as he slowly looked back at me.

"Yes, what is it exactly?" Even though I couldn't see his face, I knew Glyden had to be smirking.

"It symbolizes protection and clear thinking." I pondered at this and kept looking at the people in their armor that glistened as we walked by.

"So...they can't die?" I asked, still unsure of everything that was around me.

"Of course, they can. It just takes longer for them to die. They believe in a force that can heal them. This force relies on all four normal elements without the fifth. However, it is dangerous, so they use the rock. The legend says that the rock around their neck was found by their first kin of elves." As Glyden replied, I noticed the same glow of blue in his eyes.

"So, they are elves? I thought elves were fake."

"Well, don't tell them that, Sasi." Glyden chuckled to himself as we kept following a narrow, muddy road that led to our destination.

There was one boy I noticed, but he wasn't like the others. He had brown eyes like caramel and black hair when others had blond. His ears were pointy but not like the others. He had a better build than most of the men there. I studied his eyes as he waved to me. I looked around to see if there was someone else he was waving to, but sure enough, it was towards me.

"That right there, Sasi, is Aubrith. He helps and serves the Kendlish Elves instead of helping his own clan." Glyden spoke softly, hoping no one else would hear.

"Why doesn't he help his own clan?"

"Well, you see, he works with the blue and white who usually have a headpiece of an owl. He is mixed, half Elven and half OV. We know the OV for the rebirth of our fellow gods, but the elves disagree. They have their own belief, which I explained earlier, but Aubrith's mom is an elf and his father is OV. His father was the leader of his people, but Aubrith doesn't believe in their teachings. He still pretends for them, so they won't threaten his mother."

I studied Aubrith's face a little longer until something clicked.

"Wait, I know him. He's the one who took me after I fell out of the portal."

"Well, I'm sure this won't be awkward at all," Glyden said in a snarky tone.

Rain came down as I walked over to Aubrith. His eyes glowed through the mist, but he looked frightened to know I had still lived. He hurried his talking as if he didn't want me to stay long.

"Hello...Sasi... I believe we have met."

"Yes, we have. You tried to take me away, remember?"

He looked puzzled, as if not knowing what to do. He picked up the shovel that lay nearby so he could keep busy while he was talking.

"I didn't mean any of it. I'm glad you're alive. I tried to lead you to the clothes the villagers had on, but I didn't know Aurelia sent guards to get you. What are you doing in Jaklish?"

"My friend Glyden here told me to come here. I need answers about the kingdom. Maybe I can help you or something if you help me learn more about this place."

"Help me? I don't need your foolish help." He narrowed his eyes at me.

"No. I'm trying to let you know I am here for you and your people. I don't want any trouble."

"Ah, well, Sasi. If you must know, we need help to set up watchtowers. In the morning we will start our quest. Get some rest at my home. My mother will enjoy some company." He laughed and looked down at the end of his shovel. "It will be nice having an outsider around the house. You will have answers soon enough." He smirked and led me to his home. I had a weird feeling about him, and my gut didn't tell me it was good or bad. I unmounted Glyden and looked back at him.

"It will be okay, Sasi. Aubrith is a man you can trust. I'll be here if you need anything." Glyden responded, already knowing what I was thinking. I walked with Aubrith, who was still smirking at me. This was about to be very interesting.

I entered the small cottage that Aubrith stayed in. I noticed it was sparse. The wood creaked as I walked in.

"I know it's not much, but as long as you can sleep, that will be a plus." Aubrith set his shovel down in the corner next to books that had dust on them.

"Mom, this is Sasi. She will be our guest for tonight." My eyes followed to whom he was talking to. There stood an old woman with blonde hair and pointy ears. I noticed she was blind and used a cane to walk. She wore a blue tunic that was wrinkled and a shawl that was golden with markings on the edges.

"Hi! It's very nice to meet you," I acknowledged to the woman as I awkwardly stood in the corner with my knife.

"Child, you look scared to meet me! I can promise you I'm not a threat." Before I could say anything else, the woman hugged me and kissed both of my cheeks.

"I know I'm blind child, but it doesn't mean I can't see you." I was confused by what she said, but I shook it off.

"Aubrith's mom, thank you again for letting Glyden and I stay here," I acknowledged. She laughed and rested her arm on my shoulder. "My name is Lenia, darling. Come and sit. Aubrith will make us dinner. Glyden and I are old friends." I sat down at the table and looked around the cottage some more.

"Wow! You have a lot of old books and jars of things everywhere." Aubrith set down a wooden cup of water, and I sipped it.

"Yes, child, that's because I can heal people." I spit out my water, then quickly tried to wipe it.

"You what?" I asked as I tried to clean up the water I spilled everywhere.

Lenia laughed and clapped her hands. She lifted one hand, and all the rest of the water in my cup levitated.

"How are you doing that?" My voice went quiet, just watching in amazement. "The Goddess has been great to me even though our realm is quickly decaying." Aubrith stopped cutting up vegetables and looked over at us.

"I'm sorry my mother likes to tell lies," he said sternly, looking in our direction. His mom waved him off and looked at me again.

"I'm not lying, he's just mad he didn't get to tell you why exactly you're here." My eyebrows knitted together.

"Why am I here?" I asked the fragile woman in front of me.

"I can't tell you that. I know you're here for a reason." Aubrith set down what looked like rice and vegetables on a wooden plate in front of me. I stared off into the distance, wondering what she meant.

"You must eat. The food will get cold." Aubrith nudged the food over to me. "Right." I reached down for a fork, but I noticed there were no utensils here. I ate the rice as delicately as I could since I didn't have a fork. I looked over at Aubrith and his mother, and they had rice everywhere.

After dinner, Aubrith showed me to my room, which comprised a bed with dust-covered sheets. "Thank you again for everything, Aubrith." I looked back into his caramel eyes.

"Of course." Aubrith bowed then shut the door to my room.

I tore off my fur coat but took out the owl pin and stared at it. I stripped off my boots and set the pin inside of my boot. I quickly laid down and tried not to think too much about the day. I looked up and saw a crack in the ceiling of my room. I followed it with my eyes until I spotted an opening. I got up from my bed and saw that there was a journal kept at the bottom of the crack.

I looked around, trying not to disturb anyone with the crackling under my feet. I flipped through the pages of the journal. I noticed Aubrith signed at the bottom of every page. "This was Aubrith's journal." I quickly kept scanning through until I landed on a familiar date. The date I won the national championship.

"There was an opening in the aura today. I saw a blue light coming down, but I didn't know what to do. None of us did. I thought it was Aurelia's doing since she has been trying to control everything."

Aurelia? The queen? I kept reading:

After a while, I tried to go to where the light was, but I couldn't see anything. All I saw were the markings from the Goddess. I tried to find any life but nothing was there. I went through the village. I had to disguise myself or they would kill me. I didn't want to startle anyone. I saw a girl. She had brown hair and light brown eyes. She was covered in dirt. She had to be the reason all of this started. I tried to help her however, she got spotted by another.

So that's why he grabbed me? I put the journal back where it came from. I didn't want anyone to think I was snooping around, even though I was. I went to lie back down until I heard the front door creak open. I grabbed my knife from my pants and held it closer to me as I heard the footsteps echo. The sound stopped before my door, and I saw the shadow underneath it.

I held my breath and slowly got out of bed to reach for my shoes and my coat. I quietly hid underneath the bed as I slid my boots back on. My door opened to reveal an enormous man who wasn't Aubrith at all. He had armor on, just like the guards at the castle.

"She's not here," he whispered.

There's more than one.

As soon as they left, I took a deep breath and made my way to the door. I looked outside my bedroom door and didn't see the men anymore. I made my way to Aubrith's room and jolted him.

He drew his sword at my neck and pressed it on my skin. When he saw it was me, his eyes softened. "What are you doing awake? It's time for bed." He rubbed his sleepy eyes and put down his sword.

"There were people looking for me. I don't know what to do. I'm scared. What if they try to take me?" I ran my fingers through my hair.

"Hey, hey calm down." He pulled me towards him and guided me to sit on the edge of his bed. "We will leave in a little while. I didn't think they would try to locate you this fast. We need to move. I'll explain every-thing, but right now I need you to promise me you will be alright."

He looked me in the eye, waiting for an answer. I softly nodded, and he wrapped his arms around me. The moment didn't last long, and before I knew it, he grabbed his armor and all of his weapons. I followed behind him as he woke up Glyden and his mother.

"We need to go now. Let's go to the woods. It will be hard to find us there," Aubrith declared as he shook Gylden's antlers. Glyden woke with a jolt and took a deep breath.

"Aubrith the woods are too dangerous. I don't know what lies there except beasts."

"Listen, Gly, they're coming. Whether we like it, they are. We need to move." Aubrith and his mom grabbed a saddle that was hanging on their wall and packed up food on Glyden.

I mounted Glyden and looked at Aubrith. "Aren't you coming?" He hesitated before he finally spoke.

"I'll meet up with you guys. Get her safe, Glyden. I'll see you two soon."

I looked at Aubrith, and he gave me a weak smile. Lenia grabbed my hand before we left. "Always look up, child." I didn't know what that meant. She whispered something in her own language. Her eyes glowed blue as she gave my hand one last squeeze. With that, Glyden took off, and all I saw was fog and darkness in front of us. I hoped all of this was a dream. I wanted none of this. I held onto Glyden's soft fur and let him take me where we needed to be.

CHAPTER

FIVE

All I could see was fog. There was fog everywhere, and the humidity made it hard to breathe. I gripped Glyden tighter as he kept walking. Although I don't know how he could see anything because all I could see were his horns.

"Sasi, we're almost there, don't worry," I heard Glyden say in a hush tone.

"Why are you whispering?" I asked as I sat up to see anything past the fog.

"They're watching," he urged. I felt his body tense below me.

My instinct was to lie lower and to not make a sound, but something told me to be more intuitive, and I turned around.

There was a man dressed in all black standing in the middle of the road in front of us. He had a sword and a mask to where you couldn't see anything. The way he was standing looked as if he was going to strike us.

Glyden kept walking as if nothing bad was happening, even though my gut said otherwise.

We reached a bridge, and you could hear the water below us, but I had no clue what Glyden was going to do.

"Well…?" I sighed as I laid on Glyden's back.

"Well, what, Sasi? It's not like I can maneuver over this preposterous thing."

I felt Glyden tense again, and I knew behind me was the man.

"I know you're a part of the Hogg Len clan, but you must make peace with us. We want no trouble, and I know you don't either." Glyden said, still facing the bridge.

"*Poalikus mikgreglan,*" the shadowed figure replied. Whatever he said, it sounded vile.

"We need to get to Elggland," Glyden muttered.

The man slowly walked closer to us, still uncertain if we would attack. The closer he got, the more I realized what he looked like. He had two heads and four arms. It threw me off guard, because from a distance, it looked like something completely different. The man wore a white chest piece and dangled a sword that was pure white.

He pointed in the direction opposite of the bridge and said something in his language again that I didn't understand.

"What was that all about?" I asked Glyden as the intruder left.

"Passfinders. They try to be whatever you're afraid of.

They morph into what terrifies you. You can't look at them, but you can still talk to them."

I kept thinking about what I saw and remembered the Passfinder was just a man dressed in black. I didn't know what that fear of mine could mean. I shook my head and cleared my throat.

"How long would you say it will take us to get to the place you want to show me?" I asked, gently petting Glyden.

"Not long at all. Lift your head."

I glanced to see a massive castle that was bigger than the one in Bolithium. There were plants overtaking the castle, engulfing the stone walls with the green vines. The stone arches looked ancient. The castle had a mystic vibe to it, which wasn't shocking considering this entire place was mysterious.

We made our way slowly through the courtyard that surrounded the front of the castle. The ground was soaked from the rain that trickled down on us. I removed my hood, letting the droplets run off it and onto my hair. I slowly got off Glyden and analyzed my surroundings to notice that we were close to the main entrance. I was about to push the massive wooden doors with a design of a snake coming out of a rose, but someone cleared their throat next to me.

"May I help you?" a bald man in a silk-patterned robe asked. He had tattoos of strange markings that even covered his head. He had a certain posture to him. He kept his hands in his robe and looked confident, even though he wasn't that tall.

"I'm sorry, my name is Sasi. This is Glyden. My friend sent us here, Aubrith. There were attackers from the village we came from, so I honestly have no clue what you would do for us," I rushed, noticing I didn't take a breath that whole time I spoke.

The man looked behind me to, I assumed, examine Glyden, who was just eating grass. *Typical.*

"I suppose you could come in, but make sure your friend over there eats nothing inside." He hushed. At first, I thought he tried to make a joke, but it didn't seem like he did. He was serious about what he'd meant.

I grabbed Glyden to lead him inside the castle. All I could see was a long hallway with candles alongside the wall. This place differed from the castle I'd first been in.

"What do you do here?" I asked, trying to catch up with the man in the robe.

"You can ask questions later, but right now we need to get you to a part of the palace that would actually be of some use to you two."

I looked at Glyden questionably, and he kept his head high as he walked behind the man. I hope we were in the right place because I didn't feel like traveling again any time soon.

We stopped at a door with locks that led all the way to the ceiling. The door was as big as the stone wall outside the courtyard. I wondered what we were doing here until the bald guy started mumbling something. I couldn't make out the words, but his eyes rolled back. His whispering bounced off the walls of the hallway we were in. I had an uneasy feeling because it's not every day you see someone mumbling something and looking possessed.

He returned to his original self and bowed towards the door. As he did that, each lock started unlocking each other.

"This way." The man led his hand out for me to follow through the door. As soon as the door completely opened, a vibrant aura welcomed me. The castle was white all around. Even the floor had white marble. People walked around in robes like the man wore. I felt out of place with my clothing when everyone was in fancy attire.

Glyden and I got weird looks from the people walking by. *Where the hell did Aubrith send me?*

I felt a hand on my arm, and the man's eyes were staring into me.

"This way." I felt my legs move on their own without me knowing I was moving them. We made it to the main building of this place. I could tell it was the wealthiest looking area considering the exquisite silk used for the banners around the room. A man in a white fur coat with a spiky bone crown met my eyes. His skin was so pale, it almost blended in with the marble floor. He was wearing maroon armor under the fur coat and had on maroon shoes. His olive eyes stared deeply into me, and he smirked towards me. He descended the stairs as the fur coat dragged behind him. He pulled his long, straight blond hair back. His jawline protruded out distinctively.

He was standing in front of us. He bowed before me and picked up my hand. He kissed the back of it.

"What a pleasure to have you," he complimented and smiled at me.

"Hi...?" I squeaked out. I hoped he'd tell me his name.

"Ah yes, my name is Prince Justorah of Elggland" His voice was so crisp and clear. This man was intimidating, but he didn't look any older than me.

"What is this place?" I wondered, trying to get the awkwardness out of the air.

"What? You've never heard of this place? The legend of my father, who defeated the enemy of the south. The 'powers' we possess here are part of our beloved legend. The mystical well at the base of the mountain. It is the source of everything here," he explained arrogantly. His charm faded when he kept rambling how great his family was.

After what felt like an hour of him explaining to me about his wealth, I had to stop him. "Okay, so Aubrith sent us here. Do you know him or not?" I interrogated.

He looked shocked by my demeanor, but I didn't want to listen to another hour about how "great" he really was.

"Yes, of course..." he gulped.

"Aubrith is an old friend of my family. Well, his mom is. But any person related to Lenia is our friend. She is an excellent witch."

My eyes widened at the end of his sentence. "She's a what?" I took a step back, trying to process everything that was being told to me. It couldn't be true, could it? "She told me she was a healer?" My mind was racing with thoughts that I couldn't keep up with.

"A witch, a healer, all the same thing. She was one of the best in her time, but her power was fading. She used it to save me from dying when I was a baby. I owe her my life." He looked away from me for a brief second, then returned to meet my gaze.

"Why did he send you here, though?" He changed the subject and readjusted his armor.

"There were these people who attacked the village we were in. I don't know who they were, but he sent us here to get answers about the kingdom and to warn you of what is coming your way, I believe."

He stroked his chin, grazing over the stubble that was there.

"Guard... Send out a dozen soldiers towards the mountain pass as well as two Links in the trees. We need to be on high alert. Can we also get the witches to track a friend of mine? I need to make sure him and his mother are still alive."

The last sentence made my stomach uneasy. *Aubrith couldn't be dead, could he?* I tried to focus on the problems at hand.

"What exactly are 'Links'?" I asked Justorah, which caught him off guard.

"They're powerful wizards, who can process their magic from the nature around us and cast it from far away. Why?" he probed. He looked more stoic.

"So, they're like snipers, but with magic?" I replied. His face turned from stoic to pure confusion.

"What is this sniper?" he asked and got closer to me.

"It's nothing. I'm sorry. I forgot." He gave me a strange glance and walked out of the room.

I followed behind him, hoping not to miss anything. I wanted to know more about this place. I wanted to know more about Aubrith. I knew his mom had powers but not like this, and I didn't know that an elf could be a witch, too. This place kept getting weirder and weirder, and it was just getting started.

CHAPTER

SIX

We explored more of the elegant palace, which was lined with red and white all around. Vast banners hung down with a rose symbol all over. I was waiting to hear anything about Aubrith, but there was no news.

"Do you want something to eat? Anything to drink?" Justorah's voice was laced with concern. For a person who looked like he could end someone's life in a split second, he was very nice.

"Can I get something to drink, please?" I shyly asked. We were in his throne room that overlooked the foggy mountain pass.

"Fetch her something to drink," he demanded to a servant that was standing to the side of him.

"Yes, sir. Right away, sir." The man hurried off to get something to drink for me.

"If I may ask, why did you leave Aurelia?" Justorah probed as he stood next to me.

I looked up at him, and his gaze was fixed on the mountain pass overseeing his guards.

"I don't know why. Glyden found me wandering the garden, and before I knew it, I'm here. He convinced me I would learn more about this place, and I felt safer with him than I did with her." I let out a slight chuckle and looked at the ground.

"Well, there must've been a reason for you to follow Glyden." He shifted his gaze at me.

"Yeah, there was this flower that I saw—" I stopped mid-sentence and looked around the throne room, straight to his banner.

"The rose. It was the rose on your banner."

Justorah smiled and let out a hearty laugh.

"I know. I was the one who set up the flower. Gly is actually a friend of mine. I asked for a favor to retrieve you."

I was stunned. I stumbled backwards to look at him.

"Why?" That was all I could get out.

"Look, we need you. In the legends, it is said that someone will come from the other world and help us. I hate to say it, but the queen is starving out the entire kingdom. Although we left that part of the kingdom a long time ago, every day we hear reports that more people are dying. She is destroying the land and killing those who possess any magic. Here we accept the unordinary, those that possess magic or are ancient beings, such as Glyden.

"Sasi, I never brought you here to hurt you. I need your help. The owls have been sensing something, and I can't just ignore them. I need to know what's happening and how to stop it. I can't ignore it anymore." He said all of that with seriousness. *But how was I supposed to save them?*

"Why did I even come here? Why was I sent here? Was the owl in the garden you, too?" I questioned as my voice quivered.

"I do not know why you are here. But I know you must possess some power or else you wouldn't be here. The owl reported back to me that you were with Glyden." His eyes softened, and he took my hands.

"We need you more than ever. You must help us defeat whatever is making some of our people with healing magic sick. Also, you must help us destroy Aurelia." He looked at me with pleading eyes, and I felt like everything he was saying was the truth.

It was hard to wrap my head around all of this, considering I just met him. *Why would a man with obvious power ask for help?* I looked back up at him. I didn't have any magic powers. He must be wrong, but deep inside, I knew there was some truth to it. *Why else would this have happened?*

"I'll help, but I can't guarantee it will..." I was cut off with a body colliding with me. He wrapped his arms around me and held me as I slowly felt my shirt getting wet with his tears.

"I can't thank you enough, Sasi," he stuttered out.

I hoped I could help them even though I did not know how to even start.

CHAPTER

SEVEN

I sat in the war room looking around at the pictures on the wall. It kept showing the rose symbol with the snake near it.

"Okay, I spoke with my warriors, and they confirmed they saw Aurelia's minions in the high pass of the mountain. They're gaining on you, so if you want to help us, we need to act fast." Justorah gazed at me.

"Can we wait for Aubrith? He must know what to do." I kept looking to see if his demeanor would change, but it didn't. Instead, he just nodded and left the room, not looking at me.

I don't even know why I kept involving Aubrith in my decision making. It was like I owed it to him since he helped me get away. There was something about Aubrith that made me feel like I could trust him. He'd saved my life back in Jaklish and tried to save my life when I came from the blue light.

I heard the door open, and to my surprise, it was him. In his glory, with mud of some sort on his face. He reeked of an odor that burned my nostrils. I quickly tried to hide the dry heave that was about to escape my mouth. I've always had a sensitive nose, and certain smells caused an instant reaction. The first time that had happened was at a random kids' birthday party in third grade. The smell of the food he'd brought in was so retched I started hurling. I've worked on controlling that, but still sometimes smells could get the best of me.

"I'm sorry I couldn't get here sooner. I needed to defend my village." He bowed his head towards me. I walked towards him.

"It's fine. I found out Aurelia is evil," I admitted. He looked at me and nodded his head.

"What did you find out about the beloved Aurelia of Bolithium?" Aubrith smirked. A servant brought him a towel so he could wipe his face.

"She cares about money," I admitted. Aubrith nodded his head.

"And?"

"She has a massive army. One that we cannot defeat with what we have right now."

"Well, I'd first start with getting some better armor than what you have," he smirked and looked at my outfit.

I sighed, knowing he was right. I wandered to the armor area of the war room. "After I get changed, then what do we do?" I asked, looking back at him. "Then we defeat Aurelia," he simplified, as if it was the easiest decision.

Justorah heard the comment about my clothes and put himself into the conversation.

"I heard someone needs clothing. I have a fine selection down the corridor for any gender." He smiled proudly and clasped his hands together.

Aubrith grunted and crossed his arms. "Justorah." I had a sense that they didn't really like each other. That's weird, considering Aubrith's mother supposedly saved Justorah's life. I glanced at Justorah and saw his smile drop and his eyes narrow. "Ah, yes. Aubrith. What a lovely surprise. How is your mother? I hope you made it to my home safely." A faint smile had appeared. There was definite tension in the air, but I couldn't pick up on it.

Aubrith was about to speak, but I cleared my throat before he could get a word out.

"Justorah, I need a quick wardrobe change, please. The clothes I got from the palace have holes in them now. Do you have anything more comfortable?" I kept my gaze on Justorah, hoping whatever tension between him and Aubrith would fall flat. Justorah turned his gaze to me, and his eyes softened slightly.

"Sasi, darling. You can have anything of mine." Justorah turned towards a servant and screamed at them to take me to the wardrobe room right away.

The servant guided me down the corridor to where a small courtyard was with statues of creatures I've never seen before. There were roses everywhere in the courtyard, like the ones I saw in the garden. The servant led me to a room that was all maroon inside with little blue flames, keeping the room lit.

"Let me know if you need anything," the servant announced. They shut the door behind them. I glanced at the massive room with almost every gown and suit imaginable. There were also some fresh linen clothes in one section of the closet. Each section had drawers that also had jewelry to go with every outfit. *Justorah must be very rich.*

There was armor in one section that differed slightly from the type of armor at the palace. This was black plated with maroon trim on the edges of the metal. I opened a door that was slightly ajar to see an array of swords with a rose emblem and a snake on the side of the swords. I went back to the linen clothes and opted to wear the black linen long-sleeve shirt with the matching black pants. He had black shoes of different sizes I put on, considering the shoes I came in had holes in them.

I looked at myself in the mirror that was to the side. I noticed how awful my hair truly looked. My braid was loose, causing fly-away hairs all around. I redid my braid when I heard yelling coming from the corridor.

I quickly finished braiding my hair and cracked the door. I glanced back to the weapon area, and without a second thought, I tightened the holster around my waist and took one of the light swords with the snake emblem on the side. I peeked my head out of the wardrobe room again and heard no sound. I walked quietly and stayed close to the wall to enter the war room.

"Aubrith?" I whispered as I re-entered the war room.

"Get down," he whispered back. I quickly obeyed. I wished this was some sort of twisted dream, but every time I looked at my sword, I got the sense that it wasn't. Before I knew it, the main door burst open.

A green creature with four ears and four eyes jumped

into the war room and started searching for someone, which I assumed was me. It had blood dripping from it already, and the creature started breathing heavily until it stopped above where I was crouching. I held my breath, fearing for the worst.

Lunging from its position, I ducked and dodged it. The creature came back towards me, extending its claws until I moved my sword to go the same way it was coming at me. My sword sliced through the creature's hand, leaving smoke to elude.

A loud screech came from the creature as its eyes were bloodshot. The creature came back to me with more force. I dodged the creature again and got back up, jabbing the sword in its chest. The creature stumbled back as a light came from its chest until it vanished.

I breathed heavily and tried to realize what just happened. My mind snapped back to reality once I heard more screams from the palace. I ran outside the war room and saw multiple green creatures attacking people in the palace. I sliced through one creature fighting a young boy, which led me to lunge my sword at another. They kept vanishing as soon as my sword hit them, which I didn't know why.

I felt a weight on my back until I realized one creature was on me. I ran backwards, slamming its body into the wall. I quickly grabbed my sword, but I was too slow. The creature knocked the sword from me and reached around me, grabbing my neck. My legs dangled, and everything was becoming fuzzy. I gripped at the creature's hands as they tightened around my neck, but I felt like it was no use. Justorah appeared out of nowhere and put his hand up, causing the creature blow up into dust. I clutched my throat as I dropped back to the floor and started coughing.

"Sasi, are you okay?" Justorah asked as he crouched down next to me, trying to usher me to a safer area. I saw my sword still on the ground and went back to grab it.

I saw one creature pinning Aubrith against the wall. I looked at my sword, and an idea came to mind. I threw my sword at the creature's back, which went through the creature's back and plunging out its chest. Aubrith took a deep breath and smiled at me.

"Good one," he smiled. I offered him my hand. "Looked like you needed some help," I smirked, and he shook his head.

"I had him." Aubrith crossed his arms. *God, he is stubborn.* "Yeah, it looked like you had him," I laughed and looked around the palace, realizing all the rest were dead.

"What were those creatures?" I asked as I straightened out my black linen outfit. I tried to brush off the dust.

"I do not recall knowing those creatures, but there's more coming. We must advance to somewhere safe," Aubrith said, walking away from me.

"Why can't we fight them?" I crossed my arms.

"There's too many of them, and Aurelia might want more of them. Our world is slowly dying, and she is more focused on her power than her people. She must be working with someone evil. Even though I know she hates magic, she may like it if it's for her own benefit." He emphasized and looked through the window, gazing at the sky.

"Look, the blue light where you came from keeps opening. We need to find out why." He walked away from me and walked down the hall.

"And where are you going?" I asked, running to catch up with him. "We need to talk to figure out a plan for this ludicrous time." He turned down the hall and put his sword in his belt. It was still hard for me to wrap my head around. *How could a woman who lived in a beautiful castle want to destroy the world?*

EIGHT

We entered the throne room, which caused my nostrils to burn because of the smell of the creature's dust still lingering. The marble floor had a black tint stained into it and banners had claw marks through the thread.

"Justorah, what were those...those...creatures?" Aubrith breathed heavily, and his hands were trembling as he swallowed down his own saliva. For someone who was as muscular as Aubrith, I would've never expected him to be shaken up by fighting. *I thought he did this for a living.*

"I honestly have no clue. I'm working with my men to get samples of their remains so we can locate them or at least find out where they originate from," Justorah admitted as he paced around with blood dripping from his formerly fancy apparel.

"Sasi, I am so sorry this is all happening. I wish we could figure out what is going on, but as of right now, I know nothing. All I know is we need to do something fast." Justorah finally sat on his throne and slowly took off his bone crown to run his hands through his platinum hair. He slicked his hair back and rubbed his eyes.

"There has to be something. My mother might help, or Glyden can get some information through other realms with his own powers. There has to be something!" Aubrith flailed his arms around, shouting in the empty stoic throne room. His voice echoed throughout the throne room, causing me to flinch.

The silence after Aubrith spoke felt like ages. I couldn't help but stare at the black dust stained on the marble floor. I still didn't know how I was a natural fighter when in my realm, I'd never fought a day in my life. I looked outside to the purple sky and saw that the blue light had reappeared.

"That light is still here in this world. You'd think it'd close by now," I spoke out loud, trying to fill the silence lurking in the room.

"It won't leave until a certain magic is used to destroy the portal. The skilled warrior can save us from that magic, but I think the magic is already in this realm." Justorah sighed into his hands. I sat staring at the light until a thought came to my mind.

"What if we go to the source of the magic?"

Aubrith looked at me and broke into laughter.

"You're not serious, right? There would be a lot of magic sources all over. I don't even know where they're located. My mother doesn't even know." Aubrith crossed his arms, having an arrogant tone in his voice. I didn't get how he could be so arrogant. It annoyed me.

"Sasi, we have thought about this before in this

world. The only source of the magic is close to the light. Glyden located it before. It led him to the light and obviously we can't go into the light, so we're left here to die out and the rest of the kingdoms will fall with us."

"You may not go into the light, but I can. I mean, I came from it, so why can't I go into the light?" I shifted my posture to cross my arms. Aubrith and Justorah had this wild look on their faces, which scared me a little.

"That's a perfect thought, Sasi. We could send you something to trap the magic or to locate the magic. Glyden could help with this. One second, let me summon him to see if this would work." Justorah lifted his hand and a white energy source appeared. He whispered something in a foreign language, and the light kept getting brighter until he snapped his fingers. Glyden's antlers appeared first and shined bright enough to light up the entire room. His whole body reappeared with his white fur radiating.

"You summoned me?" Glyden questioned as he bowed his head towards Justorah. "Yes, well, we have a proposition, and I want to know if it would work." Justorah put back on his crown and moved his hand under his chin in a thoughtful position.

"Okay, go on with it." Glyden shook his body and closed his eyes, waiting to hear the news.

Justorah looked towards us, and Aubrith nodded as if giving Justorah approval to tell Glyden.

"Well, you saw the creatures that came into the castle today, right?" Justorah asked Glyden.

"Yes, of course I saw them. They had to have a witch's help or someone on the inside to get past the barrier you cast over the castle." Glyden furrowed his bushy white eyebrows.

"Yes, but they're going to come back. We need to get to the major source of the magic for this madness to stop. We can't take another attack like that, neither can any other kingdom. I won't allow it." Justorah stood up and got closer to Glyden.

"What do you suggest we do? We can't go into the light. It's too dangerous." Justorah took a deep breath and put his hand on Glyden's fur. "Sasi can get through since she came in. She's the key we've been missing in this realm. And I think you should go with her. Aubrith is going to go with her, too."

Aubrith shifted uncomfortably and walked forward. "You never said I was going with her. It is up to her and Glyden." Aubrith crossed his arms again and looked annoyed.

"Aubrith, she will need protection. Now, I will have to think of a spell or a tonic you can have to be safe for both of you to travel through, but this is our only choice." Glyden still stayed silent through all the talking, as if he was thinking through something.

"I don't think Aubrith will make it through. I know I might if I link to Sasi." My heart raced.

"Wait, what do you mean link? And I'm not letting you both risk your life for me." Justorah shifted to face me. He wasn't expecting me to raise my voice, and neither were Glyden and Aubrith.

"Sasi, I assure you; this is what I'm meant to do. It is my duty to risk my life for the greater sake of my realm," Glyden said calmly. Aubrith looked at me and looked back at Justorah. His gaze moved to the dust and ripped banners.

"I'm in. My mother would want me to do this, so here I am. What do we have to do?" Aubrith gripped his sword. He spoke with so much confidence. I knew it was an act. Behind his hard demeanor, I knew it scared him to lose his life over some portal. I guess it was a light that could tear his realm apart, according to Justorah. I still had my reservations about Justorah, but he'd saved my life against the monsters.

"I need to find this tonic. I know it's in the ancient books our Lilyas used," Justorah said as he was walking towards the door.

"Lilyas?" I asked as my gaze shifted to him walking out.

"It is the parents of our parents and their parents and their parents and—" Glyden spoke in a rambling matter, but I stopped him before he could continue.

"—I get it, it's like your ancestors." I put my hand on Glyden's fur. "Ancestors is a weird word, Sasi. It's Lilyas." Aubrith now joined the conversation. I rolled my eyes at our cultural differences and returned my gaze to the door, only to realize Justorah had already left. I hoped that there could be a way to end this whole thing. Maybe I could help them and return to my life on the Earth I knew. I stared back at Aubrith.

"You really think this could work?" I asked Aubrith and Glyden.

"I was told to watch you, Sasi. That has been my job. I have to watch you try to do this, too." Glyden looked at me and his eyes softened.

"Who even told you to watch me? I know someone had to. You said it was your duty," I walked closer to Glyden.

"It was Terra. Like I said earlier, maybe you will meet her one day. She is a very busy woman, though." Glyden smirked at me.

"I think we can do this. I don't trust Justorah. I never have. But I believe that if he gets this potion for us to try it, then it's worth it. He helped fend off those beasts," Aubrith admitted as he put his arms at his side.

"Yeah, why don't you trust Justorah? Didn't your mom save his life?" Now it was my turn to cross my arms and look at Aubrith.

"She saved his life a long time ago. It was when everyone wanted this source of magic, and she had to protect it. Justorah's family wanted the magic, but they never said why. All I know is that Justorah was there with his father, and things got out of hand. My mother lost her eyesight in the fighting. Justorah's dad was also a part of Aurelia's people at the time and had my dad persecuted for being with an elf. I have a lot of reasons to be angry with him." Aubrith kept his eyes on the white marble and breathed out slowly.

"You have a lot of reasons to be mad at Justorah's father and family but not him. I mean, he doesn't want to be with Aurelia right now. Maybe he's changed. He lives far away from her and seems to have magic, even when Aurelia doesn't like magic. Give him a chance." I tried to look at Aubrith, but he still wasn't looking up.

"Fine, I guess I judged him a little too hard. But I still

don't fully trust the guy." Aubrith finally looked up and crossed his arms.

"Well, he wants to close the portal. I think that's a win for everyone here." I looked at Aubrith and Glyden. Aubrith nodded his head. Glyden kept looking at me.

"I better go find a room for me to sleep in. The sun is already descending. I will see you guys in the morning, I guess." Aubrith exited the throne room. Glyden and I were left in the room together.

"Maybe I should do the same. What do you think of this whole thing, Gly?" I asked as I went near the elk.

"I don't have any opinion, Sasi. I just want you safe." He brushed past me and exited the throne room.

I sighed and walked into the corridor outside of the throne room. I took in the hallway's images. It was so pristine when I came in earlier, and now everything was torn apart. I walked down the hall and found a servant who was sweeping up some of the dust.

"Is there a room that I can sleep in tonight?"

The servant looked up from what they were doing and walked to the end of the hallway. I followed her since I didn't know what else to do. She pointed to the room on the right. When I entered, it looked like no one had been in there in years. There was dust everywhere and even cobwebs. I sat on the bed, which brought up more dust. I laid down as it showed the night sky across the way from the bay window.

CHAPTER

NINE

I woke up in the cracked stone room, which had a musty smell to it. This temple didn't have the best living conditions. I oddly felt at home here than I did at the original palace I was in. I scanned the room and saw books with inches of dust spread onto them. Whoever was in this room before me hadn't been here for a while.

I used my chamber pot to relieve myself. Stepping into the bathtub made of marble, I felt the stinging pain run through my body as my wounds hit the water. I took a deep breath, trying to ease my mind on the fact that I'm going to go back to my home. The place I grew up in. Even though I have a connection to this place, I wanted to get back to the dorms, or at least see my mom.

I got out of the tub and stared at my reflection in the mirror. I knew that when I went back, I wouldn't be the same person I had been a week ago. A part of me still thought this place was a dream. I gathered the white cloth that the servants of Justorah had given me. As soon as I put them on, I felt the breeze flow through from the open window in my room. I stared at the blue light as it lit up the sky.

"Sasi?" Aubrith walked in.

"Haven't you heard of knocking?" My voice came out high pitched from being startled.

"I'm sorry, but Justorah said that they made the tonic, and well, today might be the day." He awkwardly scratched his neck.

I smiled at him as we walked down the giant hall that led to the throne room. The hall was filled with men in the clothes I was wearing, but they were reading books and talking animatedly. They all cast gaunt looks our way and walked by us in hushed tones. I looked up at Aubrith, and he just shrugged as if to let me know that he didn't know why they were acting weird.

"Hello, Sasi! Come! Sit!" Justorah screamed as we walked into his throne room. His attire today was different. He looked slightly relaxed in a shirt that resembled mine, but he had red thread embodied with the rose symbol in the middle. He had leather pants and wore black boots that were stained with mud.

"Ah yes, my outfit isn't my usual one, but that's because I was sparring outside earlier. But come, I want to show you what you will do to get past the guards that are stationed on the mountain pass." He must've sensed that I was looking at his outfit. Justorah excitedly took a seat on a round wooden table with books and wooden cups filled with a blue drink.

Aubrith and I sat on the rustic wooden seats that creaked when we sat down. Justorah summoned Glyden by whispering in another language again. A bright white light appeared in the room and before we knew it, Glyden appeared and shook his antlers.

"There, I have everyone present. Anyway, I need you all to drink this." He handed us our wooden cups and held a wooden bowl for Glyden. "Not to be rude, but what is it exactly that we will drink?" Aubrith and I looked to Justorah for answers, but he just laughed.

"It's the tonic for you all to go into the portal, of course! What did you think it was?" Justorah rolled up his sleeves and crushed some sort of white plant into all our drinks. "There, now you can drink it."

Aubrith didn't waste any time and chugged the whole drink. He gagged after he drank it then looked to me. I hesitated before I plunged the smooth, stout drink down. It tasted as if it was a mixture of vomit and glue. It took everything in me not to throw it up. The lining in my eyes filled with tears from the disgust I felt.

"And Glyden, why aren't you drinking?" Justorah looked at him as he pushed the bowl towards him again. "Well, from the looks of those two, they don't seem to like it."

"Glyden, you must drink. Then I can tell you all the plan once you go to the other realm." Glyden reluctantly drank the tonic, and he heaved with every lick he took.

"Now that we have that out of the way, I must tell Sasi something very important. So Aubrith if you wouldn't mind stepping out briefly, and Glyden, you're dismissed but only for a short amount of time." Justorah waved his hands at the two of them before repositioning himself in front of me.

Aubrith went out of the throne room, and Glyden disappeared. It was only Justorah and I in this vast throne room. He leaned in and whispered, "Sasi, I saw a vision of your mom in the other realm, and I think she has knowledge of our realm. Has she mentioned anything to you in the past?" He crossed his arms and looked at me.

"My mom? No, why would you suggest that? She's busy, yes, but I don't think she would know about this place. It's hard for me to even wrap my head around." I tried to think of anything my mom could've done to be suspicious throughout my life, but nothing came to my mind. She was always a decent mother and provided for me.

"She wears a blue necklace, right?" Justorah now stood to walk around the room.

"Yes, she has always wore a blue necklace around her neck my whole life." I scrunched my eyebrows together. *What did her necklace have to do with anything?*

"Well, that isn't any ordinary necklace, Sasi. That's a necklace from Terra." He turned around to study my body language.

I held my breath and clenched my fists. *Why did this Terra woman keep coming up?*

"Well, it must be a misunderstanding then. A pure coincidence. Anyone can have a blue necklace." I tried to show that he didn't faze me, but my mind had a thousand questions.

"Maybe it is but be careful. Terra isn't, let's say, the nicest person. Her and I have some history. I want these pieces in the other realm. They're the key to everything,

Sasi. It could change this realm, for the better." He looked at me and then walked closer to me. I wasn't even sure this plan would work. I didn't even know what I was supposed to be looking for. I wanted to trust him. After all, he saved my life.

"Sasi, Terra has been around for a very long time. She is powerful. She's letting our realm fall apart, and I need to help save us all." He ran his hands through his platinum hair.

Why would Terra want this realm to fall apart? She'd asked Glyden to watch me. If she was so powerful, why was she letting it fall apart? I felt like Justorah was telling the truth, but it didn't make sense why she sent Glyden. Maybe he didn't know Glyden worked for her.

"What are you talking about? The pieces in the other realm?" Justorah looked at me with this wicked glare in his eyes.

"You'll know soon enough. When you get what you're looking for, bring them back to me, okay? I really want to save this realm. I don't want any more of those beasts coming around." He touched my arm then called Aubrith and Glyden back into the room. Before Aubrith came in, Justorah held out his hand, and his eyes glowed blue. "Give this to Aubrith. He will know what to do with it when the time comes." It looked like it was a metal straw of some sort, but one end was closed. There was golden cursive writing on it. The writing vanished before I could even comprehend it was there. I gulped, even though my throat was so dry I thought it could bleed. My breathing intensified as he handed over the device. "You're going to do great, Sasi. You wouldn't be here if it weren't true. I'll be watching you along your journey, and I'll try to keep Aurelia occupied." He gave a smirk, even though his eyes filled with sadness. I knew he didn't know if I were to see him again.

I leaned over and hugged him, taking in his aroma of pine needles and mint. We stayed like that for a while until he pulled away to find Aubrith and Glyden staring at us.

There was a man in a dark-maroon hooded cloak by the doors. He was the same man who had let us in the other day. His markings were still the same, although they looked like a fresh tattoo. I walked over to Aubrith and Glyden.

"Are you ready, Sasi?" I gazed into Glyden's honey eyes. I noticed he was thinking about something.

"As ready as I'll ever be." Aubrith smirked at me and shook his head. I handed him the object that Justorah gave me. "Justorah told me you have to take care of this and that you'd know what to do with it when the time comes." Aubrith examined the object and put it in his satchel. "It's a Tetyr. It's made for opening specific objects that aren't made to be opened. I don't know why we will need it, but I'll keep it."

Justorah whispered something to the bald man with the markings and walked over to us. "Farewell again. My good friend here will show you out of the palace. Watch your step and watch out for the wolves."

I gave Justorah one last wave goodbye. We walked with the man in the hood. He opened the mountainous door, and we walked through the corridor. I noticed that the banners that were barely hanging on the wall the other day were perfectly in place. The walls of the corridor were wet from the humidity and the corridor smelled of mildew. The man in the hood held out his hand and touched one stone, which opened another part of the palace. It amazed me that this palace seemed to keep growing every time I walked through it.

We walked down the curving stairs that seemed to never end. I tried not to look down because it would make me nauseous, which I didn't want to happen, considering I barely started my journey.

He got to the end of the stairs and whispered something under his breath. The wall opened, moving stone after stone.

"This way, Sasi. There should be a group of Links ready to assist you down the path. I wish you luck. May the Goddess bless you." His eyes glowed blue as he put his hood back on. He walked back up the steps. I looked outside the opening and realized it was where we came in from but from a different angle.

The mud seeped into my boots as I felt a slight mist of rain coming down. I pulled up my hood and slowly started walking on the path, trying not to slip from the mud on the stones. We got to the end of the path, and there wasn't anyone there.

"Where're the Links?" I peered at the tree escaping above the fog and saw a faint figure camouflaged in the tree with gloves on.

"I think you answered your own question." Glyden smirked and walked past me. I realized that the end of the path was on the side of a mountain. There was a dirt path going in a zigzag motion, disappearing under the clouds.

"This doesn't look dangerous at all," I sarcastically mentioned. Glyden went first and went slowly, making sure not to hit any rocks still stuck in the gravel. Aubrith gestured for me to go next. I sighed and tried to follow the step Glyden took, but it was hard considering he had four footprints.

The squishing sound under the shoes I wore was all I heard going down the mountain as we slowly descended into the cloud. The air was cool around me and for a moment, and I forgot I was in another place. It felt like I was on a hiking trail back in Earth. I couldn't see the Links in the trees anymore, which I thought was strange.

"Glyden, are we still, okay? I haven't seen the Links for a while." I stopped. I motioned for all of us look around.

"Do you hear that?" Glyden whispered. I stayed silent to hear whatever Glyden was hearing. The fog was so thick that I could barely even see Glyden in front of me. Aubrith must've felt the same because I felt his hand on my shoulder.

"Get down!" Aubrith pushed me down as I saw an arrow whiz through the air, barely missing Aubrith. Glyden walked down the hill faster, and I followed in suit, considering we couldn't see anything. More arrows kept passing us, and one ripped a piece of my clothing as it went by. Before I knew it, I felt one of my knives from my side escaped the hilt. Aubrith threw the knife in the middle of the fog, earning a grunt from whatever he hit.

As we ascended further down the hill, the thing

Aubrith hit was one of the queen's soldiers. He laid flat with the knife in his chest, and his bow and arrows lay beside him. Aubrith took the knife out of the man and wiped it with his shirt.

"Here you go." Aubrith held out the knife in his hand.

I reached over and grabbed it from him, putting the knife back in my hilt.

"How did you know he was there?" Aubrith smirked and picked up the bow and arrows. "I didn't. I was just trying to see if he was in that area, and I guess he was." Glyden rolled his eyes and kept walking on the trail.

"We have to be careful. There will be more. I'm guessing he was their scout." I nodded my head in response and followed Glyden.

We kept walking and finally reached a stream. Glyden went first to investigate the area to see if anymore of the queen's guards were there. As he started walking out into the open, I noticed there were foot-prints on the other side of the water.

"Glyden, it's not a good idea. Let's keep moving, and we will settle down in another area." Glyden moved his antlers in agreement and started following Aubrith and I down the path again. There was smoke coming from the end of the stream.

"I'll go first, Sasi. You go towards the back and Glyden try to find a safe area," Aubrith pleaded. Glyden looked slightly annoyed but obeyed anyway and lay down in the grass's rough.

I went off the path and headed into the forest area. I saw Aubrith approach the camp slowly with his dagger drawn, ready to strike. He looked around and kicked a branch that was laying there out of disappointment. He put his dagger away. As he was turning around, there was a figure standing in front of him.

He panicked and tried to reach for his dagger, but he was too late. The attacker put him in a chokehold and yelled out, "Where is she?" Aubrith shook his head, notifying them he didn't know where I was. I took a deep breath and closed my eyes, hoping that they wouldn't kill us before we even started this mission. I slowly stood up with my hands in the air, approaching Aubrith and the attacker. As I got closer, more soldiers appeared out of the grass. They pulled out their swords, making a slick noise as the blade came out from their hilt. The sound alone sent a shiver down my spine as I kept walking straight.

"Ah, so nice of you to join us. We were just having fun with your friend here." The man wore a hood over his head and looked like he was wearing a robe of some sort, but the rest of the surrounding men were fully armored.

"Yes, it really is such a shame. Let him go, and you can take me, okay?" The man considered the idea for a moment then dropped Aubrith out of his clutch. There was a dark-red mark on Aubriths neck from the grip of the man. Aubrith slowly breathed and gasped as if he was on his last breath. I looked back up at the man, and he laughed at Aubrith's gasps. "Some protectors," the man sneered at Aubrith on the ground and motioned the other men to grab him.

"What are you doing? Take me, not him. I told you not to take him." I pleaded in disbelief at what was happening. The man's hearty laugh echoed in the camp-site. "I believe you said for me to let him go, which is what I simply did." He smirked in my direction. I tried to march towards him, but it felt as if they glued my feet to the ground. "What's wrong? You can't move? Oh! What a pity, you see I'm not an ordinary soldier." He snapped his fingers and my feet moved. My stomach sank, knowing that he could control what I did. My knife dropped to the ground, and I didn't even release it on my own. He did. "Alright well let's walk to back to the castle then." He turned around and suddenly I walked with him. I didn't know what to do, but I closed my eyes and wished something would stop this from happening.

In my head, I imagined talking to Glyden. *Glyden are you near us?* I thought in my mind, hoping he could read my thoughts. *Be patient and keep him stalled, Sasi. I'm always closer than one can see.* I heard his voice echo in my mind, and a smile instantly formed on my face.

"So, you never exactly told me what you are," I told the man in the robe. "It's not important. Nothing you can do can stop me from letting me take you to the queen." He kept walking, and I realized his feet had chains on them as if he was a prisoner.

"Why do you wear chains on your feet?" He stopped in his tracks and slowly turned his head to me.

"The real question is how can you see that?" He was about to pull off his hood for me to see his face, but he cowered to the ground, as all the other soldiers did.

They covered their ears and tried to hide against something as if there was something terrifying. They all reached for their eyes, but before they could, blood oozed from their eye sockets, which caused me to gag. They all fell to the ground and Aubrith looked at me, wondering what happened.

"It's really rude of you guys to tell me to go somewhere safe when you guys need me to save you." I heard Glyden's hooves crinkle in the soil, his figure appearing in front of us.

"How did you—" but before Aubrith could finish his sentence, Glyden talked over him.

"How could I what? I am an ancient elk. Of course, I would have magic flowing through me." Glyden rolled his eyes and started walking away from us.

"Wait, where are you going?" I asked him as he turned his back to us.

"I'm going to the light, of course. That's what we came to do in the first place. We can't wait here for the night. There's more of them coming and with bodies laid here, they'll be furious and want revenge. We need to get to the other realm and find the pieces to help close the portal. We don't have time for rest."

Aubrith and I looked at each other before we started walking on the path again behind Glyden now.

CHAPTER

TEN

My feet throbbed as we kept walking. The sound of the dirt crinkling as my shoes pressed down with every step was white noise to me after a while. I kept wondering what my mom in the other realm was doing. *Was she looking for me?* I knew I'd seen her in the light back at the palace, but maybe it had been an illusion. I tried to push past the negative thoughts that kept coming in. Finally, I looked up from the ground, only to see Aubrith looking at me.

I caught him as he tried to play it off, as if he was thinking about something serious. I brushed it off, not wanting to make things more awkward between us.

I looked up and saw that it was early morning here. The sky was lilac with stars faintly showing. There was no vegetation around us. Just the red dirt that I'd landed in when I came to this realm. If someone tried to get us, we'd be easy targets.

I noticed Glyden drag his back hooves as we were nearing towards the light.

"We could stop if your legs are hurting you," I spoke louder so Glyden could hear above the breeze.

"Sasi, the light is in sight. We can't waste any time. We have to keep moving, and I will rest in the other realm."

Glyden picked up his pace, leaving Aubrith and me behind. I looked at Aubrith and noticed he had his eyebrows drawn together as if he were deep in thought.

"What's wrong?" I nudged my elbow into his side to get his attention.

"We haven't seen the queen's men since the last campsite. Isn't that a little weird?" he finally spoke up after a long pause. It was strange that no one else was near us. The queen wouldn't just back off her men. She would've sent more.

I noticed Glyden stopped a few yards away from the light itself.

"Glyden, what is it?" I drew my knife, looking around us.

"In the distance, there are some rocks. I sense the guards over there. Probably archers. I was holding back so we could all run together and hope for the best." Glyden gave his best hopeful smile and shook his antlers.

"Ladies first." Aubrith nudged me forward towards the captivating light. The light made soft sounds like waves crashing together. It seemed so peaceful, yet I knew that wouldn't be the case.

We all looked at each other wearily, not knowing if this would even work. I closed my eyes and took a deep breath. Aubrith snuck his hand inside of mine, and I unconsciously squeezed it. I patted Glyden's fur as he nuzzled into me.

"Are you guys ready?" I asked as my legs wobbled. The pit in my stomach grew as I saw a bunch of little black dots in the distance, knowing those were bows at the ready.

"Let's do this." I dropped Aubrith's hand and stopped petting Glyden, knowing what was to come next.

Those were the last words we said before we ran for our lives. Dust flew up around us, engulfing my lungs. All I remember was seeing arrow after arrow almost hitting my feet as I keep running. The whizzing of the arrows flying echoed around me as I dived into the light that had sent me here.

I felt warmth all around me and events in my life being projected in the light before everything around me turned cold and black.

CHAPTER
ELEVEN

I heard cars honking and sirens in the distance. The various sounds of people talking and calling for taxis lingered. I opened my eyes to see blurry clouds above me. It was dark outside, meaning it had to be nighttime. I glanced around and noticed the buildings illuminating the sky with endless amounts of lights. I could see a cellphone tower in the distance blinking its red light. I sat up and felt around me, realizing that I was on cement and had to be super high in the air.

The realization hit me; I was still on top of the hospital. Thoughts about Glyden and Aubrith flooded my mind. *Did they make it here, too?* A large grunt coming from Aubrith, who lay on the cement a few feet away, quickly answered me.

"Aubrith are you okay?" I quickly went to his side to see if he was hurt.

"No. Why is this realm so noisy? My head hurts, and there are so many bright things all around." He rubbed his head. Aubrith looked around, gazing at all the lights. He took a step towards the edge before he jumped back.

"What's wrong?" I went over to see if the snake was there again.

"We're so high up." His legs looked wobbly as he slowly went to sit again.

"Aubrith, are you scared of heights?" I tried to hide the laugh that escaped, but it was too late.

"No. I am not. I don't think that we should be this high up." He crossed his arms and sat for a moment, taking in the scenery again.

"Sure, whatever you say." I laughed as I saw him trying to stay far away from the edge.

"Where's Glyden?" I looked around the top of the building and noticed a dark complexion of a man's arm behind the air system. I slowly approached the man, only to realize the man was naked and seemed to be unconscious.

I glanced away from the man and walked back to Aubrith, trying to forget the mental image in my head.

"Did you find him?" Aubrith looked toward where I'd come from.

"Well, I found a man, so I hope that's him, or it's a naked man sleeping on top of a hospital."

"Wait, what? A man? Glyden is a magical elk? And what is a hospital?" Aubrith looked extremely puzzled.

"I think Glyden turned into a man to make it into this realm. I know Justorah talked to him, so maybe they talked about this. I forget you're not from my realm. A hospital is a place where people go when they're injured or sick."

It seemed like Aubrith was trying to process all that I said until he opened his mouth again.

"Why can't people just go to a healer or drink a potion? Why do they have to go to an actual place? This realm seems to have all these unnecessary things." He puffed his chest and kept looking around New York City.

"I honestly don't know. I think the main reason is because we're in the United States. Besides, you've literally been in this realm for five minutes. Stop judging it." I picked at my boots that had a tear in them.

"What? Sasi, I think you could do better on names for a realm." Aubrith chuckled to himself and shook his head.

"No, like this realm has different places in it, just like your realm has different places in it. We are just in one of those places." Aubrith seemed to process what I was telling him before we heard a grunt from where the man was.

"Glyden, we're over here!" Aubrith yelled in the direction.

A man peered over the air system. He had black curly hair and the same caramel eyes. He was very well built considering his shoulder muscles also could be seen from when he glanced in our direction.

"Guys, we made it!" Glyden exclaimed as he fully stood up.

"Glyden, please get some clothing. I have seen you in all your glory before, but you need clothes now. You don't have fur to cover you." I said, glancing anywhere but Glyden.

Glyden suddenly reached to cover himself.

"Where shall I get clothing? Is there a clothier near-by?" Glyden looked towards me with pleading eyes.

"Sadly no, but there are employee lockers and maybe a hospital gown you could borrow." I moved towards the elevator doors that were a few feet away.

"Lockers? I'm sorry, but what is that?" Glyden followed me towards the elevator with Aubrith trailing along.

Oh, this is going to be a long journey. I slightly shook my head.

The elevator dinged, and the metal doors opened. Aubrith and Glyden looked in amazement as I stepped in.

"Well, don't just stand there. Get in!" I laughed to myself and both hurried in.

"Is this a teleporter?" Aubrith asked in all seriousness.

"No... Well yes, this kind of is, but oh well." I struggled to find the words to explain to him what an elevator was.

The doors swung open again, leading us to an empty hospital floor. The walls were painted white and a little blue line on the floor following the sign that said, "employees only," which led me to pull Glyden in that direction.

There was a number pad on the door, which I quickly typed in my mom's code, hoping not to get caught. The green light appeared on the door, and the lock unlocked. We stepped into the room leading to the row of lockers. Thankfully, no one was in the locker room.

"Okay, pick a locker and we will take the clothes.

Aubrith we need to change too. I'm afraid your blood-stained tunic and my dirty clothing won't suffice the world out there." Aubrith looked at his outfit and his face fell slightly.

We picked three random lockers to unlock. Aubrith got to wear a sweatshirt, jeans, and loafers. Glyden was in a tight suit where the pants were raised to his shin. I, unfortunately, opened a locker that had a very oversized t-shirt and jeans.

"Sasi, I think this garment is supposed to be looser, don't you think?" Glyden said hopefully.

"We have to wear this until we get to my house. Once we get there, we can change into better clothes." Glyden gave a small nod as he uncomfortably walked towards the door.

"You guys follow my lead, and we will get out smoothly." They both nodded.

A woman walked by us in the hallway, glancing in Glyden's direction. She briefly smiled before continuing to walk.

"Glyden, you are already getting women." Aubrith rolled his eyes at Glyden who was completely oblivious.

"I'm sorry, it isn't mating season, and I cannot reproduce," Glyden walked to the elevator. I smiled at the two of them bickering and walked into the elevator behind them, pressing the first-floor button.

As the doors opened, I peered around the corner, making sure no one was there. I looped my arms around Aubrith and Glyden as we walked out of the elevator and towards the sliding doors. I felt a drop of rain on my face as soon as we stepped outside.

"Okay, we have to walk quickly to my mom's apartment so we can at least get better clothes than what we are wearing." I turned and looked at Glyden and Aubrith, noticing that they were taking in their surroundings.

"Do we have to walk as fast as them?" Aubrith pointed around us at random people walking to their destination.

"Yes, and also it is bad to point at people here." I grabbed Aubrith's and Glyden's arms as we walked through the streets of New York City. I noticed they were getting distracted by looking at the various people around us. They kept talking to themselves about the people they observed. I would hear comments about how people dressed.

Walking through the crowd, we kept getting pushed and shoved, which I knew was annoying Aubrith. Every time we got pushed, he would say, "I could kill them right now." Glyden was quite the opposite. Every time he got pushed and shoved, he would simply say hello and want to talk to the person about their life. Of course, this made people walk away even faster.

The rain intensified, making it hard to see what was in front of me. When it normally rained like this, I would always carry an umbrella so I could at least see where I am going. However, this was a unique situation, considering that I was in some random nurse's clothes.

After the twenty-minute walk, I found myself in front of the building that I used to call home. This place held so many memories, but the only memory that seemed to come to my mind was watching my favorite television shows on repeat. I missed lying in bed to watch them.

"Are you guys ready?" They were soaked and shivering. Glyden nodded vigorously, noting that he wanted to go inside already. I went to the side of the building and started walking up the metal stairs.

"I might be new to this realm, but I think we are supposed to use the door to get into a home." Aubrith's teeth were clicking together as he shivered.

"I know that, but I don't have a key into the home, so this will have to work for now," I continued, walking the metal stairs like I had done time and time again.

Aubrith and Glyden shrugged as they followed me up to the third floor of the apartment building.

"Alright, are you ready?" I asked as I was lifting the window to my mom's apartment. Before they could even respond, Aubrith already climbed into the window. I heard a crash and noticed that he didn't realize that he needed to step onto the kitchen counter before touching the ground. I could see through the window that he was holding his leg.

"Please don't do what he just did." Glyden laughed as he swung his legs over the window and onto the kitchen counter. He simply hopped down onto the floor and helped Aubrith up. I swung my legs over and shut the window behind me. Once I got onto the floor, I walked over to the lights to turn them on.

The room was illuminated with my mom's dark-purple walls and granite counter. The house was spotless like it always was. The painting of a tulip still hung on the wall that has been there since I was a little kid. I took in my surroundings, trying to remember what life was like when I lived here. The smell was the same: a scent of lavender and jasmine filling the room. I noticed Glyden was already on the couch making himself at home.

"Are you feeling okay, Glyden?" I walked over to the other side of the apartment to the couch. Glyden was laying down touching his head.

"Yeah, I think I am alright. Do you have any other clothes or maybe a chamber pot I can use? I need to get warm again." I nodded and made my way to the laundry room, grabbing whatever clothes I thought could fit him and Aubrith. I showed him where the bathroom was, too. He stared in amazement at the toilet and flushed several times to look at the water go away. I shook my head as I shut the door to the bathroom.

"Aubrith do you need anything?" Aubrith was too busy opening and closing the refrigerator. "Did you know your food is… cold?" Aubrith was amazed as he kept opening and closing the refrigerator, which he called the "grey box."

"Yeah, the food is supposed to be cold in there." I walked over and finally shut the refrigerator door. He smiled in amazement and ran towards the television. I sighed and went to check on Glyden. I knocked on the door to the bathroom, but he didn't respond.

"Glyden are you okay?" I knocked again, but still, there was no answer. I finally opened the door and saw Glyden gripping the bathtub and panting.

"Hey. Talk to me Glyden." I rested my hand on his back, and he jolted up and shivered.

"I keep seeing the image of a bird in my mind. A bird on what your realm calls a hat, I think. It is a bird, and the hat is very blue and there are metal statues of people coming out of a building," Glyden kept repeating this phrase as his eyes darted back and forth.

"Okay, let's lay down and talk this through. There was a bird and metal statues? Do you think this is the first clue that is coming in for us?" He gripped my hand, and suddenly I saw the image in my head as well. However, it wasn't what I was expecting. It was a person wearing a Toronto Blue Jays hat walking into the stadium.

"I know where that place is. It's in Toronto." He gulped and looked right into my eyes.

"We need to go there. Soon. How can we get there?" He stood up and walked towards the kitchen.

"Well, it's in Canada. That's a whole other country. We need passports and to get on a plane. I have no money so I don't know how we would get there." I paced back and forth, trying to get the image out of my head of the Toronto Blue Jay logo. "I can teleport us there. I could teleport in the other realm. I'm sure I could do it in this realm." Glyden quickly grabbed my hands, but I pulled away before he could do something drastic.

"We need to change our clothes and sleep here for tonight. My mom works at night, so she won't be back until early in the morning. Plus, I am starving. I will order us food and we can discuss the plan over with Aubrith tonight." I grabbed my mom's apartment phone and called the nearest pizza place for a pizza. Aubrith was still amazed by the television and kept flipping through channels. I handed them some of my basketball clothes and sweats.

The pizza arrived, and we all sat around the TV

watching a random show. Aubrith was amazed that they cut the food into triangles. "This food is amazing. I would never put cheese and sauce together. That is insane to me." Aubrith stuffed the pizza in his mouth as Glyden and I looked at him in bewilderment.

"Speaking about insane... We are going to try to teleport to Toronto, Canada tomorrow." I watched Aubrith drop his slice of pizza on the floor.

TWELVE

I grabbed some old backpacks I had and began filling them with essentials. I packed snacks and jackets inside each of the backpacks. Thankfully, I had oversized jackets and sweatshirts from when I was playing basketball, so Glyden and Aubrith could have some clothing.

"Alright, I think we should get ready to let Glyden do whatever he needs to do." I placed the two backpacks in front of them and sat down across from Glyden. I put my hair up as Aubrith grabbed his backpack to see what it was inside.

Aubrith quickly put his sweatshirt over and gripped my hand when we sat down. I blushed as I looked at him but quickly brushed off the feeling. Glyden took Aubrith and my hand in his as he closed his eyes. I got dizzy and feel nauseous. I shook off the feeling as I saw the room getting smaller and colder. Aubrith squeezed his hand in mine, reassuring me I wasn't the only one getting the side effects. I saw pictures of Canada swirling around us.

The CN tower, the Blue Jays, and the Toronto Maple Leafs. Suddenly, the world went black, and I felt like my head was going to explode.

After the pain subdued, I opened my eyes, realizing we weren't in my mother's apartment anymore. I was outside, and faint raindrops hit my face. Aubrith looked as confused as me as we took in our surroundings. I stood up and realized that Glyden was already making his way over to talk to a pedestrian.

"Is he supposed to do that? Are we really in the place of Canada? This place is cold." Aubrith admitted as he shivered.

"I don't know, but I can tell you one thing, we are in Toronto, Canada. You can tell by the baseball field behind us. Those gold statues on the wall that people are taking a picture in front of will let you know that." I brushed my hair back with my hand to smooth it out.

"Why are they coming out of the building?" Aubrith asked, looking up at the statues.

"That I do not know. I wonder what Gly is talking about to that person." Aubrith looked over to Glyden and the random man he was talking to.

"He's probably saying nonsense again and going to scare away the man," I smirked, knowing that Aubrith was probably right. And sure enough, the man walked away from Glyden with a disgusted look.

"Well, how did that go, Glyden?" Aubrith asked with a smirk on his face. Glyden looked defeated by the way his posture sunk.

"I asked where a bird and a needle were and if there was a way to get to the needle." I laughed before it took me a minute to piece together what he was meaning. I looked up and saw the CN Tower right next to us and a line of tourists trying to get their pass.

"We have to wait in that line over there. I've been to Toronto before. They take you up an elevator to the top. It's quite fascinating."

Aubrith and Glyden looked at me like I had three heads. Glyden followed my eyes and looked at the line of people waiting.

"Come on, we have to move. I keep hearing that it is here." Glyden started walking to the CN Tower and stood in line.

We waited in the line where there was a red carpet and music playing.

"So, people actually go up this thing for fun?" Glyden asked. He looked nervous as he bit his nails.

"Yeah, but you have to pay to go up. Hopefully, we can just tell them to put it on my card." The teller called us over, and I let her know three people would go. Before I could pull out my card from my backpack, Glyden looked at her, and his eyes glowed briefly.

"Okay, here are your tickets. Enjoy the view!" The teller said as she called the next people in line.

We walked to the elevator with another group of people before the elevator operator pressed the button to the top.

I gripped Glyden's arm and whispered to him, "Glyden, we didn't pay."

"Hush, I still have powers. We can do anything. The human mind is so weak. I convinced her we paid." I stared at him, even though he had his eyes closed.

Shaking my head in disbelief, I noticed Aubrith looked like he was about to throw up.

"I thought you said earlier you weren't afraid of heights?" I studied Aubrith's face as I smirked at him.

"Oh, I'm not. Maybe it's something I ate." Aubrith assured as he gripped onto the bar of the elevator.

"It's cool that the elevator here has glass all around it and the elevator in the hospital did not." Aubrith sarcastically mentioned as he gripped even tighter on the bar and dry heaved.

"Oh yeah, it's so cool that we are going up super high to see the city." I was having way too much fun with his torture of being afraid of heights.

I tried to take in the view myself. I kept thinking about what this vision would tell us. It's funny how I came here with a team once and my mom. Now I was coming here with two people from another realm, trying to save the world. I guess they were another form of a team going after the same objective. Granted, a basketball game didn't determine the end of a realm. But looking back on my life, I had always been on a team. Whether it's with going to many basketball camps over the years or my mom and I being a team.

Before we got out of the elevator, Glyden pulled on the elevator operator's arm. She looked at him so disgusted and was going to pull away before he asked, "Where is the top of this tower?"

She slowly pulled away and awkwardly smiled at us. "There is an option for the edge experience. You have to talk to the man in the red shirt over there to have that experience. It is wet outside, so I don't think they will do it today." She pushed the elevator button back down before Glyden could reply. We moved through crowds of people, briefly bumping into them just to get to the area the woman told us about.

"Are you guys here for the edge experience?" A man with curly blond hair asked in his red shirt. His green eyes were piercing. "Yes, we are. Can you take us up?" I asked, smiling at him.

"Well, it's slippery right now so we will have to wait." The man replied.

Glyden looked at him with his glowing blue eyes, and suddenly the man responded, "Actually, we can go up. Let me take you!" Aubrith rolled his eyes before we got harnesses on and followed the man.

"I don't like how this thing is fitting me. It is too tight." Aubrith tugged at his harness.

"Can you stop complaining for, like, two seconds?" I looked at him, and he stared right back.

"Do you guys want to help the other realm or not?" Glyden asked both of us. I broke my gaze from Aubrith and crossed my arms. Aubrith smirked until he realized where we were walking to.

"Um, I think you and Glyden can actually take it from here." He tried to walk back, but I shoved Aubrith forward.

"Oh no, I insist you lead the way," I asserted and laughed slightly.

Aubrith gulped and nervously kept tugging on his harness. He kept his eyes straight ahead. I was kind of hoping for another remark from him, but he stayed silent the whole time.

"Alright, you guys will be hooked to me, so please no crazy movements." The man kept smiling as he led us to the very top. The wind was noticeable right away as we climbed to the metal grates. I held onto the wet rail, realizing this probably wasn't a good idea.

We crept around the top, letting the rain and wind mixture hit us in the face and allow us to be drenched. I moved my hand to the concrete behind the railing before I felt a sensation that sent a shiver up my back.

"What is it?" Aubrith yelled over the wind. "It's here," I yelled back. Aubrith reached into his pocket and pulled out the metal straw. The more I looked at it, it looked like a regular pen. The famous pen that was supposed to help us, according to Justorah. He handed it to me, allowing me to press the pen near the concrete. As we kept moving around the edge, the pen would shake until it floated out of my hand.

Glyden smiled. He held out his hand and reached to the pen as he turned it midair. A piece of concrete came out with a tiny crystal shard. It looked like it had faint writing on it, but before I could get a glimpse, Glyden snatched it and put it in his pocket. I quickly gave the pen back to Aubrith before Glyden pulled all of us towards the area we came in. The man from the CN Tower let out a wail before he had no choice but to follow us back.

"Thank you for your time. We have to go now." I smiled at the man working as I unhooked my harness. We were drenched and water fell off our clothes. The man awkwardly waved, trying to figure out what happened. We weaved throughout the crowds in the CN

Tower. Aubrith was petrified by the little kids running around and screaming so much that he was paying more attention to them and didn't realize he bumped into a woman.

"I'm sorry." He helped the girl, who looked around my age, up off the ground. She smiled sweetly at him.

"Oh! You're okay. I have to watch where I'm going." *Seriously? She was trying to flirt with him?* I rolled my eyes and realized why I even cared? Aubrith didn't notice her flirting because he kept walking with Glyden and I. We made it to the elevator to take us down.

"Well, that was easy," Aubrith acknowledged as we got into the elevator. There was only one other man with us, and it was the elevator operator. Except I noticed he wasn't wearing a red shirt like everyone else. He was wearing a button-down and jeans. His hair was slicked back, and he looked like he'd been in a fight with fresh scratch marks on his neck.

Before I knew it, he turned around and his green eyes glowed blue like Glyden's. Aubrith quickly intervened and put himself between me and the man. He grabbed a special knife from his pocket and cut the man with it. The man's skin oozed black, and he grabbed Aubrith's throat. He pushed Aubrith up in the air, making him collide with the glass elevator wall. The man looked at me as he choked Aubrith. I quickly grabbed the pen from Aubrith's pocket and stabbed the man in the neck.

He released Aubrith as he held his neck from the outpour of black oozing from his wound. Aubrith fell to the floor, grabbing his own neck, gasping for air.

"Is he dead?" Glyden asked, opening one eye.

"Well, let's say this pen is useful in other ways." I held the pen, now covered in black liquid.

"If he's in this realm, that means Aurelia sent more of her minions to our world," Aubrith asserted, leaning on the glass. "We have to be careful. We can't let other humans see this." Before we knew it, the man's body vanished, but the black goo remained on the floor.

The elevator dinged open as we all ran out, trying to find a safe location to lay low. Blending into the crowd on the street, we walked with our hoods up from the basketball hoodies. The rain intensified, and Glyden laughed and pulled us into an old bookstore.

"Glyden, what are we doing here? No one is here! More are probably coming." I frantically said, looking around the bookstore that looked like it hadn't been touched in ages.

"I think I know the owner of this place," Glyden assured, walking around before he found an old man rocking in a rocking chair, reading a book.

"Endy?" Glyden approached the man carefully. The old man looked up from his book and looked at Glyden like he didn't know him. "Endy, it's me, Glyden. I'm a human!" Endy laughed and threw the book aside as he rushed to embrace Glyden.

"Glyden, it's so nice to see you again! Who are they? Are they also like you?" This man obviously knew Glyden came from the other realm, but I couldn't piece together the story of how they met. From the looks of the old man, he looked normal. Slightly tan, crooked yellow teeth, white, piercing hair that was parted, and an enormous stomach. He dressed in a flannel and jeans. He had a slight beard that looked like he hadn't cared for it in years.

"These are my friends. They aren't like me, but she is from this realm." I felt the man's eyes pierce into me as he took a step closer.

"You're the girl." I looked at him with wide eyes. *What did he know about me?*

"Yes, I'm a girl." I awkwardly laughed.

The man seemed to sense my hesitation as he explained he'd gotten banished from the other realm.

"How were you exiled? No one gets exiled?" Aubrith leaned against the counter with the register, looking at the old man with disgust.

"Let's just say I was in love with the wrong woman. I paid the price. I have been paying the price. I mean, look at me, I'm mortal. I have aged! I never age." He rested his hands on his stomach before continuing. "There is a tragic love story back home I resonate with. Where a man meets a very attractive and intelligent woman. They fall in love even though it's forbidden. She is a goddess. The man is a mere mortal. The goddess's family made her choose whether to protect the realm or protect the man she loves. She, of course, chose the realm. The man never wanted her to change and the goddess's love for her people was one of the many things he loved about her. Well, it turns out the family wanted her to kill him. She never wanted to hurt anyone, though, and they still never knew if the man died or not. The story is that she killed him, ruled the realm, and they live in peace and harmony to this day." He clasped his hands and gave a brief look towards Glyden before moving around Aubrith and I.

"That's a horrible story. There's no love in that. No love story ends with no real ending." Aubrith stared at the old man with his fist balled up.

"Well kid, sometimes stories just end. They never really give you the full details because no one knows the full details." The old man dusted off some books before looking at Glyden.

"Why did you come here anyway, Glyden?" he looked annoyed to be in our space.

"We are hiding from the Queen Aurealia's minions. I don't want to die in this realm. How sad would that be?" Glyden smirked at the old man, and the old man's smile faltered.

"Aurelia? God, she's still alive? I can't believe she's ruled that long. But of course, by Terra's orders, everyone can do what they will." He crossed his arms and sighed. "How is Terra, Glyden?"

"Oh, she's fine. Still in Guirra." The old man smiled and clasped his hands together. Aubrith and I looked at the two men in disbelief. *How the heck did this man know about Terra?*

"I have dry clothes in the back. You can change while I finish helping the customers." Both Aubrith and I looked around, noticing that we were the only ones in the store. We shook it off and went to the back with Glyden in search of the dry clothes. The floorboards creaked as we moved through the store. I looked at the shelves, and the books looked like no one had touched them in ages, with all the dust piling on their spines. I flipped on the light in the back room that seemed to flicker until it got to a steady glow. Aubrith dusted off the seat that was there and sat down.

The room was hardly even a room at all. There was a sink that was rusted around its edges and a shattered mirror. *How could anyone even use this room?* I took in the area again and noticed the tile had cracks. The tile also had a lot of stains in some places. The shelves contained more dust and cobwebs.

"Ah, here are the clothes." Aubrith handed me a dusty duffle bag that contained oversized Carhart button-downs and jeans. "This is a unique tunic. isn't it?" Aubrith slipped on the button down and tried to look at his reflection in the shattered mirror. "It's not a tunic, but this will keep us warm for the time being."

I turned around and examined the shelves. There had to be books or something in here to be useful for the mission.

I paced back and forth, causing Aubrith to put his hands on my shoulders. "Are you alright?" He asked and quickly took his hands off me before I could even process how close he was to me. I looked into his eyes and took in my breath.

"Yeah, I'm alright. I wanted to find at least something in this room that would help us." I shuffled past him, examining a shelf with four books on it.

Kneeling, I took a book in my hand. The book had to be sitting here for years. It smelled of mold and had layers of dust.

"That book smells so bad." Aubrith put his fingers to pinch the bridge of his nose. I dusted off the book until I noticed a faint sliver of a golden emblem of some sort.

"Do you know what this means?" I handed the book over to him.

"It has to be something from the realm, but all I know is that book has magic in it." Aubrith gave the book back to me and shrugged.

"What do you mean, magic? You can't just drop that bomb on me and expect me to go along with it." I glared at him and stood up.

He ran his hands over his face and glanced at me through his fingers. He sighed and gave me a wavering look.

"The book has that golden emblem because that's what all the books that have magic in them from the realm have. My mom has some back at her house. That's how I know. The person who wrote the book or put the spell in the book is the only one who can read it."

He picked up another book and started scraping off the dust. I examined the book in my hand and started flipping through the pages. Every page was blank except for the cursive gold writing at the very top that was engraved with "J+E."

"Would you by chance think the E in these stands for Endy?" I showed him the letter, and he squinted to see what I was talking about.

"I don't see an E. I'm sorry, I think the rush of running away from people has gotten to you."

He continued to peer down at the remaining books and kept tossing them to the side after he flipped through the pages, only to find nothing in all of them. He sighed and left the room.

He didn't see the letters? I searched the remaining books and saw that each one had the letters "J+E" on them. Endy had to know something, but why did he keep these books in such poor condition if it had a spell in it. Picking up the books, I sauntered back into the room with Glyden and Endy.

Endy gaped at what I was holding and came rushing to me.

"Put those back right now. I'm afraid those aren't for you to be looking through now." He quickly took the books out of my hands, but before he could put them back, I reached for his arm to hold him in place.

"What is the significance of these books?" My eyes glanced down at the books he held and saw sweat form on his brow. He gulped and saw that Glyden and Aubrith were looking at him with expecting answers.

"Well, I told you already. I had a forbidden love with a woman whom I cannot speak about anymore. She gave me these." He wiped his forehead with his free hand, combing through his grey hair. I examined his face and looked into his eyes, which kept darting back and forth to see if I believed him.

Truthfully, I didn't know whether to believe him, but if there was a spell in those books to help us in the future, then it only made sense but to push further.

"So, this girl? Or goddess, was it? Did she leave you anything of importance in these books? Anything to help us out in this puzzle we are trying to solve?" I finally let go of his arm and took a step back. I could tell he was thinking about lying, but his face softened, and he slightly smiled.

"She was a goddess. Well, I should say is a goddess. Glyden knows some of the story, I'm sure. I fell in love with a powerful woman. I am not ashamed to say I still love her with everything I have. I still try to look for her, you know. I wear this necklace that she gave me when we were young. She said it would protect me, and I don't know if it is by luck or this necklace that has kept me alive all these years. You know I have had health problems, and the doctors here have even told me I shouldn't be alive—"

"—Okay, we get it. She helps you. Spit it out, man." Aubrith gave an annoyed huff. I glanced at Aubrith and gave him a dirty look. This man may be the key to helping us out with this thing so I could have a normal life, and Aubrith had no sympathy for him. I rolled my eyes and returned my gaze to Endy.

"Continue with your story. Sorry about Aubrith being so rude." I did a small smile, and Endy looked up to the ceiling and back down again to my eyes.

"Right, as I was saying," he scratched at his beard. He set the books down on a nearby table. "I didn't know. She was a goddess. Or shall I say, *the* Goddess. She was a beautiful girl who was my age. She would often play with the other school kids. She would play with such tenacity it amazed me." He smiled and had a distant look. "I made a mistake when we were growing up. I developed feelings for her, and she said that we couldn't be together. I didn't understand why. This was when the realm was basically one alliance with each other." He sat down in his chair and stroked the necklace.

"It was around that time she had a meeting with her mother. The creator of all of this, and something about that meeting really took a toll on her. She told me she couldn't be with me because of her duty, and back then, I didn't understand that. I don't have powers. I was merely just someone in the realm who she went to school with. But her family wanted her with someone who at least possessed magic of some sort. I mean, later she found that person, and they had a baby girl, but the point is, I found someone else. Someone who I could love. It was her friend Jura, and we just clicked. Then, she hadn't liked that we were together and banished us here before I could even know what was going on. I mean, sometimes I hear from Terra, her sister, through my thoughts, and she tells me what's going on in the realm." He pushed his hair back and sighed.

"I mean, that is a pleasant story about our Goddess, but that doesn't explain the books." Aubrith looked at him with scrunched eyebrows. I rolled my eyes and looked at Endy expectantly.

"Right, you're right. Anyway, Jura goes by a name of Selene here, and well, things didn't work out like I wanted. She left for Ireland, and I haven't seen her in a long time. She didn't like how I wanted to start a life here. She always wanted to go back to the realm and wanted to find a way. I love Earth. Other mortals like me get to age here a lot quicker than over there. The 'J' on the book is for Jura, and the 'E' is for me. She put an enchantment lock on the spells for our eyes only. She thought that these could help us if we ever had a fight with anyone." He smiled to himself and looked down at his gold ring. "I ended up marrying someone here, though. I have children. None of them know about the life I had before this one. I lost my wife a few years ago to this thing called cancer. That's the only time I tried to use these useless spells, and nothing worked. I guess that's a downside of being a mortal." He wiped a tear that fell from his eye. He handed the book back to me and stood up from his chair.

"Maybe you would have more use for them than I did. But you will have to talk to Selene. Last, I know, she was in Ireland. She told me decades ago there was an energy source that could transport her back there. I don't know if she was successful, but if Glyden is here, then something must be wrong in the other realm." He leaned against the counter where the register was.

"We're just trying to find sources that would help close the portal." I glanced at the book and ran my fingers along the edge of the cracked spine. "Do you think this Selene was onto something?" I stared at Endy, and he looked at the ground. "To be honest, I do not know. But it's worth a try. The spells never worked for me. Maybe they will work for her and you. You can take the books. It's not like my grandchildren can read them." He smiled and looked at Glyden.

"Why are *you* here, though, Glyden?" He studied Glyden like he was really trying to read him.

"I'm here to protect her. Terra told me to do that, and here I am." Glyden stood awkwardly near me.

"Well, Glyden, if Terra tells you to do something, you

have to do it." They both laughed. Aubrith and I looked at each other and thought we were missing an inside joke.

"Also, Glyden, people are quite rude to people with a darker skin color here. It's the weirdest thing. Just be careful, don't let the mortals boss you around, okay?" Endy squeezed Glyden's shoulder before walking to the front of the store to help a customer that walked in. Glyden glanced down at his skin and looked puzzled. "That is strange indeed." He mumbled and looked at Aubrith. "I guess you need to be careful too, Aubrith. Maybe it's like their clans or something." I cleared my throat and looked at them both. "Actually, it's racism. Pretty common here on Earth. It's not okay, but yeah, I've even had my fair share of rude things said to me." Aubrith and Glyden looked at me, stunned.

"Well, if I ever meet racism, I will cut their throat for you." Aubrith put his hand on my shoulder.

"Oh, no. Racism isn't a person. I mean, kind of, but it's a way of thinking. It's taught in some families I guess." That made Glyden and Aubrith even more confused. I changed the subject.

"So, are we going to Ireland now or do we keep trying to find the sources?" I looked at Glyden, and he put his hands in his jacket pockets.

"I guess we could. I haven't seen Jura in ages, or I should say Selene. She has probably aged." Aubrith grabbed more of the books and stuffed them in his backpack. I looked at him and saw him grabbing other books in the store.

"What? I need books to read, you know?" He gave me

an annoyed look and kept looking throughout the store to find other books than just the spellbooks. I was just shocked he read books.

Endy came back over to us, looking at us with hesitation.

"If you go to Ireland, take this." He removed his necklace from his neck and gave it to me. The necklace looked in a way like the one my mom always wore. *That's a strange coincidence.*

"Are you sure? You said that this necklace has protected you for a while." I felt instantly calmer when the necklace was in my hand.

"I think you need it more than I do." Endy squeezed my shoulder then embraced me. It was strange how this old man would just willingly hand over his possessions to us. I turned to Glyden. "I guess we're going to Ireland?" Glyden smiled at me. "I guess we're going to Ireland."

THIRTEEN

We said goodbye to Endy and went back out on the streets of Toronto again. People were walking past and talking on their phones, paying no mind to anything else happening in the world. I almost envied them. They didn't have to patch up an entire realm by themselves. They didn't have to talk to an ancient elk every day. I didn't know how good I'd had it with my other life until I wasn't living it anymore. I was living an entirely different one. I missed playing basketball, and I missed my mom, strangely enough. At least being with Aubrith and Glyden helped me be a part of something. I always liked the idea of a team and helping others, which was why I played basketball. I must admit it was weird all the places where we had to go were places where my mom and I have been before.

Someone shoved me on the side of the street, which knocked me off my thoughts. As I looked up, the person's eyes glowed blue, and they smiled at me. I looked to see where Glyden and Aubrith were, and they were still walking ahead. I walked faster up to them and Glyden looked at me weirdly. The person looked strangely familiar in their leather jacket. *I have seen them before.*

"What happened?" he questioned and slowed his walking to a stop. This caused other people around us to get annoyed.

"There was a person who shoved me, and their eyes glowed blue." I tried walking again, and Glyden grabbed my arm.

"That's strange that you can see that, Sasi," Aubrith spoke up and looked around us.

"It is also strange that their eyes are glowing blue. There must be more people from the other realm here. We must lie low. I thought we lost them when we went to visit Endy." Glyden looked around the busy streets only to find a place called Pizza Pizza. He guided Aubrith and I over there, and we sat at a small table.

"Well, you guys worry about everything that is going on. I am going to order this chicken dish." Aubrith went to the counter and started ordering his meal.

I rolled my eyes and kept looking around as if someone was going to attack us.

"Glyden, I need you to do that thing to the lady that pays for this," Aubrith demanded. Glyden sighed and got up and turned to me, "I never knew my powers would get orange coated chicken."

I laughed to myself and kept looking out the window, only to find that the person across the way was the same person who shoved me on the street. They smiled at me, and I turned away to find Aubrith with hot wing sauce all over his face.

"These are fantastic," Aubrith assured, as he pointed towards his chicken wings.

"I'm glad you like chicken wings." I laughed at him, and he frowned as he kept eating.

Glyden was super quiet, pondering about something.

"I sense danger coming towards us. Aubrith finish up your food quickly. We might have to move faster than I expected." Glyden stood up only for the person to put their hands on Glyden's shoulder.

"I think you need to sit down," the person said. They had a gruff voice. I gulped as I locked eyes with them. Aubrith just looked oblivious until he realized a new person sitting at our table. Aubrith got up quickly, but with an invisible force, it pushed him back down into his chair.

"She needs to come back to the other realm, Glyden," the person said to Glyden. *How did they know Glyden's name?*

"If you're from the other realm, then what are you doing here?" I looked at them before Glyden could speak.

"You're a foolish girl if you really think you can find all the pieces of this puzzle. The pieces are hidden for a reason. Now there's no reason for this to be a thing. Go back to the other realm where we can sort this out properly," they assured. I looked at Glyden and could see him analyzing the person.

Aubrith was physically trying to reach for his

weapon, but it was no use considering the person was using magic on him.

"Look, I didn't want this to be ugly, but if you want to have it that way, then I have no choice." The person reached into their pocket, and I threw Aubrith's soda at their face. The hold on Aubrith broke, and he lunged across the table and punched the person in the face.

"Go!" Aubrith shouted and ran out of the pizza place. The three of us ran down the street, pushing and shoving people out of the way. Glyden looked back and saw the person running towards us. Glyden held out his hand and a green force was forming in his palm. I looked at Glyden, and he locked eyes with me and shot the force back towards the person. He made the green force blast on the cement as we ran down the street, startling people around us as we kept moving.

"What the hell was that?" Aubrith jumped as he almost ran into a person on their bike. I ran faster as I heard a blast get near us. One blast almost hit my foot as I kept running. Glyden shot another blast towards a car that was next to the person. The car exploded, causing the person to get tossed to the side with the explosion.

"There, that should take care of him," Glyden said. He pulled Aubrith and I into a random store and kept looking out the window.

"My god is everyone alright outside?" an older woman asked us as she was heading out the door.

"That person walked by, and the car exploded!" Glyden exclaimed.

"Oh dear, that's awful." She walked out of the store, and we started hearing sirens. People were surrounding the area of the blast and checking to see if the person who was chasing us was okay.

"We need to keep moving. There will be more of them everywhere we go in this realm." Glyden rubbed his face with his hands.

"What even were they? And since when can you shoot magic out of your hands?" Aubrith asked. He paced around the area we were in.

"To be honest, I didn't know I could do that, but it benefited us." He studied his hand, and though there was nothing there, his hand was still hot to the touch.

"That was kind of cool, I have to admit." I looked at Glyden, and he smiled.

"Cool? He could've killed innocents! He could've blown our whole cover!" Aubrith exclaimed.

"Shush! People can hear you; you know?" I told Aubrith, and he breathed in and out.

Glyden held out his hands and looked at us expectantly. There were police officers about to walk into the store.

"Grab my hands, quick."

We grabbed his hands, and before I knew it, I was being transported again. I thought about the time my mom and I went on a trip to check out stones in England. I'd been so happy then. The world faded to black before I could relive that memory.

I smelled my mom's cooking. I could smell the spices she would make and the soft music playing in the background. I remembered it was after a basketball game. She said she had to meet a friend, so she missed my game. I had to get a ride from one of my friends on my team back to my house. But when I walked in, I could smell all the spices and hear the music. I remembered being angry at her because she said she was busy, but there she was cooking and being happy. I'd set my bag down and looked at her by the stove.

"So did you win?" she'd pondered as she put the last of the chicken into the pan.

"Yeah, we won by four points. You know you could've seen it yourself." I'd been bitter. I'd been being petty, but who wasn't when they're thirteen?

"You know I couldn't do that, Sasi. I had a very important meeting." She'd sighed as she stirred some sauce in the pan.

"I know you're always busy." I'd attempted to go up to my room, but she'd caught my arm.

"I really wanted to go, but I couldn't. One day you will probably understand what I'm doing to protect us." She'd let go of my arm. She must've realized she'd still been holding it.

"Protect us? Protect us from what? You're a doctor and make good money. At least that's what other kids say to me when we are at school." I'd furrowed my eyebrows. I hadn't understood what she was talking about, nor did I care to. I'd marched upstairs and closed the door but had contemplated the last time I'd tried to slam it and had gotten in trouble.

Still, to this day, as I was thinking about a trip we'd taken to England that summer, I didn't know what she'd meant by protecting me. All I could remember was her with a person in a leather jacket earlier in the week back then. She'd been frantic and did an impromptu trip to England because she'd wanted me to learn more about history. Come to think of it, the man in the hospital had looked like the man from that summer that I saw. The person chasing us also wore a leather jacket. *That couldn't be a coincidence, right?* My thoughts faded again, with Glyden transporting us somewhere. *What was my mom up to all these years?*

FOURTEEN

We landed with a thud on the grass. It smelled of manure all around me. I slowly got up and looked around. I saw Glyden and Aubrith talking with a local man; he looked to be in his mid-twenties. I slowly got up and brushed leftover grass off my pants.

From all that thinking about my mom, I had an immense headache. Or maybe it was the fact that we'd transported somewhere. I could hear cows mooing in the distance. I walked over to them and yawned.

"Nice of you to join us. Glyden took us to the wrong place," Aubrith pointed out as he squinted his eyes towards Glyden.

"I didn't take us to the wrong place. I simply saw the pictures and went for it. I had nothing else to work with." Glyden crossed his arms and turned back to the other man, who was scratching his neck nervously.

"Where exactly are we?" I asked, wondering if anyone would tell me what was actually going on.

"You're in England," a man announced as he scratched his stubble. He was quite attractive to my initial glance at him.

"Uh, thanks. I'm Sasi, by the way. I hope they didn't cause you too much trouble." I smiled at the man.

He seemed to calm down a bit and put his hands down at his side.

"It's not a problem, really. They said they were trying to get to Ireland, but I went to go check on my cows and goats, and here you were in the grass." He chuckled. I smiled at him again, noticing that he was blushing.

I looked at Aubrith, who was glaring at the man. I rolled my eyes and finally looked at Glyden. He had someone else's shirt on. But it looked like it was a woman's shirt.

"Whose shirt is that?" I asked Glyden.

"Oh, that sweet lady over there gave it to me. I landed in manure. The people here were quite nice to us. They even asked us if we wanted to stay the night in their barn." Glyden gleamed, and he tried to pull his shirt down a little since it was cropping.

"It's no problem, really. We can even give you a good meal. Your friend here said that he wanted to see some stones. The stones are just down the road, so I can take you there tomorrow." The man looked proud of himself for talking to me again.

"Thank you for allowing us to be a part of your home." I smiled. He blushed and made his way back to his house.

"What the heck was that?" Aubrith asked me.

I shrugged and followed the man down the path to

his house. Once we entered the house, it smelled of fruit tea, and different spices.

"Oh, sorry. I make my own tea, so the house can be overpowering." He scratched his neck. I noticed that scratching his neck was a nervous tick of his.

"The smell is quite—" Glyden was cut off by me as I nudged him with my elbow. "The smell is lovely. Not overpowering at all." I smiled, and the man relaxed his shoulder. Aubrith rolled his eyes in the corner.

"Well, I don't like tea, so I won't be drinking any of the tea you have," Aubrith replied and gave a fake smile to the man.

"Oh, you could drink just regular water then. I have some water bottles here." The man opened his fridge and gave each of us water. I looked around his home, and it was very simple. He had some herbs on the counter, but it was a one-floor house. There were two couches faced towards a TV and across the way from a fireplace. He had pictures of his family all over the home. However, it didn't look like his parents were living in the house. There was a small table in the middle of the home with two chairs, and down the hall led to one bedroom and a bathroom.

"So, what is your name?" I looked at him as Aubrith and Glyden were trying to figure out how to work the TV.

"My name is Alex. I am the only one who lives here, by the way. My parents died about five years ago." He pointed to the picture on the wall that showed two men there. "I'm so sorry Alex. How did they pass?" I took a drink of my water, letting it coat my dry throat. I didn't even know why my throat was so dry.

"Car accident. They were going to my dad's birthday dinner. I was there with my aunt already, and they never showed up at the party." I nodded my head, not knowing what else to say. I was always bad in situations like these. When people would tell me something serious, I never really knew what to say or do. I would just nod. I remembered one of my basketball teammates had cried to me about her parents getting a divorce, and I'd sat there and nodded for a whole twenty minutes.

"God, this is awkward. Sorry, I didn't mean to just spill my life story to you." I smiled and shook my head. "It's okay. I was only raised by my mom, so it's not ideal either."

"So, is your mom from Ireland? Is that why you're trying to get there? England is a bit of a way from there." He chuckled and took a drink of his tea. "Actually, we want to find a woman that none of us have met before to help us find a stone of some sort." He narrowed his eyes and looked down.

"Wow, and I thought I was the weird one for making tea and taking care of my dad's farm." I laughed and shook my head. "No, definitely not the weirdest one here." I looked over in Glyden's direction.

"Well, you can stay here for the night. I have some mats in the back if you want to lie on the ground instead. Let me know if I could help you with anything. I mean, there is a festival just down the road from here in Glastonbury, so I thought you guys were here for that." He started gathering the herbs on the counter. "I love Glastonbury. I have never been to a concert, but I have seen the videos online." He smiled and started walking to the door. "You won't love it when there're thousands of people coming over the weekend." He exited the house, and it was just Glyden, Aubrith, and me.

"Well, when is the wedding between you two?" Aubrith said to me and had a smile that was devious. I grabbed a leftover leaf from the counter and threw it at him.

"Ow! What was that for?" He grabbed the side of his face.

"For being an idiot. That man is actually helping us when we're supposed to be finding that woman Selene or Jura or whatever she goes by now." I sat on the couch in between Glyden and Aubrith.

"Well, Sasi, I think we might have to stay here for a little while. My magic is low." Glyden held out his hand, and a small glow illuminated in his palm. It was a smaller glow than it had been in Toronto.

"Why don't you have powers here?" I grabbed his hand, and the glow went away.

"There must be something here blocking it or something even more powerful than me. I hope I can get us to finish finding everything we need to find to close the portal." He ran his hands through his hair.

"We'll get there. Even if we have to use actual money, we will get to Ireland," I assured him, and he smiled.

"Why are we even here in the first place?" Aubrith crossed his arms.

"I just kept seeing other images in my head when we

were transporting, and we ended up in a field," Glyden responded. He stared at the floor.

"Actually, I saw the images too this time. I was just thinking of the time my mom and I came here to see Stonehenge and Avebury. There're stones in Avebury. It always fascinated me as a kid." I smiled, remembering when my mom would tell me to touch them, and I would always feel warmth course through me. It made me feel safe strangely.

"Wow, so you have been everywhere in your world?" Aubrith looked at me, stunned.

"Not everywhere. Just when I was a kid, my mom used to take me to these places where she claimed were powerful. Or places that had a lot of energy. I just thought she was crazy or superstitious. I mean, you saw her rock collection in the apartment in New York."

Glyden looked at me, and it almost looked like he'd found out something about me I didn't know. His eyes had a sparkle to them, and he was wearing a smile on his face.

"You brought us here then," he stated. He got up from the couch and went to get another water. I stood up and followed him. "What do you mean, I brought us here? You control the teleporting thing." He sighed and took a long drink from the water bottle. When he was done, he wiped his mouth with his sleeve. "You brought us here. It's your memory that made you come here. I mean, we are linked after all. That's the only reason I'm in this realm is because I'm linked to you, remember?" I stood back, astonished by what he said.

"I can't control you, though. I can't read your

thoughts?" I questioned. He sighed and looked at me. "Sasi, I think you can do more than you think. But why don't you just pick a place to sleep, and we will talk more in the morning. I am exhausted." He went back to one couch by the TV and lay down.

I stared at Aubrith, and all he did was shrug his shoulders. "Do you want this couch or one of those mats?" he asked. I went to sit on the couch where he was, and he looked uncomfortable.

"Can I really do more? I mean, I am only a human." I looked at him, and he ran a hand through his curls. "I don't think just any human can go through a whole portal and feel completely normal." He put his hand on my shoulder and stood up to go sleep on the mat. I lay down on the couch, letting the surrounding sounds engulf the house. I focused on the wind hitting the house as it softly whistled instead of the thoughts that kept occurring in my mind.

§

I woke up to a soft breeze hitting my face. I looked around the house, but no one was there. I rubbed my eyes and yawned. Cracking my knuckles, I got up from the couch and opened the door. All I saw was greenery and goats walking around the land. I looked over to see Alex talking in-depth to Aubrith about something. I searched around for Glyden until I found him sitting on a hill just past the farm.

"Hey, what are you looking at?" Before Glyden could

answer, I saw some buses drive by on the main road to where a crowd of people were gathering.

"Alex said it's for a concert that is happening soon. Those people all come to listen to music. I think that's pretty neat." Glyden smiled to himself as he kept watching the people.

"So, about the other day, I don't think I could've held all of that power." I stared at my hand and looked up at Glyden.

"Well, we will see, since Alex will finally take us to see the stones. You showed stones in your vision, so they must have the next piece we need." Glyden dusted off his pants and got up. I got up as well, trying to look into his eyes.

"You know something I don't. I thought you agreed to give me answers since the beginning of this complete mess." I straightened up my back and looked at him. He gazed down at me and sighed. "It's not like I don't want you to know some things. It's better if it happens organically. Plus, I don't know if it is true or not. We will get to the stones, and then we will see." He walked away, leaving me stunned on the hill. *So, he knows something about my life that I don't know.*

I started walking back to the house frantically to talk to Glyden again, but a hand stopped me, grabbing my arm. I looked up and saw that the hand belonged to Alex. I shrugged him off. He looked guilty.

"I'm sorry to grab, you Sasi, but I don't think you should go talk to Glyden. He hasn't been feeling well, and I think he should just be by himself for a bit." He looked towards Aubrith and back at me.

"I know he's been sick the past few days, but I need to talk to him about some things," I replied and tried to go into the house. This time, Aubrith stepped in and looked at me.

"Sasi, just let him figure it out. We will go to the stones today. I just don't know what's going on with him, but it's Glyden. If anyone will figure things out, it's him." He softly smiled, and I relaxed a bit. I guess he had a point. Glyden has been throwing up and getting warm the past few nights. It wasn't like him to express any humanlike qualities before, but then again, I wanted to know more about the way we were linked. Every time I went up to him, he would just want to be further away from me. Alex probably just thought that Glyden and I were arguing a lot when, in reality, I wanted to know more about what he said.

After a few moments, Alex returned to Aubrith and me with his car keys.

"Are you ready to see the stones? There might be some druids in the area, so you could probably just keep on the path." He started walking towards his car.

"What? I thought you said people in this realm didn't have magic?" Aubrith questioned. I laughed and patted Aubrith on the back. "These people aren't magic like the one in your realm, so there isn't anything to worry about." He let out a breath and relaxed his shoulders. "Oh, thank the Serpents. I thought you had people like us." He laughed. *Why would he say the serpents?*

"What's the Serpents?" I asked, and he looked at me with wide eyes.

"Oh right, sorry. I forget you people have a different saying here. The Serpents are just like our goddesses. It's an old expression we say in the other realm, really. Well, people who still believe in that kind of thing. Come to think of it, there has been no talk about them since that exchange with the orb. I told you about how Justorah's family wanted something, but yeah, the goddesses protect the orbs. It is in children's books back in the other realm, too." Aubrith shrugged and headed back to the house to let Glyden know we were about to leave.

"Aubrith, I saw a snake symbol in Aurelia's castle, but it went away." He stopped walking and turned around. He furrowed his eyebrows. "Aurelia isn't a snake, though. She has the three wolves." He looked at me with wide eyes. "Yeah, I know. I told her that, and she didn't believe me. Then, I saw the rose in the garden which led me to meet Glyden." I assured Aubrith.

He shook his head and went back into the house to get Glyden, who looked sicker. Aubrith moved closer to me and whispered, "We will talk later, but we need to go to the stones." I sighed and started walking into the car that Alex had.

Glyden rolled down the window in the front seat to get air in his face. Aubrith's words kept floating in my mind. I didn't know the significance of anything, but it kept annoying me that Aubrith and Glyden kept all these secrets from me. I hated when people kept things from me, even though it was probably to protect me. I put my head back and tried to remember my mom and I at Avebury a long time ago. I remembered a little, but just that she had me touch a stone. She was super happy that day that I'd done that. *If only she could see me now that I am on a mission with two people who aren't even from this realm.*

CHAPTER

FIFTEEN

The sound of tires rolling on the gravel engulfed the car. No one was talking, but we all just looked outside of the window. All I could hear slightly in the background was Alex drumming his fingers against the steering wheel.

"It shouldn't be much longer until we get to Avebury. Those stones aren't as popular as Stonehenge, but I think they're more magical than the bigger stones." Alex told us. No one responded to him. We all just simply kept looking out of the windows of the vehicle and taking in the green scenery. Alex's drumming on the steering wheel got louder, which I noticed was irritating Glyden.

I hoped that Glyden would be okay instead of this sickness that lingered inside of him. He kept avoiding me at all costs, and it even repulsed him to look at me. I tried not to take offense, but it hurt. I heard a backpack unzip, and I looked over to Aubrith. He was rummaging around in his bag, looking for something. We all jostled up and down as the vehicle hit a rough part in the road, and a book came out of Aubrith's bag. I picked it up and noticed it was one of the books from Endy's bookstore.

I held it out back to him, and he locked eyes with me. He nodded his head and shoved the book back into the backpack.

"You know, you could organize that thing." I pointed to the backpack. He rolled his eyes and zipped the backpack back up.

"Whatever. I found what I wanted. As long as I know where things are, then it's fine." He crossed his arms and refocused ahead. I saw the sliver of the pen-like object in his hand. *Did he really think we would find part of the puzzle here?* I looked back to the road and noticed that there were more cars on the sidelining up for something. People were walking on the road with their cameras hanging from their necks.

"This is as far as I can take you, I'm afraid. Look for a woman named Carrie. She will help you get up to the stones. She usually does tours if she's not too busy in the gift shop." Alex awkwardly scratched his neck.

"Thank you. Really. It means a lot to us." I smiled at Alex and got out of the vehicle. As we walked up to the gift shop, the gravel crunched under our feet. Glyden dragged his feet faster and made his way up the hill.

"Are you sure he isn't mad at me?" I looked at Aubrith who had his hands rested on his backpack straps. Aubrith just shrugged and kept walking up the hill. I sighed and made my way behind him. We entered the gift shop which was small and crowded. I found someone who was working behind the counter.

"Hi, can you help us find a woman named Carrie?" He sighed and looked around the gift shop. "Sorry, it's been crazy in here today. Everyone wants a tour or to buy something." I nodded my head as the man kept looking. I saw Aubrith looking at a necklace, but he put it back on the shelf.

"Do you want anything in here?" I asked Aubrith.

"Why would I want anything in here? I don't even know this place." Aubrith scoffed and folded his arms.

"I was just wondering. You don't need to do that attitude thing again." I walked away from Aubrith and he grabbed my arm.

"I'm sorry. This whole thing has me stressed out, and my first response to anything is anger." He took a breath and looked around. "Do you want to get out of this gift-shop? I don't even think Glyden is in here."

To be honest, I didn't expect Aubrith to say that to me. He never apologizes, let alone admits that he has an anger problem. I realized Aubrith was right, and Glyden wasn't in the area. We exited the giftshop and kept walking up the hill towards the stones where everyone else was. There were sheep everywhere, just walking in the grass.

"Maybe he is already up there. I bet he has already seen the stones," Aubrith told me as we got to the grass field. There were puddles in the field that we had to avoid walking in. *Great, my shoes are going to be all muddy.*

As we got to the hill, Glyden was sitting by one stone. There were many people around us and some little kids roaming the area. Some kids were screaming. Obviously, it was their bedtime. It wasn't as peaceful as I remembered with my mom, however; we went on a tour with a group of eight people who had history majors from their university.

I stepped near a puddle, making my shoes slosh in the mud. That made Glyden turn towards Aubrith and I.

"I don't get it. I was supposed to feel better around the stones," Glyden told us as he coughed into his elbow.

"Maybe you have to wait a little bit. They might not work right away?" Aubrith suggested. Glyden scoffed and went to touch the stone again. I took a deep breath and walked towards the stone. I felt heat all around me. A bead of sweat trickled down my face. I quickly wiped it away, not wanting Glyden or Aubrith to worry.

"Sasi, with all due respect, you need to stay away from me," Glyden demanded. I kept walking towards the stone. I remembered when my mom was there with me when I was little. She would tell me to not actually touch the stone but to see if I felt heat around it. She'd made me hold an object in my hand. I'd thought she was just insane and using her superstitious ways again. As I kept thinking about that time, I didn't remember there ever being this much heat. Sure, my hand was hot from being near the stone, but it was never where I was sweating like I ran a marathon.

More beads of sweat trickled down my face. Aubrith gave me a weird look and looked back at Glyden. It felt like my legs weren't working, even though my mind kept telling me to move forward.

"Sasi, please stop coming near me. I don't want anything bad to happen. Know that I'm doing this for your own good," Glyden suggested. I looked up at him and drew my eyebrows together.

"You're doing this to me? You're the reason I can't move my legs suddenly?" I looked down at my legs, and as I looked down, blood ran out of my nose. Immediately, I put my head back and covered my nose with my sleeve.

I kept trying to will my legs forward. It felt like everything inside of me kept telling me to touch the stone. I had to listen to it. I didn't know why Glyden was telling me not to come close to him. He's been weird with me the past few days and even made comments that his sickness was my fault. I thought about something other than the situation we were in. I thought about a favorite moment between my mom and I.

It was when I'd been sick, and she'd made me my favorite dish of all time, posole. Posole was a Mexican dish with hominy and different spices. She'd usually made it the way New Mexican people made it, with no radish. She would just include pork, red chili powder, onions, and oregano. I smiled at the thought, but when I opened my eyes, Glyden was staring at me with wide eyes. I was walking towards the stones without him blocking me, and I held my hand out towards the stone and felt heat surrounding my hand. Glyden now had a bloody nose and kept looking at me. A part of the stone in the back slid out and dropped into the grass. Aubrith ran forward and gathered it. He quickly stuffed it into his backpack and looked towards Glyden and me.

I grabbed Glydens arm, and suddenly his nose stopped bleeding. He looked like he was getting more energy. I felt weak. Before I knew it, he pushed me to the ground with a force of air. I looked around us and noticed that none of the civilians cared about what we were doing.

"Never do that again," Glyden demanded and picked me up from where I was lying down in the mud. A sheep was near us, mindlessly eating grass, looking towards us. I sighed and touched my nose, which stopped bleeding.

"I don't even know what I did." I tried to touch the stone again, but when I did, it wasn't as hot.

"I don't care. We need to get a handle on this thing. How did you even get the elements to work with you?" Glyden asked. I looked at him confused. "Elements? I don't even know what you're talking about. I just missed my mom." I dusted off my shirt and looked at Aubrith, who looked at me like I was an alien of some sort.

"It didn't look like you didn't know what would happen, Sasi." Aubrith stared at me and backed up.

"How long have you known you could do that?" Glyden asked as he stretched.

"I already told you. I don't know what happened. I just thought of my mom and a voice of some sort kept telling me to go touch the stone. When I touched it, it got hot, and I just kept wanting my mom's food." I ran my hands over my face and noticed I had a little burn mark on one of my hands.

"You had to of used your powers before, Sasi. You

completely disregarded mine." Glyden looked like I hurt his feelings.

"I needed to touch the stone. I didn't even know I had powers, or if I have powers. I just felt hot everywhere, and when your hand was out, I touched it. I knew you would try to push me away. You've been doing that the whole week." I got slightly angry because he didn't even say thank you.

"You have powers. In case you didn't notice you pulled out a piece of the stone that will be a part of the puzzle. I also think that you healed me in a way. I don't feel as weak." He stretched out his neck and looked at me again. "But I don't want you to keep doing this unless you know what you're actually doing."

I looked down at my hand again because the pain of the burn was there. *Well, that was a delayed response from my nervous system.*

"I got the piece, by the way. Maybe the other one from Toronto will work with this one," Aubrith assured. I started walking away towards the gift shop when a woman dressed in a flowing skirt and flowing top came near me.

"Your energy is very good. I can sense it. Would you like a psychic reading?" she asked. I shook my head.

"No, I'm fine, thank you." I tried to move around her, but she grabbed my arm.

"Really, I can sense all of your energy. I think you need a reading." She tried to pull me toward other women dressed like her.

"I said I'm fine." I broke free from her hand, but she was on the ground. Aubrith rushed over to me and looked at the woman. "Sorry, she is just so unfriendly to people. I think it's time for her nap." Aubrith pushed me away from the woman. She continued to lay there, holding her head.

Glyden came up to me and steered Aubrith and I away from other people.

"What the heck was that?" he asked and looked at me in my eyes.

"I do not know. One moment she was asking me for a reading of my future, and the next she was on the ground." I shrugged and held up my hands.

He looked at the burn mark and grabbed my wrist.

"When did you get that burn?" He studied my hand and ran his thumb near the spot.

"When I helped you. I told you it felt hot. I guess now it just looks horrible." I pulled my hand away and looked at it myself. It was red and blistering on the sides.

"You need to learn how to control your powers." He rolled his eyes and walked down the path. I looked at Aubrith, and he shrugged.

"Do not bring me into Glyden and your little power thing. I do not want any part of that." He motioned with his hands towards my hands.

"How am I supposed to control this when I just learned I can do it today?" I looked at Aubrith as our feet hit the gravel.

"I don't know, okay? Like I said, don't bring me into anything. I hate magic." He rested his hands on his backpack straps. We picked up some speed walking since we were going downhill on the gravel.

"Is the magic thing because of your mom?" I asked, and he turned his head to me.

"My mom is a healer. Not whatever you and Glyden are." He kept staring ahead.

"Am I a healer? I mean, I healed Glyden back there."

"A healer doesn't just push people down with a force."

I looked up and saw Glyden already in the vehicle with Alex, talking to him.

"No mentioning of magic with that man near us, okay?" Aubrith looked at me. I nodded, and he got into the car. I sighed and sat next to Aubrith in the backseat.

"How was the tour?" Alex looked back at me in the rearview mirror. We locked eyes, and I smiled. "It was good! Carrie actually did a wonderful tour for us and showed us the stones up close." I felt bad for lying, but he didn't need to know what really happened. Aubrith was right.

Alex smiled and looked in the rearview mirror again. "She usually gives such lovely readings. She's a psychic, you know." He smiled at me in the mirror. Aubrith and Glyden both looked towards me, and we all gave each other a knowing look.

"Ah, yes. She gave us a lovely reading," Glyden told Alex as he looked out of the window of the vehicle.

Aubrith contained a laugh that was about to come out, and I hit him in the arm.

As we drove back to Alex's house, I kept thinking about the piece that fell out of the stone. I was wondering if it was anything significant or not. I never got a good look at the piece since Aubrith snatched it up so quick. I felt immense pain in my hand coming from the burn. My hand was swelling in the burn's area. I pulled down my sleeve to hide it. I noticed Aubrith looking at me with a look I could not decipher. I rested my head on the vehicle window as my head bumped back and forth from the vehicle driving on the gravel. I knew the house wasn't that far, but I was immensely tired. I closed my eyes, trying not to think of the pain that was throbbing in my hand.

CHAPTER

SIXTEEN

As we got to the house, I turned to Alex, who already had some stew on the stove cooking.

"Do you have any band-aids or anything to help clean a cut?" I asked, carefully keeping my hand covered with my sleeve. I caught Alex off guard, and he almost burned himself as he checked the stew.

"Um, yes. It is in the back hallway. In the bathroom. There is a mirror and behind the mirror, there are some essentials for you." He resumed stirring the stew and kept his focus on the pan.

I went to the back of the hallway and tried to look in the bathroom. I got some gauze and carefully wrapped the area. I went to put it back before I noticed Aubrith leaning on the doorframe. I jumped back, dropping the gauze.

"If you can heal people, why don't you just heal yourself?" Aubrith asked, keeping his arms crossed.

I bent down to pick up the gauze and stuffed it behind the mirror.

"I don't even know how I healed Glyden, so I don't even know where to start with myself." I looked down at my hand and wondered maybe I could just heal myself.

"My mom always said to think of a propitious time, and the healing you do within yourself will actually happen to others and yourself." He gave a small smile and looked at my hand.

"I was thinking of my mom's cooking when I healed Glyden I guess." I didn't even think that would influence anything, but maybe Aubrith had a point.

"So, can you heal people?" I smiled and hit him with my arm. He laughed and scratched at his stubble.

"Unfortunately, I got my father's abilities. Just to fight and not do anything with magic. Even though I was raised by my mother." He shrugged and sighed.

"Maybe you know how to help me then with all of this. I mean, I just learned today that I can do this. It's kind of nerve-wracking. I don't even know how to explain it." I took a deep breath, and Aubrith stood up straight.

"Sure. I might know how to guide you through some things, but I think the best person to ask is Glyden. Even though he's still ignoring you at the moment," he assured. I nodded my head and moved past him back into the kitchen area.

"Thanks for letting me use your aid kit, Alex." I went and sat on the couch where Glyden was.

"Sure. The stew is ready if anyone wants any. I think we are supposed to be getting a rainstorm tonight, so it will be cold in here." He grabbed a bowl and filled the bowl up with the liquid.

Glyden scooted further from me on the couch, and I whispered towards him, "You can't keep avoiding me forever." I got up from the couch and made my way towards the stew. Aubrith sat down on the couch with his bowl, and we all ate in silence. It was a comfortable silence. I appreciate times like these with them because no one needs to say anything, but we all are in our own little worlds. Alex stood up and said goodnight to all of us. It was just us three on the couch, watching the television in silence. I wasn't really paying attention before I saw, out of my peripheral vision, the remote of the television coming at my head. I put my hand up to block it, but it flew back to hit the wall.

Glyden nodded his head and picked up something else. Aubrith stood up quickly and looked at Glyden. "What are you doing? Are you trying to kill her?" Aubrith looked at me, stunned, and I was just taking in labored breaths.

"I didn't think she was this strong, but she's more powerful than she thinks," Glyden said pointedly. He threw a piece of paper in my direction, causing me to catch the paper. Glyden looked disappointed.

"Now you're thinking about things so it will not happen." His shoulders were dejected and he grabbed a book.

"Are you crazy? Of course, I'm thinking about things. I don't want to get hit in the face." I stood up, facing Glyden. He quickly threw the book at my head, and I held up my forearm. A force of wind sent the book back to him. He quickly held up his hand and gently set the book down in midair. He smiled and took my hand, unwrapping the gauze. I felt a warm glow then a cool sensation. My skin healed completely in the burn's area.

"We need to work on this some more. I think you could get better with this with more practice." He sat back down on the couch and took his shirt off.

"What the heck, Glyden? You just threw a book at my head, and now you think I suddenly can have these powers?" I stayed standing, looking at him.

"I don't think you will have better powers, I know. And we will work on them together. But for now, I am tired." He pulled a blanket over him and closed his eyes. I stood there, shocked that he would even think about going to bed after just attacking me like he did before healing me.

Aubrith shrugged his shoulders and lay down on the mat behind the couch. I went to the kitchen and opened the refrigerator to find a water bottle. I chugged it and went to lie on the couch. I felt so out of breath and tired from the day's events. *What the heck was even happening to me?*

SEVENTEEN

Aubrith stood over me as I lay in the grass. "You, okay?" He asked as I was developing another burn mark on my hand. Glyden had been trying to train me on handling my powers. However, his idea of training was just him throwing things towards me and laughing when I would push them back to him. Alex was out for the day. Apparently, he was going further into town to sell some of his tea packets and give some milk to a neighbor. Which left all day to Glyden and I practicing magic. However, it was mainly just him. Aubrith sat down on the hill, watching us bicker back and forth all day.

"Can't I get a break? I don't even think I am gaining any knowledge on anything. It's still the same stupid thing whenever you throw stuff at me, and my hand is killing me." My hand had blisters, and it was red all around it. Glyden walked over and held my hand. The blister vanished as I felt the cool sensation course through my hand again. Glyden smiled at me and went across from me again at a reasonable distance.

He grabbed a rock this time and chucked it towards me. I was too slow to interfere with it, and the rock almost missed my leg.

"Seriously, how is this even helping?" I glared at him. I tried to look to Aubrith for advice, but he just held his hands up.

"It is helping. You don't know it yet, but it is. I just want you to gain your confidence to use the powers," Glyden responded. He was searching for another rock in the grass.

"How can I gain confidence when you're throwing rocks at me all day?" I walked towards the house when I sensed something was coming towards me. I got out of the way before the rock hit me in my head. I could hear Glyden laugh again in the distance. I opened the door and smelled fruity tea again. I reached for the water bottle on the table. The water bottle moved away from me, and I turned around, only to see Glyden smiling at me.

"If you want the water, you will have to be quicker than that." He smiled as he crossed his arms. I tried to reach for the water bottle again, but it moved away from my grasp.

"Okay, Glyden, I think that's enough," Aubrith said in the doorway.

Glyden sighed, and I reached for the water bottle victoriously. I drank the cool liquid, and I could hear Glyden in the background sighing louder.

"Can I help you?" I turned to him, but he just grabbed the water bottle out of my hand and set it on the table.

"Can we restart? These powers need to be controlled, you know?" Glyden was making his way out of the door. I felt so much rage inside of me. How could he just take my water away from me like that? He was irritating me. I heard the door slam shut, and I looked up to see Glyden looking at the door and back at me.

"You did that, didn't you? Therefore, we need to control your powers before you just slam doors shut everywhere you go." He tried to open the door, but it wasn't budging.

"Hilarious, Sasi. Now open the door so that we can continue training." He crossed his arms, and I looked at Aubrith.

"I don't think she wants to train anymore, Glyden," Aubrith announced. He looked down at his shoes.

"Well, Aubrith, I am the only one who can train her, and we don't have that much time. Mind you, we still are on a mission here to close a portal that could end an entire realm." Glyden rubbed his eyes and looked at me.

I sighed and let my body relax a little. The door opened without me even thinking about it. Glyden walked outside as Aubrith stayed back.

"You know he's just trying to figure this all out like you are," Aubrith said to me as he left the door. I stayed there with my thoughts, just running my hands on the wooden table. I remembered I used to have a wooden table at my mom's house, and when I was little, it would fascinate me with the texture of the wood. It felt like everything I did made me think of my mom. She must be terrified that I left without even telling her. Granted, I didn't have a choice in the matter, considering I fell through an entire portal. I often wondered if she knew something about the other realm. She really believed in magic my whole life and told me about the differences between bad and good energy from people.

We would often have rocks surrounding the house to protect us from people. I remembered, when she went to medical school, it would amaze the school that she passed everything with flying colors. She was one of the best surgeons in all of New York. Whenever I would get hurt from playing outside, she would put a band-aid on the cut, but in a day the cut would be gone. More things like that kept becoming recurring memories in my mind, considering I had powers now. Maybe I always had them.

I looked down at my shoe and noticed that it was untied. I bent down to tie my shoe again. I glanced in the backpack's direction with the new piece from the stone. Aubrith didn't show us the piece yet, but I had a feeling it would look like the other one from Toronto. I got up and walked towards the backpack and unzipped it, looking through the books until I picked up a blue shard. I found the other shard from Toronto, and they clicked together like they were magnets. A bright glow ignited in the middle of them before I pulled back and dropped them to the floor, covering my eyes. All I saw were black spots around the room. I heard the door open, and it was Aubrith and Glyden standing near the door. Glyden ran over to me, and Aubrith rushed to the pieces of the stone.

"What happened?" Glyden helped me up slowly from the ground. I kept seeing black spots in my eyes as I slowly got up to my feet.

"I was looking at the shards, and they clicked together. Before I knew it, they basically blinded me." I quickly blinked, hoping that would help my eyes.

"Well, now, they're stuck together. I can't get them to pry away from each other." Aubrith kept trying to pull apart the shards. Glyden walked over and tried to pull them apart. The shards stayed intact before Glyden stepped back and put his hand out. His hand had a white glow to it, causing the stones to shake on the table. Another blast of bright light appeared in the house. I quickly covered my eyes this time. Aubrith and Glyden were both groaning and holding their eyes.

"What did you do that for?" Aubrith yelled at Glyden holding his eyes.

"I thought I could break them apart with my magic." Glyden blinked rapidly.

"Oh, my god. I am blind. I'm never going to see again." Aubrith blinked as tears came down his face. Glyden hit him in the arm.

"Stop being so dramatic. It will pass. We just had too much light." Glyden rubbed his eyes and opened them to focus on one thing.

I walked over the shards to notice they were still stuck together.

"Maybe they're supposed to be like this. Maybe they have to be glued together for the piece to fit somewhere." I thought back to Justorah's words about how it would help him get the realm back together. I shook my head and turned to Glyden.

"So, how many more pieces are in this realm?" I studied Glyden's eyes, but they weren't giving anything away.

"I honestly do not know, Sasi. I'm just sent to protect you by Terra." He looked at me again, still blinking rapidly. His eyes still adjusting to everything.

"Yeah, I know. You've told me that a million times already. I just don't know what she would want to do with me. And if you're here to protect me, does she know about that man who came to attack us?" I kept thinking about all the events we have been through so far, and nothing was making sense.

"I don't know. All she told me to do was that she knew you were in the realm and told me to get to you before anything bad happened. I am supposed to stay with you until my mission is complete." He looked at me softly.

"But when is your mission ending? Like, how will you know?" I questioned Glyden.

He smiled and shook his head.

"I don't. She will let me know, I guess when the time comes." He looked at the stones and put them back in the backpack.

"Aubrith, keep these somewhere safe. I don't want just anyone to find these." Glyden instructed. Aubrith just nodded and put his jacket over the backpack to hide it better.

Glyden looked at me and walked closer to me. I gave

him a weird look before he wrapped his arms around me.

"What are you doing?" I asked Glyden as I kept my arms straight down during the hug.

"I am hugging you. This is what humans do when the other human is sad, right?" He gripped tighter around me.

"I'm not really a hug person." I tried to get out of his grasp, but he just held me there.

"Come on. Hug back. I can't do this in the other realm." He stayed there with his hands wrapped around me.

I sighed and rolled my eyes, slowly moving my arms around him. I haven't hugged someone in a long time; it felt foreign to do so.

After a while, I pulled back, and Glyden smiled at me.

"We are going to get through this together." He patted my back and walked towards the door.

"Hey, do you think that guy will ever come after us again?" I asked Glyden. He stopped walked towards the door and had his back faced towards me.

"Why? Do you think he is here?" Glyden turned towards me with his eyebrows drawn together.

"I don't think he is. But what if he is here? What if he tries to come after us again?" I questioned Glyden. He stayed silent for a moment before responding. "I don't know. I will do everything in my power to keep you safe. I don't exactly know what he wants either." He briefly smiled before leaving the house. I followed him outside. I realized we were still in the middle of training, considering the number of rocks that were still on the hill.

"Do we go to the next location?" I asked Glyden, and he glanced back at me.

"We should move soon. For right now though, we need to work on your powers. You could still cause a lot of damage to others and even yourself if you're not careful." He walked to his rock pile and started sifting through to find a good rock to throw.

"Really? You're still thinking about my powers when some crazy person is after us?" I walked closer to him.

"Well, your powers started recently. They're out of control." Glyden kept looking for the perfect rock before picking up a white one. He motioned with his hands for me to be further back so he can try throwing it.

"I don't think that it is really necessary. Maybe we can still be on the move before he finds us." I backed up to the spot I'd been standing in all day.

"We know that the next spot is in Ireland. Endy told us to find Selene, even though her name is Jura. Whatever her name is, we know to go to Ireland." He threw the rock towards me, and I blocked it, sending the rock to the side as if it got knocked down by an invisible shield.

"Can we trust Jura? I mean she left Endy stranded in Canada," I replied to Glyden who was already picking up another rock.

"I think we can trust her. She came from the other realm, and she has to still be alive. Endy wouldn't put us in harm's way. He used to know Terra and anyone who knows Terra I can trust." Glyden launched another rock towards me. I quickly put my forearm up, sending the rock away at a further distance than before. Glyden smiled at that and bent down to get another rock.

"I don't know who Terra is. I don't trust her yet, so how can I trust Jura." Glyden paused this time in his throwing and looked towards me.

"Terra sent me. Don't you trust me?" Glyden looked dejected.

"I trust you. I do. I just don't trust Terra. I don't know her. I also heard many things about her from Justorah." Glyden rubbed the rock in his hands before responding back to me.

"Justorah is someone you can trust, but he also can be deceiving. I don't know what he said about Terra, but I promise she isn't like that." He sent the next rock towards my leg. I jumped out of the way, and he frowned.

"So, tell me more about her," I demanded and moved out of my spot.

Glyden put the rock down and put his hands on his hips. He took a deep breath before responding.

"She's a goddess. We have this thing in our realm. Like different beliefs, like you guys call it. The main area in our realm where I was created is in a place called Guirra. The major city, Lumos, is where Terra is. People there have magic. They were born with magic. There's another city in Guirra called Vibran. They have an army; it is very militant but the people have magic there."

Glyden sat down in the grass and patted the grass next to him. I moved over to sit by him and sat down. I looked around to see where Aubrith was, but he was by the cows. I looked back to Glyden to pay attention.

"Okay so Lumos and Vibran. I got it." I nodded my head and Glyden ran his hands over his face.

"The place where Justorah was, that's called Elggland. They have a different belief than Terra. They still have magic, but they are the outcasts. The people that Terra exiled from Guirra because they used their magic, let's just say, inappropriately. Justorah's family has ruled Elggland for years. There was a war in Guirra for a powerful source, but Terra's family took care of that a while ago."

Glyden started picking at the grass to distract himself from looking up.

"We also have Aurelia. Her realm does not want magic at all. They believe magic can corrupt people. It's kind of ironic since they have the most money in the land in the major city, Salcesia. That city is probably the most corrupt that you can get. Aurelia wants money. Wherever she can get it, she will."

I nodded my head, taking all of this information in. I absentmindedly started picking at the grass as well. I remembered the people were covered in mud, but in the castle, it was elaborate.

"There's Jaklish, where Aubrith is from. They have the OV and the Elves. The major city there is Banciff. They believe in the Goddess however, they praise Terra. In Guirra, it is very relaxed, and no one really praises her. People know about her, but there aren't set days to pray to her. Meanwhile, in Jaklish, people have a routine to pray to the Goddess. Certain people there are also healers who escaped during the war and lived in Jaklish to make a life. Aurelia wants control over Jaklish and to get rid of more people with magic."

Glyden looked off into the distance still grabbing at the grass. He closed his eyes and took a deep breath.

"Terra is in the lineage of the goddesses. The symbol of Guirra is a snake. Ancient legends used to say that the goddesses themselves created different realms, but people said they were actual snakes. Terra didn't always have her power. It is passed down when a goddess is deceased or transfers the power. That happened during the war, and Terra has been the supreme Goddess ever since."

I tried to take what Glyden said in, but it was hard to wrap my head around how their god was living among them. I leaned back on my elbows and looked up at the sky.

"So, you think that Terra also built this realm. Like Earth in present time?" I glanced at Glyden, and he just stared at me.

"She probably didn't, but other people in her lineage, yeah. The other realm has different methods of time. People there age quicker than here. I think the goddesses did that to create a balance, but I am not sure."

"So, her family is the one to blame for all the craziness in our world?" I laughed and Glyden laughed, too.

"Oh no, you humans did that all by yourself. Our realm isn't perfect by any means, but regular people here with no magic cause way more problems." He laughed louder. I just smiled at him.

"So, do you think someone has traveled through the realms before?" I thought back to my mom and how weird things used to happen when I was little. Even her necklace was apparently the necklace people around Terra wore. According to Justorah, of course.

"It is possible. Terra's family created the realms so I can see they could move through them." He looked deep in thought. I cleared my throat before I spoke again.

"My mom used to wear a blue necklace. She would keep rocks around the house. She even has taken me here before and told me to be near these stones. I always thought she was crazy, but maybe she had magic?"

Glyden laughed harder than before and clutched his stomach. He fell backwards in the grass.

"Oh, that is so funny. A mortal having powers? You are hilarious, Sasi. I think your mom is just unique here. Someone with magic living here out of all places is absurd."

I laughed with him and shook away the idea of my mom having powers. Glyden had to be right. Anyone here with powers would be insane. *Of course, there is me.* I stared down at my hand to see if I had any more burns.

"So how do you think I got my powers?" I looked at Glyden, and his laughing died down a bit.

"Maybe just passing through the realms, you got something from them." He shrugged. I was about to speak, but Aubrith sat down next to us.

"Hey, what are you guys talking about? You laughed pretty hard over here." He put a hand through his disheveled curls.

"I was just telling her about the realm. She thought her mom had powers. Can you believe that?" Glyden almost started laughing again. Aubrith tilted his head back laughing, and I suddenly felt embarrassed.

"Okay, that's enough guys. I was just thinking about it." I felt heat on my cheeks.

"I'm sorry, but that is hilarious." Aubrith laughed louder before wiping at his eyes.

I stood up, brushing off the grass from my jeans.

"Oh, come on, where are you going?" Aubrith asked.

"I think I'm just going to nap a little. I feel tired suddenly."

Aubrith and Glyden shared a look, and Aubrith rolled his eyes.

"Okay, whatever. Have fun napping," Aubrith said as he refocused his attention on Glyden.

I rolled my eyes and walked towards the house. I lay down on the couch and pulled a blanket over me. *How could I be so stupid to admit that to them?* My cheeks felt hot again as I pulled the blanket over my head.

CHAPTER

EIGHTEEN

"Do you guys think that people actually enjoy this?" Aubrith questioned as he held up a tea bag. It was later in the week and Alex invited us to go to the market with him.

"I think people enjoy tea. I enjoy tea." I looked up at Aubrith as I brought a new box over to the table Alex was setting up at. Alex was talking to some local people in the area.

"Why are we helping him if he's just going to stand there and talk all day?" Aubrith said, bringing me another box.

"Well, he has let us stay at his house for more than a week, so I would say that it is nice. The least we can do is help him with his herbs and tea," I replied as I used a box cutter to cut open the box to get the herbs out.

"Where's Glyden when we need him?" Aubrith said as he grunted, picking up the last box. Glyden insisted on going and find materials for our travel. We were planning to go to Ireland soon to get the next shard. To get out of helping Alex, Glyden wanted to do anything else other than lugging boxes of plants across a small town.

"He just told me today that he wanted to get some materials. Probably new clothes. We've been wearing the same two pairs of clothes for around nine days. They stink horrendously." I sorted out the herbs like Alex said to organizing the different spices in different piles.

"Well, Alex said we could use that thing that cleans clothes, but it scared me. I tried to wash my clothes out in the rain, but that didn't end well." Aubrith shook his head.

I laughed and opened a fresh box to sort. Alex walked over to us and smiled.

"So, how are you liking my job?" He asked, trying to hide his smile towards Aubrith. Aubrith rolled his eyes and grabbed the box cutter from me. He aggressively opened the box in front of Alex. I tried to hide my smile.

"I think we respect what you do here. Thank you again for letting us help. You've helped us so much so we thought we could repay you this way." I replied to Alex. He laughed and ran his hands through his wavy hair.

"Thank you. That means a lot." He stared at me for a while before a customer came up to him to ask him the price of his tea.

Aubrith scoffed at me and continued mauling the box with the box cutter.

"I think you're just supposed to cut the box with the box cutter, not demolish it." I nudged his arm, and he stared at me with a straight face.

"You like him, don't you?" He kept staring at me. I blushed and gathered the herbs.

"He's been nice to us." I kept it vague. The truth is, I didn't know Alex that well. Sure, he was attractive, but he barely talked to us.

"Is that what it takes for you to like a man? Them just being...nice?" Aubrith made a disgusted face. I didn't know why he always put up a guard about things when, in reality, Aubrith had showed a softer side to Glyden and me.

I rolled my eyes and continued to sort through the herbs. A man in front of me cleared his throat to get my attention.

"Do you guys sell anything with cinnamon?" he asked.

"Actually, sir, I don't think he has that today." I was going to keep talking but looking at the man in front of me was the same man who had been chasing us in Toronto.

"Hi again. Sasi, is it?" He asked and picked up a herb. He put it up to his nose and inhaled the plant.

I gulped and stared at him. He was still in his leather jacket, and he had a cut on his head. His head had an old gauze pad attached to it. Aubrith must've noticed my body language and looked up. He immediately stood back.

"Look, we don't want any trouble. We are just here to get the pieces for the other realm and go. We will leave this realm soon." I kept my breathing steady, even though I was terrified of this man.

"Oh, I know you have your little scavenger hunt. You just need to give the stones to me before you to end up giving them to the wrong person." He held out his hand and gritted his teeth.

"How can I even trust you? You're the one who chased us around Toronto." I tried to keep my voice down so other people around us didn't get suspicious.

"Look, kid, I can't even trust you. That's why I need the stones. You were the ones who tried to kill me remember?" He pointed to his head wound and cracked his knuckles. He cleared his throat before he spoke again. "I'm not going to ask you again. Give me the stones or we are going to do this the hard way." His eyes glowed blue, and I gulped. Before I could respond, I felt Aubrith next to me.

"Hard way it is then," Aubrith said as he flipped the table towards him and threw cinnamon in his face. The man immediately grabbed his eyes.

"We need to go, now!" Aubrith pulled me away. He picked up his backpack, which was behind the last box, and we ran through the town. People kept looking at us weirdly. I heard Alex's voice in the background asking where we were going.

We ran to a clothing store and dodged the clothing racks as the clothes jingled against the metal. Glyden was trying on a new jean jacket and had several clothes in his hands. Aubrith ran over to him and pulled him away.

"Hey! I have to pay for these!" Glyden shouted at Aubrith as he was being pulled out of the store.

"You never pay for anything anyway!" Aubrith yelled back and moved us through the town. The store clerk came running out, yelling at Glyden about the clothes.

"Sorry!" Glyden yelled over his shoulder.

The man was on our trail and kept running behind us. I looked over my shoulder and saw a glow in his hand. He moved his hand towards Aubrith, and I immediately tackled Aubrith as he was running. We broke through a window of a store as the magic flew by us.

Aubrith held his head, and he looked at me with wide eyes.

"What the heck was that for?" he groaned as he shook off the glass.

"He was going to kill us! I saw the power forming in his hand." I noticed I had a gash on my arm. I was bleeding. The store manager of this store looked at us. She was in shock just holding a pair of flowers in one hand and a pair of scissors in the other. I looked at her and waved.

"Sorry about the mess." I told her as I grabbed Aubrith's arm to resume running down the street. I found Glyden in the middle of the street, shooting magic back at the man. There were bystanders watching the whole thing.

"I know I hurt my head, but they aren't supposed to watch this, right?" Aubrith motioned his hands over to the people in the street, watching everything. I shook my head. I tried to think of Glyden's training, but nothing was coming to mind. I held out my hand and gripped Aubrith's arm. I felt Aubrith try to get my hand off him, but I kept holding on. I pulled Aubrith with me as we ran towards Glyden, who was in the middle of a fight. As soon as I touched Glyden, I thought of Dublin.

All I could see were memories floating around me, and I sighed. I knew I could transport us. I kept Dublin in mind before everything went to black.

CHAPTER
NINETEEN

Car noises echoed around us. I looked around and saw Aubrith leaning on the side of an ATM. Glyden was looking at a large spindle across the street. I looked at the wall of the building, trying to see what street we were on. A gust of wind pierced through my flimsy coat. I shivered and tried to pull my clothes closer to my body.

"Aubrith, are you okay?" I shouted over the wind.

All Aubrith did was hold his thumb up. He bent over and vomited near the ATM. The people behind him waiting to get to the ATM all shouted at him. I ran over and pulled him away from the ATM. I rubbed my hand on his back instinctively, but he pulled away.

"I don't need your help, you know," Aubrith said as he clutched his stomach.

"It looks like you do. I mean, you threw up over there." I pointed towards the ATM. People were still avoiding the area and hopping over the scene.

He shook his head and kneeled on the sidewalk. He

clutched his stomach again and did a dry heave. I looked away quickly. As much as I was trying to help, I hated these instances. I hated everything about vomit, and it even made me want to gag. Another gust of wind came in, and I instantly shivered.

"Are you okay?" a man in a suit asked me. I nodded my head, and he smiled.

"If you're looking to go to Temple Bar, it's just down there. Go past the bridge, and once you see overpriced cider, you know you're in the right spot." He smiled and kept walking down the street.

I must look like I'm a tourist. Or, I am the only person in a summer jacket. Glyden crossed the street and gave Aubrith a disgusted look.

"You know, people here have an accent. How fascinating." Glyden smiled and started walking down the street.

"Where are you going?" I asked and went to help Aubrith up.

"A place where we can stay and get food." He kept walking down the street, not even waiting for us. I tapped Aubrith on the back, and he nodded his head, knowing it was time to walk. As I walked ahead, Aubrith clutched my arm. I looked up at him, and he gave me a glare. I knew he grabbed me because he was still feeling the side effects of the teleporting, but he would never admit it. I ignored him and let him hold on to my arm. We walked over the bridge and passed many fast-food places.

I saw Glyden, in the distance, take a sharp turn down a street. I rolled my eyes and pulled Aubrith with me as we increased our speed. Many people were walking and singing in the street, obviously intoxicated.

"They look like they're having fun." Aubrith pointed to a group of people singing a song together outside of a pub.

"Yeah, they do." I smiled. We found Glyden looking at a menu one hostess gave him, who was standing outside of the restaurant.

"Do you know what a shepherd's pie is?" Glyden looked at me with a confused look. I laughed and nodded my head.

"Why don't we actually try to see for ourselves." I gestured him and Aubrith up the stairs into the restaurant. The hostess seated us, and we ordered our food. Glyden ordered himself and Aubrith a cider.

"This juice is fantastic, Sasi. You must try it," Glyden suggested as he chugged the whole glass and wanted another one. I laughed to myself as I kept seeing Aubrith and Glyden drink more ciders.

We left the restaurant and Glyden and Aubrith were holding onto each other as they swayed down the cobblestone. Aubrith hiccuped a few times and kept laughing at everything. I saw a hostel was near us; I tried to guide Glyden and Aubrith down the path towards the hostel so we could sleep somewhere. The man at the front desk was yawning and scrolling on his computer.

"Hi, do you have anything for three people? We preferably don't want anyone else in our room." I asked. The man looked over my shoulder to see Glyden and Aubrith laughing with each other at a plant in the lobby. The man rolled his eyes and scratched his chest.

"You're American right?" He asked and looked me up and down.

"Yeah? Does that change anything for the room?" I looked back at Aubrith and Glyden who kept laughing at nothing.

"No, it just explains a lot. Anyway, we have a room available. Will that be cash or credit?" He coughed to clear his throat and looked over his glasses.

I smiled and went and grabbed Aubrith's backpack. I was searching for my wallet since I already felt bad that Glyden used his powers on the server at the restaurant.

I went back to the desk only to see Glyden staring at the man, and the man handed us a key, convinced we paid for the room. Glyden dangled the key in front of me and laughed. I rolled my eyes and lugged Aubrith's back-pack up the stairs. The hallway smelled of mildew, and Aubrith covered his nose.

We opened the door to see three beds with metal railings. I sighed and took the bed closest to the window. Glyden laid down on the bed closest to the door and closed his eyes. Aubrith jumped on his bed before laying down.

"Why is everything spinning?" Aubrith said as he held his head.

"Everything seems to move. Are we moving?" Glyden looked at me.

"No, you guys are just drunk." I laughed, and Glyden shook his head.

"I don't even know what that means. I am not what you say." Glyden put his head on the pillow and clutched his head.

"Is there a bathroom?" Aubrith looked at me. I nodded my head and gave him the key.

"The bathroom is down the hall." He nodded and ran out of the room. I took off my jeans and got under the covers. Glyden still had his eyes closed. A breeze came through the window, and Glyden immediately opened his eyes. He ran across the small room and shut the window.

"None of that wind. I'm cold as it is." He settled back down on the bed and grabbed the small blanket. He shivered and tried to control his breathing.

"It's cold here. I thought you brought jackets for us?" I looked over to Glyden.

"Yeah, that was before we were getting chased by that killer in a leather jacket." He rolled his eyes and held his hands out. He formed a yellow glow in his hands and smiled contently. Aubrith opened the door, and the glow went out.

"Can't you see I'm busy over here. I'm trying to get warm," Glyden said and tried to do the glow again, but it didn't happen. He sighed and stared at the ceiling.

"I lost my concentration, and I'm too tired to do it again." He rubbed his eyes and shivered again.

Aubrith took off his sweatshirt and got into his bed. He shivered as well as his teeth clattered. Glyden shivered more, and he got up.

"Okay, we need to huddle together." He had his hands on his hips. I leaned on my elbows and looked at him.

"Are you crazy? It will get warmer during the night." I

turned over and faced the wall. I heard Aubrith get out of his bed and move to Glyden's bed.

"The major ground rule for this is we cannot move throughout the night. I am not getting hit by your arms. Also, no stealing of my blanket. I brought mine over here, so you have yours and I have mine," Aubrith said to Glyden as he laid down on his back. I looked at them and rolled my eyes.

"We're already warmer over here, Sasi. Don't be ridiculous. You're going to freeze over there," Glyden said, and I knew he was right. I was already shivering. I put my pride aside and grabbed my pillow and blanket to lie next to Glyden. I had to admit, between the three of us, I felt like I was getting warm. I clasped my hands over my stomach and stared at the ceiling. Glyden was already snoring.

"Thank you for saving me in that town," Aubrith admitted quietly. I almost believed I imagined he'd spoken.

"Yeah, no problem," I replied. I kept looking at the ceiling. I could sense Aubrith wanted to say more, but he didn't. I just heard him breathing on the other side of Glyden.

§

We woke up and made our way down to the buffet of food. And by food, I mean bread and tea. Aubrith gave a disgusted look towards the tea and grabbed his bread. Glyden put some jam on his bread and went to sit at a table with another group of people at it. I walked over to where Glyden was sitting and awkwardly nodded at the other people at the table.

"What's the plan today?" Glyden asked me. I was about to answer when a man from the other group responded.

"We were going to go on the Hill of Tara tour. You guys should come!" the man exclaimed. I gave Glyden a confused look, and he shrugged his shoulders.

"Is the tour open to anyone?" Glyden asked as he took a bite of his bread. Aubrith sat down and already had his mouth stuffed with bread.

"They said there were some openings. We must walk to the bus pickup location, though. It's just down the street," another man in their group said. Glyden nodded and looked at me. I was shaking my head, and Glyden smiled.

"We'd love to join you on the tour," Glyden insisted, and one man in the group patted Glyden on the back.

"What are we doing?" Aubrith asked with his mouth full. I looked at him disgustedly and closed my eyes.

"Apparently, we are going on a tour. Isn't that right, Glyden?" I looked over to Glyden, who was talking with the rest of the group, oblivious to me and Aubrith, who rolled his eyes and kept shoving food in his mouth. *This is going to be great.*

We met the group outside as we grabbed the rest of our gear. One man looked at us and then looked around.

"I think you can get a coat in that shop over there?" The man pointed across the street.

"Oh, we're good. Thank you, though." I clutched my

shirt, trying to stay warm. Glyden gleamed at the information and went in and got us three coats.

"Wow. Did you even pay for those?" one man asked from the group. Glyden looked at me with wide eyes.

"Yeah, he has that app on his phone. That lets you pay," I responded. All the men seemed to nod and left the topic alone. Glyden looked at me again, and I shook my head as if to tell him it was not the time.

The bus arrived, and we sat towards the back of the bus. The tour guide seemed pleased to have more people on the tour. The other people from the hostel were in the front of the bus. I whispered to Glyden, "Why did you want us on this tour?"

Glyden looked around before he leaned in and said, "I think Jura is going to be there." I drew my eyebrows together. *Jura? Who the heck was Jura?* Then I realized Jura was Selene's other name. It was hard to remember. I nodded my head and sat back in my seat. I glanced at Aubrith, who was sleeping with his head all the way back on the bus.

The ride comprised some history about the place, but I was looking out of the window and not paying attention to the tour guide. It just shocked me how everywhere I looked was so green. I didn't think I'd seen this much greenery in my life. I didn't even know there would be such different shades of green to focus on. Rain hit the bus window. This place had a weird, calming effect on me. It was a weird sensation. I think Glyden felt it too, since he kept looking at his hands. The bus pulled up to the parking spot, and we all got out. The tour guide did a headcount before leading us towards the hill.

"We have to pass through this cemetery. It holds many people. The tombstones can have inscriptions all the way to the 1700s." Other people on the tour gasped and kept walking. Glyden gave me a weird look, and I shrugged my shoulders. He whispered towards me, "Why would anyone be fascinated by a cemetery?" I tried to contain my laugh. He laughed and kept walking ahead of us.

"This mound you see here. Some say that it was a burial site. It is called The Mound of the Hostages," the tour guide announced to the group. People immediately took out their cameras. Glyden looked over at me again. This time I couldn't hold in my laugh. Some people glared at me, and my cheeks heated.

"Kings often used the Hill of Tara. They would go up that hill to hold a ceremony for the new king of Ireland." The man pointed up towards the hill that was still far away. Aubrith almost tripped over a dent in the ground. He gripped his backpack straps.

"Are you okay?" I asked, and he walked ahead of me. *I take that as an okay?* I shook my head and walked behind him.

"The legend is that if you touch the coronation stone at the top, you could hear a great roar put there from the ancient gods in Ireland," the guide said again as we climbed to the top. I looked at Aubrith and Glyden, who were sharing a water bottle.

"This is pretty high up. You could see a lot from up here," a man in the group said. The tour guide nodded and announced that apparently you can see half of the counties in Ireland from this spot.

"The Hill of Tara is one of the most sacred places. It is said that gods from another world used to come through here as if it was a portal. In fact, the kings of Ireland had to symbolically marry the goddess Medb to be king." All the people on the hill gasped and were talking amongst each other. I walked over to Glyden and Aubrith, and they gave me a look.

"You think it's here?" I asked Aubrith and Glyden.

"If it's a portal to the otherworld, it might be worth a shot to try to see if a shard is here. This place feels like it has a ton of power. I'm actually a little terrified by it," Glyden admitted. I nodded my head. The whole time we've been on this property, I felt a cool sensation around me. I sighed and looked around to see all the people on the hill.

"There's too many bystanders here to do anything." Aubrith grabbed his backpack and was searching for the pen-like object.

"Do you think we should use this?" Aubrith held up the pen. I shook my head and looked back at the coronation stone. The stone looked like it was a rounded-out rock shot up from the ground.

"I think I can do it when we all get to touch the stone," I told Aubrith. He nodded and put the pen in his pocket. I went towards the tour guide.

"So do you know anything about the goddess Medb?" I asked him. He laughed and looked at me.

"She was a little insane, if you ask me. She had three criteria for her suitors: no fear, kind, and without jealousy for her—since she had a lot of lovers. Her father was a high king of Ireland, however, her enemy was

Conchobar. He was the king of Ulster. They got married, but it ended badly. She went onto other lovers, who would often challenge each other then die, so she got to hold power for a while. A druid gave her a prophecy that one of her sons named Maine would kill off Conchobar, so she named all her sons the same name. Isn't that quite the story?" The tour guide looked at me with a crazed smile. I smiled back at him, but when I returned to Glyden and Aubrith, my smile faltered.

"I don't think Medb is a goddess like Terra." I looked at Glyden, who crossed his arms and sighed.

"You don't think the stone is here?" His voice faltered.

"I think this land has something powerful on it, but this coronation stone is a decoy." I pointed back to the stone everyone in the group was touching.

"Where do you suggest the magic lies, then?" Glyden looked at me, and I shrugged my shoulders.

"I have no clue, but it has to be here somewhere. You don't feel this much power and not have a single thing of magic on this land." I crossed my arms. It felt like we were close, but we just didn't know where to look.

"I'm going to let you all get your pictures, but we need to get back to the bus in thirty minutes," the tour guide said before walking away.

"We need to find the shard on this land—and fast," Aubrith said. I just hoped that we could do that considering we were on a time limit.

CHAPTER

TWENTY

We searched the grounds quickly, starting with The Mound of the Hostages. Glyden held out his hands to see if any magic was there but shook his head. We kept making our way around the property. Glyden and I even went back to the cemetery, but we didn't feel as much power as we had when we'd walked up the hill. I overheard someone ask if this place was even magical. The tour guide sighed.

"It was believed to have the Arc of the Covenant here at one point. They tried to dig up whatever they could here, but unfortunately, they found nothing. People often say this place is magical, though." I ran over to Glyden, and he looked at me with wide eyes.

"We have to find it here. It has to be here somewhere." He nodded his head. Aubrith was just walking around since he couldn't really help us. I noticed he was sitting under a tree. Glyden and I kept looking but still didn't find any luck. We walked back to where Aubrith was sitting and found him asleep under the tree.

169

"Sasi, it's the tree," Glyden assured. I slowed my steps, walking up to Aubrith.

"Aubrith wake up," I demanded from him. He kept sleeping, and Glyden tried to go over there, but as soon as he got near the tree, he got forced back.

"There's a protective shield over this tree. Someone definitely does not want us near this thing," Glyden said as he looked at his hand, which was already blistering. I yelled Aubrith's name a little louder, and he jolted awake.

He squinted his eyes and gave us a confused look. "Why are you both over there instead of over here?" He stood up, and his head hit an object that was tied around a tree branch.

"We can't get to you. Glyden just tried, but it damaged him," I replied.

"You think the stone is over here?" Aubrith looked around and pulled out the pen-like object. The pen was shaking rapidly in his hand. "Guys, I think this pen is going to fly out of my hands. I can't hold on any longer." Aubrith's hands kept slipping off the pen.

The pen flew towards the tree, but an older woman grabbed the pen in midair. She analyzed it and smiled at the object. When she looked up, she had the bluest eyes I had ever seen. She walked towards us, leaning on her walking cane. Her frail hands gripped the grooves in the cane steadily. She was wearing a green raincoat and jeans with comfortable-looking shoes. Her hair was white as snow, cut short with a few curls.

"Glyden. It's been a while." She smiled up at the man. He smiled warmly at her and hugged her gently. She held out the pen towards Aubrith. "I believe this is yours." Aubrith grabbed the object and yelped when his hands touched it. The pen dropped into the dewy grass, from which steam abruptly rose. He quickly picked it up and put it in his bag.

"So, Glyden, are you going to introduce me to the friends who have brought you so far?" The older woman studied me and squinted her eyes. I felt like she was trying to look into my soul. I tried to look anywhere but her eyes, but they were captivating me.

"Ah, yes. This is Sasi. She is here on a very important mission. She is trying to close the portal between the two realms. And this gentleman over here is Lenia's son." Glyden gestured to us both. Aubrith and I were just awkwardly trying to look at the older woman. Something seemed familiar about her, but I couldn't figure out why.

She smiled at Aubrith and tried to stand up straighter than her previous position of being hunched over.

"Lenia was a wonderful healer. It's a shame she went blind during the chaos at that time." The older woman shook her head and gave Aubrith a sorrowful look. He cleared his throat and nodded his head. I could tell something was bothering him about this woman, but he seemed to collect himself.

"And you, Sasi. I haven't seen you in a very long time." She smiled warmly at me. I narrowed my eyebrows. *Had we met before?* I shook my head at my own thoughts. There was no way that I had met this woman before. I stood up straighter and shook her hand.

She raised her eyebrow at me and looked towards

Glyden. "You don't remember me?" she asked and looked back and forth between me and Glyden.

"I'm sorry. I wish I did, but I don't even know your name." I awkwardly scratched my neck as we stared at each other.

"Let's just say I used to be a friend of your mom." She looked away from me, and I studied her. A gust of wind blew, and we all shivered.

"Come. You are more than welcome to visit my home." She gestured us back towards the graveyard. I stared at the tree. There had to be a shard here. The magic was too powerful otherwise. I gathered my thoughts and looked at her again.

"We would love to, but we are in the middle of something." I smiled at her, hoping that she wouldn't be offended.

"It would just be until the storm passes." The older woman walked with her cane.

"What storm? The sky is clear?" Aubrith spoke finally. He looked up towards the sky, and there were drops of water trickling down.

"Not anymore. Come now." The older woman gestured towards us with her arm to follow her. The rain intensified the more we kept walking. There was a small house near the entrance of the cemetery.

Aubrith looked at me with wide eyes, and I looked back at him. I knew he was thinking the same thing I was: *We both didn't see that house there before when we were walking up the path.* Glyden seemed to trust her, so that pushed some of my worries away. We entered the small cottage, and there was a hole in the roof. The hole seemed to seep individual raindrops through. The drops echoed throughout the cottage.

"Jura, how has your life treated you in this realm?" Glyden asked her. My eyes bulged with this information. *That was Selene?* Aubrith seemed to ask himself the same thing because his jaw hung open.

The older woman laughed as she shuffled her feet towards a ratted chair.

"I can tell you, being old in this realm sucks. I miss the other realm. I have been trying to get back there for centuries, it feels." Jura's hands dug into the grooves of the cane.

"Endy told us we could find you here, in Ireland," Glyden replied. Jura's face visibly twitched at the mention of Endy's name.

"Is he still a prick? He left me, Glyden. He left me to live out his days in this dreaded realm." Jura spoke calmly, but her tone cut like ice. Her voice sent a chill down my spine. I gulped, suddenly feeling immensely thirsty.

"Well, speak up, child." She turned to me. I looked at Aubrith and Glyden, wondering what she possibly could've meant.

"You're thirsty, aren't you?" Jura looked at me with narrowed eyes. I slowly nodded my head, and she crossed her arms.

"Very well." She motioned her finger towards a box, and a water bottle floated out of it. The bottle swayed in the air as it came to a stop in front of me. I looked at her, and she looked at me expectantly. I held out my hand. The water bottle dropped as I caught it.

"Do you want it cold?" she questioned me. I nodded my head again. I felt unable to speak to her. She was highly intimidating, especially since I knew she was far more powerful than anyone we had met so far.

The bottle formed crystals on the sides of the plastic. My hand that encompassed the water bottle felt a cool sensation. I opened the water bottle and drank. It was almost as if there was ice in the water. Condensation was forming on the bottle as streaks of water dripped down the side.

Aubrith looked amazed, whereas Glyden wore a smug smile on his face. I rolled my eyes towards him, and he just smiled wider.

"So do you talk or do I have to keep reading your thoughts?" Jura asked again. I cleared my throat and tried to look anywhere but her eyes.

"Yes. Sorry. My throat was dry and I couldn't speak to you." I tried to look in her eyes, but I kept looking everywhere else. She had fair skin and light freckles below her eyes. She turned her attention back to Glyden.

"I see you have come to Ireland on a mission. A mission to close the portal, you say?" She shuffled her feet again until she leaned on her chair. Glyden smiled and nodded.

"Yes, she is the key to closing the portals." Glyden gestured towards me. Jura was eyeing me up and down. Out of nowhere, she started laughing. I felt slightly embarrassed—not to mention a little offended. My cheeks heated as her laughter filled the cottage.

"I'm sorry, love, but you? You looked in amazement at me just getting you water. How could you possibly be the one to close the portal? Not to mention the portal I have been trying to get through for years?" The grip on her cane tightened. I cleared my throat.

"I have learned some things. I mean...I have powers." I tried to sound confident, but she kept laughing harder.

"What powers? Let me guess, Glyden made you light up a room?" She wiped her eyes as tears formed in them from laughing so hard. Glyden now looked offended and stood back from her.

"Oh, Gly, you know I meant nothing by that comment. It's just that she has mortal blood in her. What could she possibly know?" Jura ran her frail hand through her white hair.

"I've been training her on basics. Our time got cut short by someone chasing us in England. We almost died," Glyden responded. He looked annoyed.

"Yeah, like Terra's mythical elk would almost die from someone. Especially from this realm. Aren't you one of those immortal creatures?" Jura asked Glyden with a small smile on her face. He sighed and looked at her again.

"Look, we have some books you probably can read. Endy gave them to us. I was just wondering if you can help us. Especially if that man comes back to take our lives." Glyden rubbed his face.

Jura sighed and stood up.

"Alright, I guess I can help her figure some things out. Also, what was that device you had, kid?" She moved her head to face Aubrith. He looked at me and gulped.

"We got it from someone in the new realm," Aubrith said as he nervously played with his backpack straps.

"Oh, it's an official device. Whatever you want, obviously more people want it. You guys might be the bait, you know." She leaned further back into her chair. I sat there thinking about what Jura said.

"You think other people know we are looking for things?" I questioned her. She smirked and let her hands roam across the handle on her cane.

"I think the same person is going to come back and find you all over again." She slowly got up and gripped her cane. She shuffled her way over to her table to get a banana. I studied her. I looked over to Aubrith who was doing the same thing. Glyden seemed to act completely normal. In fact, he didn't question her at all.

Aubrith put his backpack on the floor and rummaged through it. He pulled out the books and placed them on the table. Jura looked at the books and started laughing again. I was getting highly annoyed with her. I rolled my eyes and crossed my arms.

"Look, are you helping us or not?" I stared at her. Her laughing stopped, and she looked at me with crazed eyes.

"Know who you're talking to, girl." She grabbed the books and whispered something. The writing in the book magically appeared.

Aubrith grabbed the book and tried to read it. "It's all in Drudian language?" He scrunched his eyebrows together.

Glyden took the book from Aubrith and kept turning the pages.

"Druda wasn't supposed to have anyone who could do magic?" Glyden looked at her and she smiled.

"Well, I am here. I took a boat across Moonlight Bay and lived in Vibran ever since. Endy visited Vibran on important matters. The rest is history." She kept eating her banana, not caring about why Aubrith and Glyden were looking at her like she had ten heads.

"I'm sorry, but what is Druda?" I looked at them. Now all three of them looked towards me.

"See? You expect me to believe *that* is the savior of our realm?" Jura tossed her banana peel into a wooden basket.

"Druda is another place in our realm. It has insane creatures, but the people there aren't supposed to have powers. But they didn't denounce everything like Aurelia did. They had a religion of some sort that believed in their creatures and not the Goddess," Aubrith explained. I tried to make sense of everything and looked towards Glyden.

"Why didn't everyone just believe in the Goddess? I mean, I thought everyone in your realm knew she created everything?" I asked. I leaned against a chair.

"I mean, it is true. She made everything, but some people just wanted to use power against their people. They didn't want their people to all run to Guirra to be closer to her. They wanted some control over their people. I mean, here in your realm, they don't even mention the Goddess. You guys created other religions instead," Jura replied. She opened another book and revealed more words on the pages.

"Anyway, that's just a spell to teleport. These are a

variation to move somewhere. I even have a spell that said it summoned the Goddess here. I thought a long time ago, I could just summon her, and she would take me back to the realm." Jura hunched over, looking at the books on the table. She sighed and picked up one book to look through. "None of these books worked, obviously. I was at a dead end. I still am at a dead end. Ireland is said to be super powerful. Especially this hill. But I found nothing relevant in my search."

Glyden looked through the books and sighed. He set the book down and leaned against the wall. He looked at me and shook his head. I was hoping these books would tell us where the shards were, so I didn't have to keep thinking about where to teleport next. I looked down and sighed.

"Well, I guess we will be out of your way. I thought these books would be useful for something," Aubrith said as he gave the books back to her. She smiled. As we were leaving the cottage, she slammed the door before I could exit.

"They can leave but not you. You are the reason I have been trapped in this dreaded realm for such a long time. I could've had the shards already. But I didn't possess enough power. They said only someone with ties to the Goddess could have access to open and close the realms. I've been looking for the shards for my whole life. I tried everything to cut those dreaded things out, but they never worked. There's a spell on them for only you." Her eyes glowed blue, and suddenly she could walk normally. I stepped back. Glyden and Aubrith were yelling outside for me, but the door wouldn't budge.

"I swear I didn't know I could do anything. I just found out about this." I held up my hands, and she laughed. I felt my legs lift off the ground. It was like I had no control over what was happening. My body flung into the wall and the air got knocked out of me. I wheezed, trying to catch my breath. Jura picked me up and held me up off the ground, pinned to the wall.

"Give me the shards," Jura demanded. I nodded and reached into my pocket. I knew the shards were outside with Aubrith, but I had a rock in my pocket I'd taken from my mom's apartment. Maybe she wouldn't know the difference. I gave her a rock. It was always one of my favorite rocks as a kid. It would shine in the light because it was orange and yellow.

Jura took the rock and immediately dropped it. She shrieked as her hand started forming blisters. I tried to concentrate on the task at hand. I thought back to a calm moment with me and my mom. We were sitting on a lake, and she was trying to teach me how to fish. I always sucked at it, but she wasn't working, and we were traveling a lot. I thought back to her laugh. I felt warm inside. Jura was distracted, still looking at her hand and only holding me up with her other hand. I lifted my hand, and I used all my strength to push her off of me. Jura went flying into the other wall of the cottage, making a crack in the wall.

She started laughing and looked up at me.

"Is that all Glyden taught you?" She gave a wicked smile. She shot an orange blast from her hand. I ducked and started crawling over by her table. Glyden's voice was muffled through the wall, but I think he said to keep fighting her. *How was I supposed to fight this woman who has had magic all her life?* I kept crawling then hid under her table. I lifted the table and put it on its side to act as a shield. A blast went right through the table. The table was sizzling. I quickly stood up and tried to use all my strength in my hands. Little white glows were coming out of my hands, and Jura ducked. As she ducked, one of the white glows hit her arm. She shrieked, and the white glows kept coming out of my hands. *How do I stop the power?* I positioned myself towards the door, and the white glows kept firing.

The door had multiple holes. It creaked open. I used my foot to open the rest of the door since my hands were occupied. I stepped out into the grass but got blasted by a gust of air into the gravel surrounding the cottage. Glyden and Aubrith looked at me with wide eyes. I gripped the loose rocks in my hands. I felt like I had minor cuts all over my body. I turned over, letting my elbows hold all my weight. Jura emerged in the doorway, clutching her arm. Her arm was bleeding as the blood soaked through her shirt.

"You won't get away with this!" Jura walked towards me calmly. Before I could get my hands back up, Glyden stepped in front of me. She shot a fire blast out of her hands. Glyden held up his forearms, making the blasts sizzle out. He peered over his shoulder. "Get up!" he demanded. I scrambled to my feet and grabbed Aubrith's arm.

"Where are we going?" Aubrith shouted as our shoes crunched in the gravel.

"We need to get that shard before she does." I pulled

him back up the hill where there were civilians sitting underneath the tree. Aubrith looked at me confused, as I put my hand on the tree. A piece of the lower branch fell out holding a purple shard. I quickly grabbed the shard and threw it to Aubrith. He scrambled to get his backpack off and placed it near the other shards.

I looked over my shoulder. Glyden and Jura were still fighting. Glyden shouted over his shoulder, "Go now! I'll meet with you later!" Aubrith and I looked at each other before running back towards the bus.

"We are a little early to take off from Hill of Tara, but you can sit in the bus," the tour guide said as we ran onto the bus. Aubrith was sucking in his breath. I looked at him strangely. "Do you have asthma or something?" He looked at me weirdly before he coughed. He slowed his breaths and held his head down.

"I don't know what word you used. Sometimes after running a lot, I feel like I can't breathe." He rested his head on the back of the seat and closed his eyes.

I kept looking out of the window for any sign of Glyden. More people sat down on the bus and talked amongst themselves.

"I still don't see Glyden," I notified Aubrith. He looked out of the window.

"He will meet us. He said he would. I mean, he is Terra's key person, after all. I trust him," Aubrith assured me.

The bus engine turned on. Aubrith and I both looked at each other.

"How will he get to Dublin?" I asked. I could tell Aubrith was trying to act tough for the both of us, but I knew he was also getting worried. Our bus creaked across the gravel as we turned onto the main road. The Hill of Tara got smaller in the distance as the tour bus drove away, along with any chance of seeing Glyden soon.

TWENTY-ONE

Aubrith and I entered the hostel exhausted. Aubrith set his bag down on his bed. I jumped down on my bed. I sighed and looked up at the ceiling.

"Should we have left him?" I questioned. I looked over to the empty bed in the room, already missing Glyden's presence.

"If he said to trust him, I trust him. He will be back." Aubrith untied his shoes. I looked outside the window. It was already dark outside. I got up out of bed and started grabbing some of my toiletries to take to the bathroom down the hall.

"You're not leaving to go get him, right?" Aubrith stood up abruptly.

"No, I'm just going to the bathroom." I looked at him crazily. His shoulders dejected as he sat back down on his bed.

"Okay good." He leaned back on his bed to look up at the ceiling. I rolled my eyes and walked down the hallway. I realized now would be a good time to have a phone. To at least call Glyden and see where he was at. Him being gone put me on edge. He wouldn't just leave us on this mission.

I ran my toothbrush under the water and brushed my teeth. I looked around the bathroom, taking in all the stains and dirt in the grout between the tiling. *Well, you get what you paid for, I guess.*

The thoughts of the day kept replaying in my head. The shard came out of that tree way too easy. Maybe it was my adrenaline rush that made my powers come on quicker than usual. I remembered with the other shards at least I felt relief when they got out of their position. Today, with the shard in the tree, I only felt antsier. Jura was not in any way going to help us get the shard. She said she tried over and over, but nothing ever happened.

I continued with my bedtime routine and splashed some water on my face. I noticed my braid was very loose. I took my braid out and looked at all the waves and curls in my hair. I put my hands on the edge of the sink and put my head down. Today had been exhausting. I think using my powers drained me. I collected my hair back up and put it in a bun. I stared at myself in the mirror again. I had severe bags under my eyes. *That's always great.* I sighed and packed my toiletries in my smaller bag to make my way back to the room.

Jura's voice kept echoing in my head. She kept repeating how I wasn't ready. She also let me know that I was not the right person for the job at all. I doubted my power until I saw what I did to her arm. I'd never meant to hurt her like that. It'd just happened. The blood kept replaying in my mind. I shook the thought away and walked down the hall into the room with Aubrith.

He was already tucked away into his bed. I put the stuff that I had and put my little bag in my jacket.

"You know, you can put your things in my backpack. I know you lost your backpack in Toronto," Aubrith said in the abyss. His voice startled me.

"It's okay. I have a toothbrush and comb, so it's not a big deal." I laid back in my bed after taking off my shoes. I was debating on taking off my jeans to get into bed, but I decided against that when a gust of wind hit the window. I wished I hadn't lost my backpack because at least I had an extra pair of clothes in there.

"You know, I never properly thanked you for saving my life in England. So, thank you." Aubrith kept his head facing the ceiling. I gulped and recounted the memory of pushing him out of the way.

"Yeah, of course." I didn't know why things with Aubrith sometimes were so awkward. This was why I liked Glyden here. He would be our buffer for this awkwardness.

I cleared my throat. "Jura said I wasn't ready to be doing this kind of mission. She also said that only a person in the Goddess lineage can transport. But that's not true, you transported?" I lifted my head slightly to see Aubrith's face. It was too dark in the room, though; I couldn't even see my hand.

"Well, you said your mom was a mysterious person. Maybe she was a part of the lineage, and you just didn't know. Moms have a way of keeping things from people," he replied silently. I didn't know why he talked in such hushed tones. No one else was in the room with us.

"Is that what happened between you and your mom?" I questioned. It was almost as if I could hear him thinking of a response to that.

"She hid a lot of things from me, yes. I think they think they're doing it to protect you. I had to find out because, you know, my mom is blind. She said she was going on a business trip. Nothing too crazy. I was young at the time. She had the most beautiful eyes too. After she came home over a week later with a soldier from Guirra, I knew something was wrong. I was too young to understand the extent of the war. All I knew was that my mom tried to help, and she failed. She ended up giving her vision for the cause—whatever it means." Aubrith's voice carried through the room. I sat there, taking in what he said.

"I'm sorry about your mom. My mom would often leave for business trips, but it ended up with me being alone for extended periods of time sometimes. I knew she loved me, but there was always something she wasn't telling me. She is very good at changing the subject on things." I laughed, remembering that I had tried to ask my mom about different parts of our family. I'd always found it weird that it was just me and her. I didn't have any grandparents or cousins. She would always say it was just us and change the subject quickly. I sighed, thinking about her.

"She might've been in that family with the Goddess. Maybe there was some truth to what Jura was saying. Or, she could've just said that stuff to get to you," Aubrith mentioned.

"That doesn't explain my powers, though. I don't know anyone on earth with that kind of power." I pulled my blanket over my head.

"Okay then, yeah. I don't know how to help you there," Aubrith replied.

"Whatever my mom is, I just wish she would've told me. I could've been learning all of this stuff instead of wasting all my time on basketball." I sighed. That life of me playing basketball for a division-one team felt like a lifetime ago. It didn't even feel like me.

"I thought you loved that sport, basketball?" Aubrith questioned.

"I did, but I have bigger things to worry about right now."

"So how does the sport work?"

"Basketball?"

"Yeah, that sport that you play."

I pulled the blanket down from over my face and thought about it for a minute. It was still hard for me to wrap my head around that some people didn't know what basketball was.

"You have a ball and you try to get it into this circle with a net. You can bounce the ball and pass it to other people too. When the ball goes through the net, it counts as points." I hoped that helped Aubrith understand the sport more.

"So it is like the sport, Kirsevk. You put a ball in the hoop, and you get a point." I propped myself up on my elbows to face Aubrith, but it was too dark.

"I guess it is like that," I replied to him.

"Very team sport, Kirsevk. It is quite exciting," Aubrith replied to me.

"Basketball was exciting. I guess I've always been a part of a team. I mean, I would consider you and Glyden my new team now." I laughed to myself.

"It is nice being a part of a team. You aren't alone that way." Aubrith whispered into the dark room.

"Yeah, I agree. I don't enjoy being alone." I pulled the blankets up higher as another gust of wind hit.

"Me neither," Aubrith said. We both lay there, stuck in our thoughts. It was nice to have a civilized conversation with Aubrith without him grunting at me or being highly annoyed. I thought about my old team. I wondered if they were doing well without me. It wasn't like I could text them. They probably already ruled I was dead back home.

"I seriously thought I was going to die today," I admitted to Aubrith. I heard him clear his throat.

"Yeah, I thought so too."

Both of our breaths evened out, causing me to imagine the most horrible things that could be happening to Glyden right now. I sighed, knowing I couldn't do anything.

We must find a way to get Glyden back.

TWENTY-TWO

I pushed around my potatoes on the plate with my fork. I scanned the restaurant and saw everyone in their own little world. People were talking to one another, or they were involved on their phones. Aubrith's slurping brought me back to the reality I was living in. I gave him a disgusted face as he kept slurping from his coffee cup.

"What? This is way better than that other brown drink we had the other day." Aubrith continued to slurp.

"The other brown drink was tea. Tea is amazing." I rolled my eyes at him, and he gave me a disgusted look.

I continued to push around the food on my plate. I didn't feel like eating because I was imagining every horrible thing that Glyden could go through.

"Hey, he's going to be okay. Plus, eat something. The eggs here were amazing." Aubrith nudged my leg. I looked back down at my plate and decided he was right. If I had to fight anyone today, I might as well get in a good meal.

"You liked the eggs so much, you ate three," I joked with Aubrith. It was weird that we had gotten along ever since the night that we talked about our families. I could barely stand him, but I guess I could say we were getting closer to the friend thing. He slurped his coffee again, which made me cringe.

We both finished our meals, and I paid with my debit card. I still had some money in my account. Aubrith kept telling me to do the mind control so we wouldn't have to pay. I didn't feel comfortable doing that. We stood on the corner of a busy street in Dublin. The brisk air made me pull my coat towards me.

"So, what do we do today?" Aubrith asked as he stretched his legs on the side of the street. I shook my head at him and took a deep breath.

"Glyden still hasn't contacted us, and I'm getting a little worried." I shoved my hands into my coat pockets. Aubrith looked at me and gave me a comforting smile.

"We could always go sightseeing. I asked to do that to kill time, but you said we couldn't leave." Aubrith looked towards the college across the street. Aubrith had been learning how to use the community computer in the hostel. He looked up things to do in Dublin and found out that the Book of Kells was a touristy area. I told him we shouldn't go that far in case Glyden came back, but now that it had been three days since the incident, I felt like killing time was all we could do. I didn't know where to go next and without Glyden; I really didn't have a clue.

"Fine. We can go see the book." I rolled my eyes as Aubrith cheered. People who passed by us on the sidewalk looked at us strangely. I tried not to laugh at Aubrith. We walked into Trinity College. Aubrith kept looking at people as we walked through the entrance. He gasped when he saw the arches as we walked in. I rolled my eyes.

"I'll go get us tickets." I went to the student section to buy tickets for me and Aubrith. When I stepped outside, I couldn't find Aubrith at all. My initial thought was not to panic, but my increased heart rate said otherwise. I kept looking around, only seeing faces I did not know. I was considering asking people if they'd seen him until I felt a hand on my shoulder. I spun around and hit the hand away.

Aubrith looked at me, stunned, as he held his hands up.

"I was trying to let you know I was here. You didn't hear me calling you?" Aubrith questioned me. I drew my eyebrows together.

"You didn't call me?" I looked at him, confused.

"Yeah, I did. I said your name, like, four different times. Are you going deaf or something?" Aubrith asked as a joke. But I was worried because I didn't hear him.

"Of course. Yeah, I heard you say my name. Sorry I didn't respond." I gulped, hoping he wouldn't pick up on my lying.

"Well, let's go check out these books. I've been wanting to do this ever since I saw it in that box at the hostel." Aubrith had already started walking away from me. I sighed, knowing Aubrith had just called the computer a box.

We waited in line for a while. I learned Aubrith was not patient. He kept tapping his foot and would look around to see if anyone else was moving in the line. I laughed at him as other people in the line looked at us strangely.

"This is not funny," Aubrith replied with a straight face.

"Right. Just the guy who said we should waste time doesn't enjoy wasting time." I laughed again, and he crossed his arms.

Finally, someone ushered us inside, counting the number of people who'd walked into the room. There were books in cases encompassed in glass. Aubrith looked amazed as he tried to read every informational note on the sides.

I got a headache as we kept walking more into the room. I shook my head and looked up to the room, spinning. My vision kept getting blurrier. Aubrith tried talking to me about a book but noticed I wasn't feeling good. He gripped my arm to get me to look at him.

"I'm fine. I just don't know why I'm feeling like this." I kept trying to shake the feeling, but the room kept spinning.

I looked around, and my eyes seemed to only focus on the major book in the room. It was like I had tunnel vision for this book. I walked closer to it, despite Aubrith trying to get me out of the building. The book was glowing on its sides. I focused on the lettering until I realized the letters were rearranging.

"Do you see that too?" I asked Aubrith. He looked at

me, confused. He followed my line of sight and noticed the book.

"What am I supposed to be seeing?" He looked around the book.

"The letters. They're rearranging themselves. And moving all around the book." I squinted my eyes to see the book clearer than what my eyesight was allowing me.

"Nothing is happening. Are you sure you're okay?" Aubrith asked me.

"My head hurts. But the letters they're rearranging. I swear." Aubrith set his hand on my shoulder. He looked around the room to see if anyone was noticing the effects too or if it was just me.

The letters stopped moving only to reveal the message: "Don't willingly trust so easily. Some people aren't who they say they are."

The letters vanished, and the book went back to normal. I looked around to see if anyone else had seen that. The noise in the room started increasing. I realized that my hearing had gotten worse during that. I gulped down my saliva.

"Are you okay?" Aubrith looked at me worriedly.

"Yeah. It just had a weird message." I shook my head. Aubrith led me out of the room. The sunlight was sensitive to my eyes.

"What was the message you saw?" We sat on a bench outside looking at the quad.

"It just said not to trust so easily. And how some people aren't who they say they are." I kept staring out at the quad area. People were throwing a frisbee.

"What is that supposed to mean?" Aubrith looked confused as well.

"Maybe it was about Jura? I mean, that's a little too late. She tried to kill me."

"Maybe. I mean, that would make sense. She was supposed to help us, but she wanted revenge on you." Aubrith agreed with me. I ran my hands over my face and sighed.

"Is it just me or does that coffee shop have an owl symbol?" Aubrith asked.

I glanced up and noticed the white owl symbol for the coffee shop. *That's weird.*

"Maybe it's just a cool design for a coffee shop, you know?" Aubrith said. I shook my head.

"Not if I'm getting weird messages, then I see that as a symbol?" I looked back to the coffee shop.

"Well, I don't even know how my mom or anyone from my clan would do that." Aubrith picked at a scab on his hand. I stood up and walked over there. Aubrith was right behind me. I felt like my head was pulsating as I got closer to the poster of the owl. I gripped the brick wall that was near the poster. I tightly shut my eyes, trying to block out the searing pain in my head. Aubrith stood next to me, looking at me concerned. I felt something pushing on my hand against the wall. I opened my eyes to see a part of the brick coming out of the wall. I pulled my hand away and looked back at Aubrith.

"What the heck? We already got a shard from Ireland. Why would there be two?" Aubrith grabbed the piece out of the brick and gave it to me. I looked at the shard as it glistened in the sunlight.

"The piece from Hill of Tara didn't do that." I looked up at Aubrith. He quickly took the shard and pulled me with him.

"We have to get back to the hostel. The other shards aren't safe there. I knew I should've brought my backpack with me here." We ran through the crowds of people entering Trinity College. Aubrith pushed his way through. We got to the street, and a bus nearly missed us.

"Can't you slow down a bit? My lungs are burning," I yelled to Aubrith as we walked up the hill from Trinity College.

"What if someone took our shards?" he yelled back as he kept walking at a brisk pace.

We turned the corner to the hostel. The desk person was trying to get our attention, but we ran up the stairs. I pulled out the key and opened the door. Aubrith barged in, going straight to his backpack. He searched the backpack multiple times before dumping all the contents onto the floor.

"They're not here." Aubrith looked at me worriedly.

"No, they have to be here. I saw you put the shards in the backpack." I searched on the ground with all the scattered contents.

"It's not here, Sasi. All the shards are gone." Aubrith leaned against the wall. I kept frantically looking, trying to find something that obviously wasn't there. I noticed a sticky note on the floor.

"Did you have a sticky note in your backpack?" I got up from the floor. I grabbed the sticky note. The sticky note wavered in my hands as they shook.

"No. I didn't." Aubrith and I looked at each other before I flipped the note open to reveal writing:

Turn the other shard in and you'll get Glyden back.

-J

There was an address on the bottom of the note. I crumbled up the note and tossed it on the floor.

"This can't be happening." I gripped my hair. Aubrith looked worried too, as he ran his hands through his curls.

"Well, I mean we have to get Glyden back," Aubrith suggested.

"And she wins? She gets all the shards, and we are just stuck here waiting for our worlds to just vanish?" I yelled. Aubrith looked at me with enormous eyes.

"So, you want Glyden to die? He's obviously in trouble!" Aubrith exclaimed.

"No. That's not what I meant. I think there must be another way. I just can't see our mission ending this quick." I looked around the room, holding my arms above my head.

"We have to get him. The primary aim has to be him." Aubrith looked at me. "He would do anything for the both of us. You know that." Aubrith grabbed the contents that fell out of his bag. He shoved them all in the bag and started gathering everything.

"What are you doing?" I asked.

"I'm going to that address—with or without you," Aubrith said as he grabbed more things to shove in his backpack.

"We need a plan. We can't just rush in there. She will

kill us. I'm not strong enough to take her out," I tried to reason with Aubrith.

"So, we will get there, then figure out a plan when we get there." Aubrith zipped up his backpack, hesitantly putting in the recent shard.

I took a deep breath and looked around the hostel room.

"Okay. When we get there, we will create the plan." I looked at Aubrith.

"Yes. When we get there, we will create the plan," Aubrith agreed with me.

We both stared at each other, knowing that when we leave the hostel room, there would be a lot of uncertainty awaiting us.

TWENTY-THREE

We got out of the taxi and walked towards the address as it was raining. Aubrith kept readjusting his backpack numerous times. I glanced around, noticing that there were no lights or people in the area. I hoped we could come up with a decent plan before going into a trap. I pulled Aubrith aside, and he looked annoyed.

"What? We need to hurry. Who knows what she did to Glyden in there." Aubrith pulled away from me abruptly. I pulled him back again. He turned around to look at me, highly annoyed.

"We need a plan. Did you forget we can't just go in there and expect her to hand over Glyden?" I replied angrily. Aubrith huffed and looked back towards the dirt road.

"Fine, what do you want to do?" Aubrith obliged. I looked up the road and noticed a barn.

"That barn is probably where they are. Try to find an alternative entrance. I can walk in with the shard and try to distract her." I suggested. He studied me for a bit until he nodded his head.

"I guess we can do that." He continued to walk in the darkness up the road. I was shivering. I didn't know if it was because of the rain or because I was terrified of what I was walking into.

My shoes filled with water by the time we got to the barn with the amount of rain that was coming down. I looked around, trying to find another entrance. Aubrith walked around and put his thumb up towards me. I grabbed his backpack and nodded my head. *I hoped this worked.*

I composed myself by taking a deep breath. *Terra, I swear if you are real, you better help me out here.* I opened my eyes, staring at the wooden barn door in front of me. I gently pushed it open, revealing only a few lights in the barn.

"Hello? I have the shards." I raised the backpack in the air and looked around. I couldn't see a single person in the barn. I felt the hair on the back of my neck stand up before I felt myself being blasted by a cold force into the haystack in front of me. My head was pounding. I moved my hand to touch my head and felt warm liquid on my hand. *Great, I'm bleeding.* I looked up to see none other than the woman herself, Jura. She was already looking through the bag for the shard. I stood up shakily and held my hand out.

"Oh, what are you going to do?" Jura asked me. She laughed as she pulled the shard out of the backpack. I saw her reach around a grab a burlap bag that looked to have the other shards in it. Instead of adding the new shard from the backpack into her burlap bag, she dumped the other shards into Aubrith's backpack.

"I am keeping your bag too. It is easier to carry around." Jura snarled.

"Okay, where is Glyden?" I demanded. I looked around the barn, realizing no one else was here.

"Glyden and I had a little chat. I have him in a safe place. Don't worry." She smirked and held up the shards to the light.

"No, the deal was to bring Glyden and we give you the shards." I clenched my fists. I felt rage filling up my body.

"Who said I had to keep my end of the deal? How do you think I can get these shards to work? I need Glyden to get me back." She turned around, and her laugh seemed to intensify in my head. I felt hot all around me. I noticed the barn got increasingly brighter before I looked down at my hands. I had fire up to my forearms, and I was rising off the ground.

Jura paused her steps to look back at me hesitantly. Her eyes widened before she put her arms up in defense.

"Hey kid, we got off on the wrong foot." Her voice was faltering as I kept rising off of the ground. Never in my life had I felt so much rage. I felt like someone else was taking control of my body. My hands raised without my command, and they shot towards Jura. She jumped out of the way and shot back at me. I dodged her attack, and my hand shot out another fire ball towards her. She rolled on the ground to hide behind a haystack. I kept firing even though I tried to command myself to stop.

I noticed the barn was burning down. This was not

what I'd intended to do when I came here. I tried to think of a favorable moment, but nothing was coming to mind. It was like my mind blocked off everything except rage. I looked at the backpack with the shards. I noticed Aubrith was in the corner, staring at me amazed. Or, his face was in pure horror. I couldn't tell.

"Aubrith grab the bag!" I shouted. Aubrith stopped looking at me and ran after the bag. Jura tried to shoot at Aubrith, but I hit her hand when she reached out. She yelped in pain. I didn't want to cause any harm to anyone. I felt my rage slowly disintegrate like the haystack next to me. I was falling back to the ground.

When my feet hit the ground, Jura shot a white orb towards me. Everything happened so fast and before I knew it, I saw Aubrith on top of Jura with his pen in her neck. He crawled off her and looked towards me with his hands shaking. I felt an increasing amount of pain in my right arm. I looked down to notice I was bleeding. Aubrith rushed over to me and took off his coat. He tied his coat at the top of my arm to stop the bleeding.

"You killed her?" I asked in disbelief. Aubrith's hands were shaking as he tied his coat on my arm tighter. I repeated myself and he just looked at me.

"Consider this as me paying you back for saving my life in England." He inhaled a shaky breath.

He grabbed the bag and carried me out of the barn. I almost forgot that it was burning inside of there. I started coughing as soon as we hit the wet grass. The smoke filled my lungs. I coughed up phlegm and looked back at Aubrith. He grabbed the shards and tried to click them together. Only the two from Toronto and England clicked together. The shards from Ireland didn't click to the other ones.

"Come on, this has to work!" He tried to click them together again, but nothing was happening.

"She probably gave us a false one to lead us here," I whispered. I looked back towards the barn. Where the pen protruded from her neck, there was blackness surrounding the area. I looked back at Aubrith and saw him still trying to connect the shards.

"Hey, it's okay." I tried to reach out but hissed when my arm moved.

"No, it's not. We have nothing to go off of. We can't fix the entire realm with just two shards." He ran his hands through his hair. I realized he had blood all over him. It was probably mine.

"Where's Glyden?" I asked Aubrith. He immediately looked up and looked around.

"He has to be here somewhere. Hold on, I'm going to look. Just stay awake," he commanded. I nodded my head and lay down in the wet grass. It was oddly peaceful to know that Jura was gone. I stared at the sky as I heard Aubrith's footsteps squish in puddles in the distance.

I looked at my arm and noticed it kept bleeding. I looked up at the moon and felt calm all around me. I felt a cool sensation course through my body. I shivered uncontrollably. Suddenly, Glyden appeared out of the shadows. He ran over to me and smiled. He took off Aubrith's coat on my arm. I noticed he had a cut on his face. I looked up towards him as he tried to focus on my arm by laying his hands gently on my wound. I yelped out as the cool sensation pulsated through my body once again. I tried to focus on Glyden again but all I saw was a yellow glow coming from his hands.

"Hey, she needs that on her arm, or else she can bleed out," Aubrith said as he breathed heavily from running back over to me.

"When did you learn you could do this?" Glyden kept his hands on my arm, and I shrugged.

"What are you talking about?" I looked at both of them. Aubrith and Glyden exchanged a look with each other. Aubrith cleared his throat.

"Your arm is fully healed, Sasi." I got up quickly and looked at my arm. There wasn't anything there, not even a scar. It was almost as if I didn't have a wound, but my shirt said otherwise with all the blood.

"No, I did nothing. I just felt cold, but I thought that was because I was bleeding so much." I ran my hand up my arm. My arm felt sore when I lifted it. Glyden stared at me with wide eyes.

"Aubrith said that you levitated, and you had fire?" He looked at me hesitantly.

"Yeah, I did, but I don't even know where that came from. I swear. I didn't even command myself to do that." I looked at them nervously. Aubrith took a step back and sat in the mud.

"I didn't think your powers would develop this fast." Glyden looked at the ground.

"Where were you? Why couldn't you escape from her?" I asked him. He showed me his wrists, which had burn marks on them.

"She held me captive with power, and I couldn't get

out. There was a spell lock on it." His shoulders faltered. He looked at me in my eyes. "I will never leave you again, okay?" I nodded, and he patted my back. He walked towards the barn to inspect the remains of Jura. I noticed he'd taken the pen out of her neck and lifted her arms. Her body now looked like it was hundreds of years old.

"How old was she?" I asked Aubrith. He shrugged.

"Time is different in our realm. Like Glyden is probably seven hundred, give or take." I was about to respond before Glyden called us over.

We walked into the barn and saw a strange marking on her arm.

"Is that a tattoo?" I asked. Glyden nodded.

"Not just any tattoo, though. It is a saying in Khmer." Aubrith and I looked at each other.

"What is Khmer?" Aubrith asked.

"People usually speak it in Asia. I think it was influenced by Sanskrit." Glyden kept looking at her arm.

"You mean like the language of Hinduism?" I asked. Glyden looked at me, confused. "What? I took a lot of history classes in school." I shrugged my shoulders.

"It says, 'Go with the three snake heads,'" Glyden revealed. Aubrith and I looked at each other.

"What's that supposed to mean?" I crossed my arms.

"I'm not sure. I mean, back in the other realm, the Goddesses were called the serpents, but I don't get the reasoning behind it being in Khmer." Glyden kept examining her arm.

"I mean, how far away is this, Khmer?" Aubrith asked. I scratched the back of my neck.

"Khmer is spoken in Cambodia, Thailand, and even Vietnam. So, yeah, pretty far from us." I looked at the two of them. Glyden got up and brushed his hands on his jeans.

"Well, we should go there. Do your little teleport thing," Aubrith suggested. Glyden shook his head.

"We shouldn't leave unless we know we are absolutely sure why she even has that tattoo." Glyden walked back towards a small house.

"Where are you going?" I asked. Aubrith and I were getting hit with the rain.

"Somewhere warm," Glyden shouted at us. Aubrith and I looked at each other and shrugged. We started following Glyden, who knocked on the door, but no one answered. He put his ear to the door.

"We're clear. No one is in the house." He opened the door and walked in.

"Do you want to get yourself killed?" I whispered. He laughed as he turned on the lights in the house.

"No one is here. And Jura is not coming back for us. Might as well get out of that dreaded weather and relax before our next move." Glyden took off his coat and set it on the couch. He walked to the refrigerator and ate an apple. I shook my head at him.

"What's wrong?" Aubrith asked me as he drank some water.

"I just feel weird breaking into people's houses. That's all." I had to admit, the warm house was already feeling amazing on my damp skin.

"They won't be back for a few days," Glyden said as he bit into his apple.

"How do you know that? Where did you get that power?" Aubrith questioned Glyden.

"It's on this note." He pointed to the calendar on the refrigerator. I closed my eyes and shook my head.

"These days are weird. Who names something 'Monday'? Maybe it's their kid or something," Aubrith pointed out. I laughed and walked upstairs.

I didn't have the energy to correct them on what a calendar was. I found the bathroom and closed the door. I looked at myself in the mirror. My face was covered in spots of mud and blood. I had old blood caked into the side of my head. I sighed. I really looked like I was dying. My shirt was covered in blood, as well as my pants. I shed off my clothes and went into the shower. As soon as the hot water hit my face, I felt all the stress from the day wash away, with all the muddy water coming off of me with leftover blood. *What has my life come to?* I closed my eyes as the events from the day replayed in my head.

TWENTY-FOUR

"What are you doing?" I asked as I came down the stairs in fresh clothes I'd found upstairs. Aubrith and Glyden were sparring in the living room. They moved the couches and tables for extra space.

Glyden leaned over and gasped for air. He was trying to talk, but he was wheezing.

"I think he said he needs a break." Aubrith smiled at me.

"What are you doing up? I thought you would want to keep sleeping?" Glyden finally said. I shrugged my shoulders and went into the kitchen.

"So, how is the sparring?" I asked the two of them. Aubrith looked to Glyden.

"It is going well. I was teaching Glyden how to fight in case his powers went out again. You should join us. Your powers might not always be there, you know," Aubrith replied as he ripped off some tape.

"Where did you even get those gloves?" I asked

Glyden. He was taking off his gloves to reveal some tape underneath.

"The owner of the house had these in the closet. There are also more coats in there!" Glyden exclaimed. I shook my head as I went to the kitchen to look for something to eat. I found some bread and put leftover meat in the sandwich. I put some mayonnaise in the sandwich, hoping it would taste better.

"Maybe I'll join your sparring event." I bit into my sandwich, tasting too much mayonnaise. I scrunched my face and looked back at my sandwich. I hate too much mayonnaise, but I was starving, so it would do.

"Alright, well you're up next. Besides, we can't really do anything outside. There's another rainstorm." Aubrith looked disappointed. Glyden went to the kitchen and grabbed more bread.

"He's intense. I thought he was going to kill me in the sparring, so good luck." Glyden patted my back. I laughed and looked at Aubrith.

"So, what else did you two do while I was sleeping?" I set down my sandwich and made my way to the living room.

"We found out this owner has one of those boxes that tells us things." Aubrith looked at me excitedly. I tried to think about what he was saying.

"You mean they have a computer?" I asked.

"Yes, that thing." Aubrith pointed to me. I laughed and taped my hands.

"So, what am I supposed to do with this sparring thing?" I asked, putting on the gloves.

"You just have to do a simple punch into my hand, that's all," Aubrith replied as he pointed to his hand.

I clenched my hand into a fist and punched into his hand.

"Good, now do a combination and hit faster." Aubrith pointed to his hand again.

I hit his hand again before hitting it with my other hand. I was about to cheer until he hit back. I dodged it and looked at him.

"What the heck was that?" I looked at Glyden, who was already laughing.

"Do you think your defender is just going to sit there and let you hit them?" Aubrith started walking towards me. I stepped back and put my hands back up.

"Again," Aubrith demanded.

I hit his hand, and he moved his hand towards my head. I ducked down and aimed my punch at his abdomen. He backed up and swung his fist towards me again. I dodged his fist but missed his other fist that came towards my stomach.

I doubled over and tried to catch my breath. I looked back up at Aubrith, and he was walking away. I lunged towards him. He moved at the last second, making my fist collide with the couch.

"Be quicker." Aubrith held up his fists again, ready to fight.

I swung my fist at him again, this time a little faster. He dodged and moved back towards the couch. He laughed and swung towards me. I ducked and hit him in his stomach. He coughed, and I moved to the side.

"Good hit. You really nailed that one," Aubrith acknowledged as he sat on the couch.

Glyden came over and sat on the couch as well. I took off the glove and unwrapped my hand. I sat next to Glyden. A drop of sweat fell down my face. I wiped the sweat away and took a deep breath.

"That was exhausting. I feel like we didn't even do much." I put my arms above my head.

"We need to work on using your legs. A kick can go a long way," Aubrith replied as he clutched his stomach.

"Are you seriously eating my sandwich?" I asked as I looked back to Glyden on the couch. He took the sandwich out of his mouth and offered it back to me.

"Ew, get that thing away from me!" I exclaimed. Glyden shrugged and put it back in his mouth.

"Can I ask about the pan with water and grass in the kitchen?" I asked them both. Aubrith looked at me, confused.

"Oh, that was me. I put grass on my burns on my wrists. It takes off the heat from the burn from her power she used on me." Glyden showed me his wrists. I gasped as he showed me his wrists. I noticed he also had a Band-Aid on his face.

"Can't you heal yourself?" I asked Glyden. He shook his head.

"No, not with the spell she used. She did that on purpose. I have to wait this out." He pulled his sleeve back down and sat back, eating the sandwich.

"What did you find out on the computer?" I asked Aubrith, who laid his head back on the couch.

"I found nothing yet. I was waiting for you to wake

up." Aubrith pointed to the corner of the house. "The computer is on that table over there."

I stood up and stretched my back. I walked towards the computer and sat down in the chair. Glyden and Aubrith followed me.

"So, you said snakes, right?" I asked Glyden. He nodded. I Googled the significance of snakes and pressed enter on the keyboard. I clicked on some websites as Aubrith and Glyden looked amazed.

"Isn't the box amazing? It tells you everything." Aubrith nudged Glyden, who nodded. I rolled my eyes as I clicked on another website.

"It says that snakes can symbol rebirth and healing. Actually, snakes aren't bad, but I beg to differ; they're ugly looking," I said as I clicked on another site. Aubrith laughed, and Glyden gulped.

"Maybe don't say snakes are ugly in front of the Goddess if you ever meet her." Glyden patted my back.

I kept looking for different websites until I landed on one that spoke about snakes in religion.

"In Hinduism, snakes are viewed as superior status. They are called Nagas in Sanskrit. They are depicted in many statues around Cambodia and in Thailand."

I kept scrolling down the website trying to find something else about snakes.

"Snakes even were prominent with some Native American cultures with the Snake Girl, who was an underworld spirit. The Maya vision serpent from Yaxchilan. Snakes were also prominent in Peru. This is so interesting." I kept scrolling, looking through more of the site. Aubrith and Glyden kept looking at each other.

"So, snakes are huge in Cambodian culture?" Aubrith asked.

I scrolled down to the section about Cambodia.

"It says that they were a part of Cambodian mythology. Also, they are big in Hindu mythology. In India, they play roles in legends where Manasa is the queen of the snakes. It also says that the festival nag Panchami is a festival for snake worship and on the fifth day of Shravana."

I clicked on another website and did more research. I found anything about other cultures interesting, considering that not a lot of cultures are shared in school. I'd always been a history nerd at school. If it wasn't basketball, I was reading about history.

"Ah, here's one on Cambodia. It was a love story. A prince was supposed to kill the naga princess, but they ended up falling in love during the battle. It says that the woman, Soma, agreed to marry the man, Kaundinya. They ruled during the Funan era. The Khmer people believe they are descendants of them. Nagas are also depicted in Buddhism." I was talking aloud. I heard Aubrith pace back and forth. Glyden kept gripping the chair behind me.

"I don't know why Jura would be so intrigued by this, though," Aubrith spoke as he paced.

"I don't really know either. She had to have some connection to Cambodia. It wouldn't just be a coincidence." Glyden stood up and went to the kitchen. He pulled out a bag of chips and started chewing rapidly.

"Stop stress eating. Plus, the people are going to be

back in a few days so we should leave soon," I yelled out so Glyden could hear me in the kitchen.

"But you went through something traumatic. I didn't think you could teleport just yet." Glyden stuffed some more chips in his mouth.

"I'll be fine. As soon as we figure out why she was there, we can teleport," I replied to Glyden. I kept looking up more information about Cambodia and snakes.

"This website says that snakes were divine and can sometimes be half-human, half-god. The Khmer people are very in touch with this idea. Many people have different depictions of what the naga was from, but they all agree they derive from them. The naga statues can have a different amount of snakes but they're all over temples. The amount of snakes seems to have different notions too."

"What does it say about three snakes? Jura's tattoo said three snakes on it, so it has to lead us to something," Aubrith asked as I kept scrolling.

I typed in 'three-headed snake' to see if anything would come up.

"It just keeps talking about Greek mythology. I don't think we want that." I kept scrolling to see if we could find anything else.

"I'm sorry, guys, all I can find about the snake is that a seven-headed snake in Cambodia usually is a good omen. It can represent water, fertility, and even protection." I tried to research some more about the topic, but my eyes were burning from the hours we'd wasted on this.

"Great. We have nothing." Aubrith fell onto the

couch. I closed down the computer and looked at Aubrith and Glyden.

"Maybe she had someone there?" I suggested.

"Someone else from the other realm that would know about the Goddesses?" Glyden asked. He scoffed as he sat down on the couch next to Aubrith.

"I don't know. I was just trying to suggest something." I looked up at the ceiling and yawned.

"Well, if you think of something, just let us know. We need more to connect Jura to this place. If there's nothing on three heads, I don't know what to do." Aubrith got up from the couch and made his way to the bed he'd claimed.

"I think if we just let him process everything, he will be fine." Glyden looked at me.

I sighed, knowing that we were at a loss for our investigation.

"I wish that we could figure something out. She couldn't have that tattoo for nothing? She was powerful in the other realm," I told Glyden. He nodded his head and stood up.

"Maybe you're right. Someone would've had to be there to help her. Her whole aim was to get to the other realm, right?" Glyden questioned. I nodded my head and tried to make sense of what Glyden was suggesting. "So, what if that was the location to get to the other realm? Like, a source to the portal?" he asked. He locked eyes with me, and I settled back into my chair.

"She said she needed your help to get back to the other realm. So, she would've needed someone powerful,

I'd imagine." I got up and paced around the room. I bit my nails to ease my anxiety.

"She would've. But if she had a plan for me, maybe the powerful person would not help her anymore. She needed someone else to get her out. Which would've been me considering the fact she pinned me up against that tree outside with a spell block." Glyden rubbed his wrists, still looking traumatized by what Jura did to him.

"She had you on that tree? I didn't know that. I was lying on the ground, so I didn't know where Aubrith found you." I gave Glyden a small smile.

"Yeah, it's no big deal. I just felt like I betrayed you. My duty is to protect you, and I couldn't be there with you and Aubrith." He looked down at the floor.

"You protected us! You risked your life for me and Aubrith. We got the other shard because of you." I smiled at Glyden. He nodded his head.

"Where is the shard, anyway?" he asked. I looked around the room and found Aubrith's backpack. I pulled out the jade-looking shard we got from the coffee shop near the Book of Kells.

"The one we got at that tree on the Hill of Tara didn't click to the other ones. Aubrith tried to click it together with the other ones but it didn't work." I handed over the shard to Glyden, and he smiled at it.

"Yeah, she put a fake shard in the tree so she could track you. I didn't really know what else to do but wait there in the tree." Glyden grabbed the other shards and then grabbed the jade shard. The jade shard merged with the two other shards.

"It's weird that the stones are forming a little circle."

Glyden looked at the shards more closely. Glyden handed back the shards to me. I put them in the backpack on the side.

"I have no clue what to do about this Jura business. I don't know what she was planning." Glyden rubbed his eyes and laid down on the couch. I peered over at him.

"We'll figure it out. We can go adventuring in Cambodia soon." I smiled at Glyden. He nodded his head and pulled a blanket over him.

"Goodnight, Sasi. We also need to work on your control with your powers. I don't want you to feel you're not in control." Glyden looked at me seriously. I nodded my head and walked up the stairs. I rested my head on the pillow.

I ran my hand down my arm, trying to feel a bump of some sort from the attack by Jura. I couldn't find one. I sighed and looked up at the ceiling. I wondered if Terra actually heard my plead at the barn. I would never admit to Glyden or Aubrith that I secretly asked for her help back there. I couldn't determine if that was really me or her helping me. I looked at the full moon that was shining into my room. *There had to be something connecting Jura and Cambodia.*

I tried to think about the common thread between all the places we'd gone to before. I mean, I had visited Ireland with my mom when I was a kid. I went to England with her. I even went to Toronto with her. I had no connection at all to Cambodia. That's why it didn't fit the criteria of my original thought process. There couldn't be a shard there. I had nothing there to connect it to. The only thing I knew was that Jura had some connection, and each place didn't have a piece of her there.

I rubbed my eyes. They were burning from being awake for so long. And from staring at a computer. It'd been a while since I'd even looked at one of those. During this entire mission, I hadn't even had my phone with me. Sometimes in my life I'd thought I couldn't live without my phone. Now here I was, laying in some random bed in Ireland, trying to save a whole other realm I barely even knew. I missed college life. I missed going to practice and seeing my team. I thought about Glyden and Aubrith. *I guess they were my new team now.*

I closed my eyes, trying to sleep. The past few days were getting to me. I didn't want to think about the headache and whatever happened to me at the Book of Kells. I definitely didn't want to think about me levitating with fire. That one was hard to wrap my head around. I could just see Jura bleeding. I never wanted to cause harm to anyone. Jura had been broken. She'd wanted to see her old life and family again, for which she would do anything. I felt her pain oddly enough. I missed my teammates and friends back home. Most importantly, I missed my mom.

It felt weird being in these places that she and I traveled to. We'd really never done things without each other. Well, unless she'd travel for work to save people in other states, and even other countries. I desperately needed to sleep. The punch Aubrith had thrown at me earlier was hurting again. I'd never fought in my life. It was strangely nice for someone to teach me how to fight. Aubrith was right. I couldn't rely on these powers forever. Especially since I didn't even know how to control them.

I put a pillow over my ears so I could focus on the silence. I hated when my thoughts overtook my mind like this. I took a deep breath and thought of all the good times I had growing up. I felt my hand get warmer. I looked down and noticed I had a little white glow on my hands. I laid back down to focus on sleeping and thought of the wonderful childhood memories I'd had until everything faded to black.

TWENTY-FIVE

I saw my mom's face clear as day. Her brown hair had a braid down the side, like always. She smiled at me as she kneeled to my level. She brushed down my flyaways in my hair with her hand. She looked at me with so much love, but I knew this trip was going to be longer than the other ones.

The airport was busy with everyone trying to get somewhere. People were rushing past us, fading into the background. I could see her looking around like she always did. She always looked over her shoulder as if someone was coming after us.

"I need you to be good. My friend DJ is going to take care of you. He's nice. You've stayed with him before," she whispered as she kept running her hands down my denim jacket.

"Yeah, I know DJ. He makes tortillas." I laughed. She smiled at me and nodded.

"I won't be gone that long. I'll be back to help you with that jump shot before you know it." Tears rimmed her eyes. I nodded my head and knew she would be missing my basketball tournament this week.

"Why do you have to go on this trip again?" I asked her. She wiped her eyes and took a deep breath.

"It's important. I need to figure some things out. The hospital is paying for the trip, anyway. I'll be with other doctors. I need to help people in other countries, remember?" She looked at me, concerned. I nodded my head as she fixed the loop on my overalls.

"Okay, well, I have to go to my gate. Remember to keep your necklace on, okay? I don't want you to lose that. Promise me, you won't lose that," she demanded. She stood up and looked down at me. I nodded my head and touched my necklace.

"I never take it off, Mom. You know this," I said and showed her I was wearing the necklace. She laughed and kissed my forehead.

"Good. Now you go be good for DJ. I will see you in a few weeks after I settled everything. If I'm not back in time, DJ will take care of you." She looked at me seriously. I couldn't understand why she was telling me this. She left for other places before. This time, it was just with multiple doctors and a longer time. I didn't know what she had to do in the other country, but I knew it had to be serious.

She hugged me one last time before she turned towards her gate. Her button-down shirt swayed as she walked down the hall. I stared at the back of her head, wishing she would come back and say that she could stay for my basketball tournament, but she never did.

I woke up in a cold sweat, gasping for air. I looked down and realized my shirt was drenched. I ran my hands over my face, trying to get a sense of what I'd just dreamed of. I put my hand on my heart to feel the intensity of how fast it was beating. I looked at the clock and realized it was four in the morning. I sighed and laid back down on the bed. The moon was still shining into my room. I rolled my eyes at how ridiculous that dream was.

"Really? When Mom used to go on Doctors Without Borders? Why was I thinking of that?" I asked myself. I stretched my arms above my head to get some sense back into my body. I stared at the ceiling, trying to make sense of that dream. *That felt so real.*

I'd remembered that time because I had to stay with that man DJ. He was nice. We would always work on my basketball skills, and he would help me out with homework. He had salt-and-pepper hair. I always wondered why he offered to help me and my mom out. He seemed normal and would even make cookies with me sometimes. I hadn't thought about him in a while. Actually, that time when my mom went on her trip, that was the last time he'd helped us out.

I'd always thought it was maybe because I ate too many cookies or played too much basketball. But it turned out, he'd just been getting older. He had his own life. It was hard for a nine-year-old to figure that out.

I sighed and sat on the side of the bed. I took my hair out of the braid. My hair was super wavy. I just ran my hands through it to massage my scalp. I stood up and made my way down the stairs. Of course, Aubrith and Glyden would still be asleep, but I wanted tea, desperately. The wood floors creaked as I walked across them. I silently hoped that Aubrith and Glyden couldn't hear my footsteps.

I made my way to the kitchen and turned on the stove. I leaned against the counter as my dream kept replaying in my head. My mom had been so sad that day. It was hard to wonder why she was so sad. She'd never been that sad before when she left on trips like that. She'd even packed extra things that time. She would sage the house every day that month and tell me to take different rocks to school and to basketball practice. Come to think of it, she was a very weird person.

The water was boiling. I turned off the stove and poured the hot water over the teabag I had sitting in my cup. I let the tea sit for a moment before taking a sip. The warm liquid went down my throat. I sighed in contentment and looked at the sunrise that was coming through the house.

My mom loved sunrises. She would always wake up early in the morning in order to see a new shade of orange in the mix. I smiled at the memory. *Why do I keep thinking about her today?* I yawned and sat at the table. I knew that we only had a few more days where we could be in this house. We still needed to find something that connected Jura to Cambodia, but I just didn't know what. There somehow had to be a connection to the Goddesses, to Cambodia and to Jura. I knew Jura wasn't a Goddess because she couldn't gain access to the portal. At least, that was what she told me. She also said she knew my mom when we first met each other. Which had to be a stretch.

I laughed to myself, thinking about how my mom and Jura would get along with each other. I silently let Jura's words soak into my mind for a while. I got up and went to the computer again. This time, I searched for Doctors Without Borders in Cambodia. Sure enough, there were links to lead me down the path of Jura's twisted mind. *She said she met me before?* If my mom was gone, I wouldn't have met Jura before. I kept looking before I found pictures of doctors in the program helping people. *Maybe if I found a picture of my mom in Cambodia.* I scrolled down to the bottom of the page. I didn't see my mom in any of these pictures. Maybe she was just on a bathroom break, or on the year they went to take pictures, she wasn't there.

I was about to turn off the computer before I heard someone behind me.

"What are you doing?" Aubrith asked me. I jumped in my chair, spilling some tea on myself.

"Oh, nothing. I was just bored." I frantically tried to wipe off the tea on my leg. Aubrith stared at me for a while before he went to the kitchen to make himself some coffee.

"All I can say is thank the Goddess you are using that magical box and not me. That thing is confusing." Aubrith pointed towards the desktop. I laughed and met him in the kitchen.

"How did you sleep?" he asked. He was in a cheerful mood from his usual hating-the-world attitude.

"Horrible. I had strange dreams," I confessed.

Aubrith looked up at me as he poured some coffee grounds into the mixer.

"Do you want to talk about it?" he asked before turning on the machine. I shook my head. He shrugged. He pressed the button, causing Glyden to jolt off of the couch.

"What's going on?" Glyden screamed. I laughed as Glyden rubbed his head before walking over to the kitchen.

Aubrith stopped the coffee grounds mixing and added some water. I looked at him in disgust.

"What was the dream about?" Aubrith looked at me again. Glyden now looked at me, shocked.

"You had a bad dream?" Glyden looked surprised. I nodded, and he put his hand on my shoulder.

"What was it about?" Glyden asked. I finally gave up and told them the entire dream.

Aubrith stared at me with a confused look as Glyden stared at me in shock.

"Wait, your mom missed your basketball tournament?" Glyden asked. I looked at him with a incredulous face.

"Seriously? That's all you got from the story?" I asked. Glyden smiled and shook his head.

"No, of course not. I also got the part where she had her hair in a braid. That sounds like a classy woman. Kind of like you. You always have your hair in a braid." Glyden took a sip of Aubrith's coffee that he'd just made. Aubrith shoved his arm, and Glyden laughed harder.

"So, what do you think the dream is about?" Aubrith questioned. I shrugged.

"I don't know. Jura said she'd met me before. She also said she knew my mom. I didn't know what that was all about until I started realizing that I had a connection to where all the shards are. I never have been to Cambodia, but my mom has. Do you think my mom had something to do with all of this?" My hands shook. The coffee cup that lay on the table also was moving. Glyden put his hand on my shoulder, and everything stopped moving.

"Thanks." I looked to Glyden.

"No problem." Glyden patted my back and sat at the table.

"Your mom is a part of all of this? I highly doubt it. I think it was a coincidence to her being in Cambodia. I mean, that was her job, right?" Aubrith replied as he took a sip of his coffee. I looked over to Glyden, who was quiet.

"Glyden, you have to say something," I pleaded. He scratched his head and took a deep breath.

"I don't know. I mean, it sounds like you're onto something, but I don't know how your mom could even do that. I think Jura was trying to get in your head, and obviously, it worked," Glyden spoke.

I leaned against the counter again and crossed my arms. *Maybe I was being too paranoid about this.*

"Yeah, you're probably right. It was a long shot anyway." I slumped my shoulders.

"Fine, why do you think your mom has something to do with everything?" Glyden asked as he got up from the table.

"First, you mentioned the necklace. How people in

the other realm used to wear a necklace of some sort?" I looked at Aubrith and Glyden.

"Yeah, the lapis stone." Glyden nodded.

"She used to have that necklace. I even have a necklace like that one. I lost it in the other realm, but she custom made mine." Glyden rolled his eyes.

"A necklace can't prove anything. You guys have the stone on this earth. What else?" He crossed his arms.

"When I took a rock out of my pocket that my mom had given to me when I was little, Jura jumped back. The rock burned her. That's how I could even escape her the first time." I crossed my arms. Glyden drew his eyebrows together.

"I don't know. Isn't that a stretch to say your mom is connected to all of this?" Glyden looked at me and Aubrith, who shrugged his shoulders.

"I think we can say that. What else do we have?" Aubrith said aloud.

Glyden huffed and walked back to the table. Aubrith laughed.

"Seriously? You're throwing a tantrum? Also, you've been rolling your eyes at me this whole time. " I asked Glyden.

"I don't even know what that is, so those words mean nothing to me. Besides, I'm trying to be human like you, and you roll your eyes all the time." Glyden bit into a piece of bread at the table. I moved back to the computer and clicked on the website again.

"My mom went to Cambodia before. But she's not in any of these pictures. I think we should look there. Maybe we will find something, maybe we won't. Do you have a better idea?" I looked at Glyden. He rolled his eyes and huffed.

"I guess I don't, but don't complain when we find nothing in Cambodia. Also, how are you feeling? When would you be able to teleport?" He looked at me carefully.

"I think we can prepare. I'm still tired, but hopefully, that will go away soon," I admitted. Aubrith nodded his head and put the furniture back to how it was. Glyden kept looking at me.

"Yes?" I asked him. He looked at me and slightly smiled.

"Maybe we should train some more. You need to control your powers." He brushed past my shoulder. I scoffed and followed him.

"Why do you say I have no control?" I asked him. He stopped in his tracks and looked back at me. My hands were clenched and the picture frames in the hallway were shaking on the wall. He pointed to the shaking picture frames. I let my hands dangle at my sides. The frames stopped shaking.

"You were saying?" he questioned me. I rolled my eyes and made my way outside the house. It was even colder today than yesterday. The wind pierced through me. *I don't think I will ever get used to this.*

"Now where were we?" Glyden looked at me and smirked. I knew what was coming. He shot more air out of his hands. I held up my forearms to block his hits.

This was going to be a long day.

TWENTY-SIX

I tied the jacket I had around my waist. A drop of sweat rolled down my face. I quickly wiped it away as we kept moving through the crowd of people. Aubrith and Glyden were getting stared at since they had their jackets still on. Aubrith was fanning himself. The air felt dry, making my skin want to beg for moisture.

I bent over and put my hair up. I couldn't be walking around with my hair down. It was way too hot. The red dirt kicked up on my shoes before we got to the paved sidewalk.

"This place is very hot. I don't like it." Aubrith fanned himself. I negotiated with some of the local people to get us better clothing, but the best I could do for Aubrith was a long-sleeved shirt.

Glyden had been quiet ever since we'd teleported here. He was acting strange. Aubrith was more than happy to be in a warm place at first, but now he was hating it. I laughed at both of them and moved in front of them. I lead them back to our hotel, which kept trying to offer us green drinks, but we kept refusing.

"So, first day in Cambodia, how is it so far?" I asked Glyden and Aubrith. They glared at me.

"The only reason we left our hotel is to get more water. I feel like I am dehydrating." Aubrith poured his water bottle over his head.

"Was that necessary?" I glared at him as he left puddles all the way to our room.

This place was not like how I imagined. Everything seemed like it had a story and a relation to their religion. It was beautiful. Even as you walked down the street, you could see structures that represented their own culture. We saw monks walking around amongst their citizens, which was entirely different from the places we have been seeing.

You would think, with the amount of times we'd teleported, that it would be smoother each time, but that was not the case. We were all feeling the effects of this teleportation. Especially me. I felt more fatigued than I had from the other times. My body also ached. Glyden and I had to look up pictures of Cambodia before we even teleported here. Which could explain why we all hit the ground harder than usual. I kept trying to massage my neck, but it seemed like no use.

Aubrith sat on his bed with the portable fan the front desk had given us. This place was hotter than the other places we have been. The local people, at first, laughed at us for wearing winter-like clothes when we'd first gotten here. That quickly changed when we felt the effects of the heat.

I laid down on my bed and quietly observed the pamphlet the front desk had given us. There were a lot of temples and places we could visit. We just had to find out what Jura had been up to. There was the most famous site in Cambodia, Ankor Wat. That seemed to be the main attraction here. However, we would need to go with a group of some sort. I sighed and rubbed my eyes. It was a risk to come here, considering we didn't even know where the shard would be—or if there would be one here.

I looked over at Glyden, but he was already sleeping again.

"Is it just me or did that teleportation mess with you?" Aubrith asked me quietly as he held his head. I nodded and used the pamphlet to fan myself.

"No, you're right. I feel exhausted and like everything is drained from me." I looked over at Aubrith, and he nodded his head.

"Well, what's the plan for this place?" Aubrith looked at me with a hopeful smile.

"I do not know," I replied. His shoulders slumped and went back to paying attention to the fan.

"Well, this is great. We're in your realm but don't know where the heck we should go." Aubrith turned on the portable fan.

"We could just start exploring again?" I glanced at him. He was facing the ceiling, angling the fan at his face in a new direction.

"Yeah, we could. Or we can sit in this pleasant room with air," Aubrith replied. I shook my head and looked at Glyden again. He was snoring.

"We could venture outside without Glyden," I suggested. That caused Aubrith to turn his head towards me.

"Are you crazy?" he asked. I looked towards him, and he had the fan in another direction again.

"I mean, he's still sleeping. We won't be long. I want to see if there're any clues to this place. So far, we just know there are snake structures almost everywhere we go." I looked towards Aubrith, and he sighed.

"Yeah. It reminds me of Lumos back at home. That city has snake structures everywhere. But that is the birthplace of the Goddess, so it makes sense." He looked back at the ceiling.

"Your realm had snake structures too?" I held myself up on my elbow to get a better look at Aubrith across the room.

"Yes. Of course. The Goddesses are the creators of everything. It would be an insult to not have them. Especially in Lumos." Aubrith turned the fan off to look at me.

"What are you thinking? I can't read your mind, but I feel like I can hear your brain thinking." Aubrith sat up fully, waiting for me to answer.

I had a feeling that Cambodia had some connections to the other realm. There were too many connections now. I didn't know how to let Aubrith know my thoughts. I felt like I was being crazy.

"That's kind of weird, don't you think? Like the structures in your realm and the structures in this realm. And how people here think the snake or naga is divine?" I carefully asked Aubrith. He looked to be thinking. He kept his eyes on the floor for a bit before he had a response.

"I guess it is a little weird. So, you think the other shard is in Ankor Wat?" He ran his hands through his wavy hair.

"Maybe? But I don't know what else can be there. That's why I want to get a start in Cambodia." I repositioned myself and sat up in the bed to face him. He carefully looked at me and looked towards his backpack.

"Would this be the last one?"

"I do not know. But it's a start, right?"

He slowly nodded his head and reached over to his backpack. He pulled out the shards that were all connected to each other.

"The last piece has to be big. There's too much space here for just one shard," he noticed. I got up and walked over to where he was sitting.

"I suppose you're right. Maybe there's two in Cambodia?" I asked carefully.

He shook his head rapidly.

"That's what we thought in Ireland, and one was a trap. If there are two in Cambodia, we shouldn't trust one." Aubrith looked carefully at the stones. They glimmered in the sunlight.

"I guess we should wake Glyden up. We need to see how to get into Ankor Wat." Aubrith sat up and nudged Glyden, who was still snoring.

I nudged Glyden, and he snored louder.

"This is the most I have seen him sleep, to be honest." Aubrith laughed and nudged Glyden again. Glyden stirred in his sleep and rubbed his eyes.

"What do you want?" Glyden asked angrily. Aubrith and I both laughed at him.

"We need to find a way into Ankor Wat," Aubrith told him. Glyden laughed to himself and put his head on the pillow again.

"We can just teleport in there. It wouldn't be a big deal." Glyden was repositioning himself to go to sleep.

"No, you can't go back to sleep. That is exactly the reason we can't teleport anywhere for a while." I nudged Glyden again. He sighed and got up.

"Okay, okay. This Ankor Wat place, let's go, I guess." Glyden walked to the door. Aubrith and I moved quickly to follow him.

The hotel tried to get us to try the green drinks again as we stepped outside. Glyden looked around. I noticed that there was a man waiting by a carriage of some sort. The side said "Tuk Tuk."

"Hi, can we get a ride into town?" I asked. He looked at me strangely. Glyden rolled his eyes and crossed his arms.

"Use your powers to translate your words." Glyden looked to me and motioned towards the man.

"How the heck do I do that?" I whispered to Glyden. He pushed me aside and asked the man in Khmer to take us somewhere. The man motioned for us to get in the Tuk Tuk. I hopped in. I felt unsteady in the Tuk Tuk. It swayed back and forth as the man rode us into town.

Cars and motorbikes swarmed past us. I looked around and realized there were no lanes in the road. Everyone just went where they pleased.

"I can't watch this. I'm going to be sick." I closed my eyes just hearing honks all around us.

"Sasi, this is fine. I actually like this style of moving around. Quite effective." Glyden crossed his legs and looked around like he was having a lovely stroll. Not to mention other people near us were trying to get in front of our Tuk Tuk. It appeared multiple accidents could've occurred, but nothing happened. In fact, we made it to the center of town without crashing or dying.

Aubrith laughed at Glyden and me before stepping out of the Tuk Tuk. Dust swept up into our faces. I coughed profusely.

"Wow, you are struggling here." Glyden looked at me with a disappointed face. I gave him a glare.

We walked through the main town area. People were selling clothing and artifacts again. I kept looking around, trying to find some sign for us to be here. Glyden got intrigued by some artifacts. Aubrith walked over to where it said tourist. I followed him, leaving Glyden to get his mini temple artifact.

"I think people meet up here to get on that tour you were talking about." Aubrith stared at the building. I nodded my head and knocked on the door to the building.

No one was answering. A woman came around the building and tried to speak to us. Aubrith and I looked at each other. Glyden came out of nowhere and started speaking to her. Glyden and the woman were laughing, and he obviously made a joke about me and Aubrith.

Glyden looked back to us and glared but looked back

to the woman and smiled. Aubrith and I went to sit on the bench outside of the building.

"What do you think they are talking about?" Aubrith asked me.

"Probably about us. Maybe Glyden will remember we need to get to Ankor Wat." I crossed my arms looking towards Glyden.

It seemed like forever until Glyden walked towards me and Aubrith.

"So, I got us into Ankor Wat. We leave soon. A simple thank you would be nice." Glyden crossed his arms back at us two. Aubrith scoffed and stood up.

"So where do we go?" I asked, looking for a bus or some sort to take us there.

"That amiable woman is going to take us. She has to get her car from her brother, and we will be off. We will need to go to this place where they will take our pictures. That's the only way to get in. They also will hole punch our card." Glyden smiled proudly.

"Great. We have to trust another random woman. That didn't go wrong at all last time," Aubrith said sarcastically. I tried to hide my laugh but ended up coming out like a snort.

"Never do that again." Glyden looked at me grimacing. Meanwhile, Aubrith was laughing hysterically.

"I think the heat is getting to us," I admitted.

Aubrith nodded his head as he wiped his eyes from laughing so hard.

The woman came around the corner again and motioned towards Glyden.

I guess this is it.

CHAPTER
TWENTY-SEVEN

I laid my head against the window in the van. It took a while for us to wait in the lines to get a necklace with our picture on it. The security already hole punched our cards. Glyden and Aubrith thought it was so cool that we had special cards to get into somewhere. Meanwhile, everyone had to get one to enter, I guess.

The woman came to a stop towards a crowd of people. She motioned us to get out of the car and talked to Glyden some more. I stretched, hearing my back crack. I felt like I hadn't had a good sleep in weeks, which was probably right.

"She said to go up this path with these other people and to follow the road," Glyden explained. I smoothed my hair back into a braid. I looked at Glyden and Aubrith who were already ahead of me. *So much for waiting.* I quickly moved through people in the crowd, trying to reach them. Aubrith gave me a weird look when I was out of breath next to him.

"Are you okay?" he questioned. I nodded my head and took a deep breath.

"How far do we have to walk?" I asked. Glyden shrugged his shoulders.

We were walking in a forest-like area with bugs that echoed through the trees. The red dirt still coated the pavement. We kept moving with the flocks of people going to the temple. Tuk Tuk's were everywhere, trying to drop people off or take people back to the parking area.

"This place is super busy," Aubrith commented. I kept seeing all kinds of different people from all over the world. Couples took their cameras to get an excellent picture of the temple. Others had kids and were showing them the pamphlets to read. There were tour guides holding up a flag for their groups so no one got lost.

We got to the start of the temple. The path to the temple was all paved. You could see to the main temple. There was a massive moat that surrounded the entrance of the temple.

"I guess we have to walk through that?" Glyden gulped. We all walked on the bridge. There were statues at the front representing the naga from Hinduism. People kept taking pictures with the other stone structures on the bridge that were deteriorating.

"This place has to be super old. The stonework is falling apart." Aubrith touched the stone, running his hands over it.

"I think the temple was built in the 12th century or something like that," I answered. Aubrith looked towards me.

"What? I said I took history classes. I also looked up a lot of pictures of this place. It's not one of my realm's most famous places for nothing." I tried to keep walking ahead, but there were so many people in front of us. Aubrith nodded his head and took off his jacket. I held the backpack as he wrapped his jacket around his waist.

We weren't leaving anything in the hotel anymore, not after what happened in Ireland. We got to the entrance of the temple after crossing the bridge. There were intricate markings all over the stone. It amazed me that back then, people could do these amazing designs on sandstone.

Aubrith and Glyden sighed as they saw we had to keep walking to get to the main entrance of the temple.

"This path is so long. My legs are already getting numb." Glyden huffed and reached for his water bottle.

"I think that was the protection part of the temple, and now we're technically inside the temple," I explained. They both nodded at me, and we slowly kept walking through the crowds.

People were taking pictures of the trees on the side of the temple. I had to admit, this temple was vast. That's why it kept amazing me how they built this structure with the tools back then.

There were palm trees towards the entrance. Several tour guides stopped at the entrance for people to take pictures of even the more intricate markings on the wall. Glyden stopped at one marking and looked at it.

"Are you okay? We still have to go in," I announced to Aubrith and Glyden. Glyden nodded but kept staring at the markings.

"What's wrong?" Aubrith and I stepped aside so people could walk past us.

"Nothing. It's just that there are some markings on this temple that I have seen before. I can't place where I have seen them, though," Glyden noted. I walked over to where he was pointing toward.

There were some warriors fighting each other with another man in the sky. I looked at Glyden then at the markings.

"Is it in Bolithiem where Aurelia lived or another part of your realm?" I asked. Aubrith now came over to look at the markings for himself. There was a rope blocking us from touching the markings to preserve the temple itself.

"I've seen that before too. I think it is actually in the Goddess's Book," Aubrith announced. Glyden and I whipped our heads towards him.

"How do you know that?" Glyden asked him. He stepped closer to Aubrith and stared him in the eyes.

"My mom. She used to have the book in our house before the soldiers came and banned it," Aubrith replied. He held his hands up when facing Glyden, who had this weird glare of anger towards Aubrith.

"Whoa, guys. Think about where you are, Glyden. You can't expose yourself here." I put my hand on Glyden's shoulder. He seemed to calm down before looking at Aubrith again.

"That book was supposed to be banished. I have only ever seen it once. That was next to Terra." Glyden cleared his throat. He looked at me apologetically and kept walking into the temple. Some people around us were looking at us.

We walked further into the temple, and there were halls that looked slightly disheveled over time. I saw some monks walking around. People were adamant about taking pictures of them, but they kept walking.

The further we walked, the more markings we seemed to observe. There were monks sitting in areas with candles. People kept going up to them to get a blessing. Aubrith and I kept looking around to see more people waiting for a blessing.

"Do you think we should get one of those?" Aubrith asked. I shook my head. We kept moving through the temple. It was strange how the entire temple had an open ceiling but also had such beautiful markings all over the walls.

People were lining up to go up these stairs that took you to the tallest point of Angkor Wat.

"The pamphlet said it can take you up seventy feet. What does that mean?" Aubrith questioned.

"It means it's very tall." I looked up the stairs that were rocking side to side as people were going up and down.

Glyden and Aubrith looked up and nodded. Two little kids came up to us to ask for money. They were selling some magazines about Angkor Wat. Aubrith was about to give in until I pulled him away from them.

"You know they could try to get to you, right? Like they might steal something?" I looked at Aubrith seriously.

"Oh, Sasi. A child would steal something? That's

cute." Aubrith pushed past me to go talk to the kids again. Glyden stood by me, shaking his head.

"What do you think they are going to steal from him?" Glyden asked.

"I don't know, but the pen he usually keeps in his pocket for emergencies might be one thing they steal," I acknowledged. Glyden nodded his head as we kept looking at the exchange between Aubrith and the kids. Aubrith set his backpack down as he was searching for some money. One kid snuck his hand in Aubrith's pocket. He grabbed the pen and took off.

Aubrith looked at me and Glyden.

"He grabbed my pen!" he exclaimed. Other people around us were looking at Aubrith. Glyden and I were laughing.

"Well, go get it!" I yelled back to him. Aubrith started running after the kid. I picked up Aubrith's backpack off the ground and slung it around my shoulders.

"Want to see if the shard is up there?" I looked up the steps. Glyden was debating until he shook his head no.

"I don't think I will be able to do that. I'll wait down here for Aubrith. We will be here when you come down. If nothing is up there, we did our best. We tried to find the shard," Glyden assured me. I nodded my head and got in line to go up the steps.

There was a limited amount of people allowed to go up the scaffolding steps at a time. The woman, who was to handle the amount of people, motioned me to step on the steps. The steps swayed even with one foot on them. I took a deep breath and positioned myself to keep going up. I moved my feet up the steps. Someone was coming down the steps, and immediately the entire platform rocked. I gripped onto the railing and looked up.

The person hastened down the steps, causing a ripple effect to the rest of the platform. I took a deep breath and kept moving up the steps. My legs moved further up the ladder. I felt my back leaning back as I gripped the railing. *Great, I'm testing gravity right now.* I kept moving and leaped up onto the top of the platform. I looked down, and my legs got rubbery. I wasn't afraid of heights by any means but looking straight down made my stomach drop slightly.

I looked around the top of the platform. I hopped down the steps that led to a bigger opening. I noticed there were some monks up here, meditating. I gripped onto one pillar and oversaw all of Cambodia. *This place is so big.* I kept looking around, trying to find something. A clue even to what could be up here to help with the shard. Even to find the shard itself.

I put my hand out, and I felt no energy here. I thought that was strange, considering this was supposedly one of the most powerful places ever. I kneeled next to a marking. It had some of the same markings downstairs. I could tell this one might've been part of the Buddhist section of the temple. Even though the temple was originally Hindu, now it was considered Buddhist.

This marking was fresher than the older ones. I ran my hand over it. *Still cold. What the heck?* I looked around and gripped the backpack that settled on my shoulders. I noticed a monk that opened one eye and was looking at me. When I walked over to him, he closed his eyes.

"Hello?" I asked him.

"Shh," he demanded. I looked around, trying to see if anyone else saw that.

"You were the one looking at me," I whispered to the monk. He shushed me again. *Whatever.*

"No, come back," he commented. I looked back at the monk, who still had his eyes closed. I sighed and went over to him. I sat in front of him and set my backpack down next to me.

"Okay, what do you want?" I asked the monk. The monk reached out and grabbed my hand.

I gasped as I saw images in my head. The shards were all lined up and created a circle. Someone's hands put the circle inside the rays of blue shining down. I couldn't quite see whose hands they belonged to. The images faltered, and I started gasping.

The monk stared at me, and I flipped my arm over. There was a tiny tattoo with a snake. I went to touch the tattoo on my arm, but it vanished. I looked up at the man, and his eyes were glowing.

"So, you're the one." The monk looked at me. He still was holding my hand. I gulped as I nodded.

"Someone is awaiting you at the center over there." The monk pointed with his other hand. There was a person standing there in all black. I creased my eyebrows at the monk, and he let go of my hand.

"I hope you find her, Sasi." The monk got up from where he was sitting. He walked past me, back down the steps. *What did he mean by 'her'? And how did he know my name?* I looked where the monk was praying and saw he was sitting near the shard, which was black and glowing in the sunlight.

I looked back to where the person was standing and to the shard. I picked the shard up and stuffed it in my backpack. I made my way over to the figure that was standing in the middle. I jumped down some steps, and the person turned around.

I gasped.

"What are you doing here?" I asked.

CHAPTER
TWENTY-EIGHT

I looked at the figure standing there. He looked at me and sighed.

"Sasi, we need to talk," the person suggested. I could recognize that leather jacket anywhere. Especially after he tried to kill us in several places.

"Stay back!" I exclaimed.

Other people in the temple looked towards me. I clenched my fists and looked towards the man in front of me.

"I'm not here to hurt you. I was never trying to hurt you." He slicked back his black hair.

"Yeah, you have a funny way of showing that." I kept trying to keep my cool. I noticed that the man had distinguished features. He had a scar that went through his eyebrow.

"I want the stones. I need them, actually. It's my mission to get them. They can't be taken out of their place." The man walked back and ran a hand through his hair once again. I stared at him, trying to see what he would do.

"Well, I need them for my mission. And my mission helps save a lot of lives." I stood my ground.

"Sasi, I do not want to argue with you. I need the stones." He held his hand out. I looked up at him and shook my head. *How did he know my name?* I remembered he might be the same man from the room with my mom in the hospital.

"How do you know my mom?" I questioned.

He seemed stunned by this information. He looked around and kept fighting with his zipper on his jacket.

"I don't know what you mean." He visibly started sweating.

"I saw you. I saw you at the hospital with her. You don't work at the hospital, though. So how do you know her? Did she tell you to come and get me or something?" I was getting confused. I didn't know why my mom's presence had led me to every place for a shard. I didn't know why'd she never told me about this man. I wanted answers.

"No, I don't know your mom." He gulped.

Liar. I kept staring at him. More people were coming up the stairs to see the view of Angkor Wat. I looked towards them. "You're losing time if you wanted the shards," I smirked at the man. He looked around and noticed all the people coming up the steps. He grabbed my arm quickly. The grip on my arm was burning. I looked into his eyes. They didn't turn blue at all. *What are you?* I wanted to ask him, but the more he held onto me, the more powerless I felt.

"Your little magic won't work here." He smirked as he gripped harder.

I remembered Aubrith's training when no magic was available. I aimed for his stomach and punched as hard as I could. He stumbled backward, clutching his abdomen. People audibly gasped. I made my way to the stairs and ran down them, even though it shook the entire scaffolding. Other people on the stairs gripped the metal railing.

"Sorry!" I yelled out. Once I made it down the stairs, I scanned the temple area for Glyden or Aubrith. Glyden was still in the same spot. I ran towards him, and he immediately pushed off of the wall he was leaning on.

"What's wrong?" he asked me. I grabbed his arm and led him down one of the empty hallways of the temple. I looked around before I started speaking.

"That psycho man is back. He wants the shards. He said it was his mission to get them from us or something. What if Jura was working with him?" I rambled. Glyden put his hands on my shoulders and breathed in and out. I followed suit and looked at him.

"Everything will be okay. Although, I found out we don't have powers here. I don't know why. This has to be the one place in your realm where powers are useless." He looked around, trying to find the man.

"Where's Aubrith?" I questioned.

"He's fine. He got the pen back. He was looking for a restroom to use." I nodded my head. A crowd of people started gasping, and I turned to look. The man was running down the steps as I had.

"Okay, Glyden, we have to go." I pulled Glyden away

towards where Aubrith would be. We squeezed in between people, apologizing as we went.

We found Aubrith, who was fixing his jacket around his waist. I grabbed him, and he was surprised.

"Oh, it's you. How was the shard?" Aubrith asked me. I looked over at him as we were all walking quickly around Angkor Wat. Glyden led us down another hallway. We all leaned against the wall to catch our breath.

"I take it someone is after us again?" Aubrith commented. He took a deep breath.

"Yes. Our favorite person, the Leather-Jacket-Man," I replied sarcastically. Aubrith groaned and leaned further against the wall. I laughed and looked towards Glyden.

"Hey, are you doing okay?" Glyden was breathing heavier than normal.

"Yeah, I'm okay. It's just hard to breathe." He coughed into his arm. I narrowed my eyebrows at him. He shook his head, and I let it go. I glanced towards where the man had gone. He was walking in the opposite direction of where we were.

"He went the other way. Come on, let's go before he changes his mind." I pulled Aubrith and Glyden with me. We blended in with the crowd of people that looked to be going to another temple that was close by. We kept walking and stumbled over ruins from the other temple.

"Well, this temple looks like someone has not kept up with it over the years," Aubrith commented. I nodded in agreement. I scanned the temple to see any sign of any person trying to harm us.

"So, what did the guy have to say?" Aubrith asked.

"He said he was on an important mission and

wanted the shards. By the way, I got the shard. It is all black this time." I patted the backpack. Aubrith nodded.

"Why does he want the shards so badly? Do you think he and Jura worked together on this?" Aubrith questioned. I shrugged.

"It would make sense. I do know though; we have no powers here. It is all physical fighting. He gripped my arm so tight it left a mark. I couldn't use any power on him, so I had to hit him." I lifted my sleeved shirt to expose my arm. Aubrith looked at me and looked towards Glyden.

"I'll kill him. Next time I see him, I will," Aubrith assured. I laughed and pulled down the sleeve.

"He didn't want me to leave with the stones. But I did one of those punches you taught me to do. That seemed to do the trick." I nudged Aubrith. He smiled.

"It is odd that he wants the stones so badly. What could he want to do with them?" Glyden asked aloud.

We continued walking, hearing loud bugs echoing throughout the forest. We reached a temple that had a tree growing inside of it. It looked like it should be mythical, but there was no power here. I felt nothing inside.

I glanced towards Glyden to see if he felt the same way. He put his hand on the stone near the tree and shook his head.

"Still nothing?" I asked.

Glyden sighed. "We can't do anything. I never thought I would say this, but we have to rely on Aubrith." I laughed as Aubrith glared at Glyden.

We continued to walk through the jungle area until we realized the crowd of people was no longer with us.

There were a few people around but not many. I heard footsteps behind us. Before I could do anything, I saw Aubrith punch towards the man that was coming at me.

I drifted off to the side as Glyden grabbed me. Aubrith and the man were throwing punches on the ground at each other.

"Should we help him?" I asked Glyden. He shrugged. He went over and grabbed the man off Aubrith.

"To what do we owe the pleasure?" Glyden asked the man in the leather jacket.

"Like I told Sasi, I need those shards." The man had a bloody nose. He held his head back as Glyden kept a grip on him.

"Yeah, we can't give them to you. So, go run off and tell whomever you're working for that we can't get that for you," Glyden commanded.

Aubrith got up off the ground and clutched his side. He was forming a black eye.

"You don't understand. They'll kill me. They'll kill my family. I never wanted to hurt you. But I need the shards." The man kept his eyes on us.

"Not if we kill you first." Aubrith charged to him. I stepped in front of him and stopped Aubrith from hurting the man.

"Who is going to kill your family?" I asked the man. He gulped.

"I can't tell you that. I can tell you they're serious. They heard those shards will close the portal. We don't want the portal closed," the man commented. I stepped back and looked confused. *I thought this was the major problem to begin with?* I rubbed my eyes and looked towards the man.

"Why don't you want the portal closed?" I asked. Aubrith and Glyden even looked confused. I thought everyone wanted the portal closed.

"Something dark might happen if the portal is closed. I don't know if that's true or not, but I have to take that chance," the man said. He squared himself up with Aubrith, who took a step back. Glyden grabbed the man again.

"Darkness? What darkness? We are stopping the portals from tearing. The tearing of the portals can cause devastating things to happen to our people—and even Sasi's people. There isn't any darkness left," Aubrith noted. I looked back and forth between Glyden and Aubrith. I knew little about the war that happened with Aubrith's mom. I had a feeling that Aubrith was talking about the darkness from the war.

The man started laughing hysterically. Glyden looked at him crazily.

"This man is insane," Glyden stated. I nodded my head, and Glyden kicked him so he could kneel.

"No, wait. Listen. There was something that happened in the war. Not everything can be kept away forever. You know that, Glyden. You work for Terra." Glyden took a step back and let go of the man, who looked at me and Aubrith hungrily.

"I need those shards." He lunged towards me. I took a step to the side when he got close, making him fall into the red dirt.

"Do you need help with him?" Aubrith asked with his fists already raised.

"I think I got it." I set Aubrith's backpack down and got into my fighting stance. The other man laughed at me.

"I can't believe you men pick the girl to fight me." The man spat in the dirt as he came charging again. I ducked out of the way and hit him in the head with the back of my elbow. The man's face planted into the dirt. He slowly got up from his position and looked at me.

"You're going to pay." He spat blood out of his mouth. I noticed he had his stomach open again for a punch, so I aimed there before landing one on his face. He reached for his nose again. A fresh stream of blood came rushing down.

He held his stance before he lunged towards me again. This time, I kicked his knee as he bent down, trying to grab me. He screamed out in pain. I rolled out from under him and kicked him in his side.

"Come on, Sasi. We'd better go," Glyden commented quietly. I looked up and noticed there were more people surrounding us. I nodded my head, and we all ran down the trail in the forest area. Aubrith was laughing, as was Glyden.

"Sometimes, Sasi, sometimes you can be cool," Aubrith spoke. I laughed. He nudged me.

"I think what you did back there was amazing." Glyden patted my back. I looked back at where the Leather-Jacket-Man was lying on the ground.

"I hope he doesn't follow us again," I commented.

Aubrith and Glyden nodded in agreement. We made our way back to the parking area.

"Did the woman from Siem Reap say she was picking us up?" I asked. Glyden gulped and shook his head.

"About that..." Glyden started his sentence. I rolled my eyes and went over to the Tuk Tuk men. We all loaded in, heading back to our hotel. I stared down at my hand, watching the open cuts across my knuckles ooze with blood.

"The cuts heal quick." Aubrith looked towards my hand. I nodded my head as the three of us rode in silence.

TWENTY-NINE

The sound of rocks clanking together startled me awake. I opened my eyes and looked towards the sound. Aubrith slammed the shards together, trying to form more of the circle. The rocks looked strange, considering it wasn't a full circle yet. It was a very colorful arrangement of shards. Although, the newest shard we got was black. It didn't help with the colors. I thought the colors would mean something until I heard another banging coming from Aubrith.

"Seriously? We are trying to sleep." I looked over at Glyden, who was snoring loudly.

"I can't get the Cambodia one to click with the rest. You don't think that we got scammed again, do you?" Aubrith nervously tried to click the shards together again. Still, nothing was happening.

"I don't think so. The monk was very helpful before he got up and left." I rubbed my eyes and yawned. It was so early in the morning, not even the sun was fully awake.

"Wait, a monk? You never told me a monk gave this to you?" Aubrith pulled his hands back to analyze the black shard.

"I had other things on my mind, considering we were being chased again." I rolled my eyes and went to stretch my arms. I flinched in pain until I remembered I had cuts and bruises on my hands. I tried to move my hand by opening and closing it, but it stung. I winced and looked back towards Aubrith.

Aubrith looked towards my hands and shook his head.

"What?" I questioned. If he was going to say something to me, he should've just said it.

"Nothing. You just should've put something on that. Or at least done one of your healing things." He moved his eyes back to the shard.

"Did you forget the part where my magic doesn't work here?" I got up to go to the bathroom. He was right, as much as I hated to admit it. I needed to clean my cuts. I knew we had some ointment from the beginning, but it was going to be hard to find. I rummaged through my toiletry bag before I heard footsteps behind me. I turned around only to find Aubrith holding out a tube of Neosporin.

"Thank you," I mumbled. Aubrith nodded his head and leaned against the doorframe.

"I don't even know what they put in that stuff, but it has helped me on this journey. I'm just thankful you brought it from your mom's place." I nodded my head as I applied the ointment.

"Who was the monk?" he asked quietly. I shook my head.

I recapped the ointment and set it on the counter in the bathroom. I sighed before trying to comprehend what the monk told me.

"The monk wanted me to hold his hand. It was weird. He was telling me things that I didn't know. I also saw I had a snake tattoo, but it vanished after a while. Everything was just weird with him. He tried to tell me to talk to a woman that was there. Wait... All I saw though was the man in the black leather jacket. That man had other plans and wanted all our shards. I didn't even notice a woman, though. When I saw the man in black, that was all I saw."

Aubrith had a stoic face, listening to the entire story. He crossed his arms and sighed.

"I think we got tricked again. I mean, why else isn't the stone connecting to the others. Maybe, if we find that monk, we can get him to give us the real one." Aubrith walked back towards the shards and stared at them. I walked out of the room and sat at the table.

I glanced at the shards and took them in my hands. They felt warm to the touch but not as warm as they had been previously. I touched the black shard. The shard was warm, even warmer than the other ones.

"I think we have the right shard. Do you think that, because we can't use our powers, it isn't connecting? I mean, Glyden even told me we didn't have powers. The Leather-Jacket-Man, when he grabbed my arm, told me my powers didn't work here." I handed back the shard to Aubrith.

He studied it before he set it back on the table.

"I don't know what else to do. It won't click, and we have no powers. How are we even supposed to know where the next spot is?" he rambled on. I put my hand on his wrist to make him stop talking. He looked down at our interaction and pulled away.

"I'm sorry. I wish I could help. I don't know why we have no magic here. I thought out of all places that this was the one place we would have more magic." I sighed and laid my head on the table.

Glyden stirred awake in his bed. He glanced towards the two of us.

"What happened with the shard?" He rubbed at his eyes before laying his head back on the pillow.

"They aren't connecting. I think it's because we have no powers here." I sighed, feeling the cold from the table radiate on my cheek.

"They should connect. Even if we don't have our powers." Glyden stretched and yawned once more.

"Well, they don't. Try it." I tossed the shard to him as he lay in bed.

Glyden examined the shard as he held it up. I gave him the other shards to inspect as well. He tried to click them together, but it wasn't working. Glyden fully sat up in bed and kept trying. He looked up towards me and Aubrith.

"Yeah, they don't work." Glyden handed the shards back to us.

"We could've told you that." I rolled my eyes towards him. He fell back towards the bed and laid his head on the pillow.

"Should we try to find that woman? The woman that the monk told me to talk to? I mean, it might be worth it?" I suggested. Aubrith shrugged his shoulders. Glyden sighed and got out of bed finally.

"What monk?" Glyden asked. He sat across from us as he rubbed his eyes.

"There was a monk at the temple. He's the one who gave me the shard. He told me to find a woman, but I found that man in the leather jacket instead. Something strange also happened. I had a snake tattoo appear on me, then it was gone in an instant." I looked at the two of them. Glyden's eyebrows raised as he got up out of the chair. He paced around.

"Why didn't you tell me this sooner? I could've gone back to the monk or found the woman. That was probably our way out. Back to the other realm. Maybe they would've led us to the next spot," Glyden rambled on.

"I didn't know it was that important. I only remembered it when we got back here. Plus, you were sleeping. It's not like you were ready to go fight or talk to anyone earlier," I fumed. I filled with rage towards Glyden. How could he accuse me of not doing enough? I was the one who had to go get the shard. I was even the one who had to fight the other man when he didn't offer to fight.

"Sasi. Please try to calm down. It's not that big of a deal, honestly. We will find the other shard. The woman probably wasn't a major clue or anything." Aubrith put his hand on my shoulder. He tried to calm me down, but I was filling with more rage.

Glyden looked towards my hands. There was a glint of glee in his eyes.

"Keep getting mad at me," Glyden suggested. He kept raising his voice towards me. Aubrith kept trying to calm me down. I realized what Glyden was trying to do, and I looked towards my hands. They were glowing red. I took a deep breath and snapped out of whatever trance I was in. Glyden's shoulders deflated.

"I thought this would be the time where we could control your powers." Glyden sat on the bed. My hands felt cool as they returned to their normal color. I slouched on the bed and put my hands on my face.

"I don't know what I am doing. How do we know this is going to work? This is an enormous risk. I'm sick and tired of being chased. I'm also tired of fighting. I don't even want these stupid powers." I laid back on the bed. I could feel Glyden and Aubrith looking towards me. I peeked through my hands to see both of them staring at me. I sighed and put my arms at my sides.

"Maybe you need some rest, Sasi. I shouldn't have yelled at you. I'm sorry. I know there is a lot of pressure on you," Glyden admitted. I nodded my head and turned towards the wall. I could hear both of them whispering about me.

"I think she's tired. Give her a day. She couldn't have possibly seen that woman the monk told her to talk to," Aubrith whispered solemnly.

"We should find that woman. She could lead us somewhere. We have little to work with. We should take every opportunity we have to find something," Glyden advised.

Although I couldn't see both of them, I could sense Aubrith was probably shaking his head.

"No, we can't. We can't leave her here," Aubrith stressed. I knew he wouldn't go along with Glyden. I closed my eyes, letting their whispers lull me to sleep.

§

By the time I'd awoken, I noticed the empty hotel room. I looked towards the window and realized that it was night out. *How long was I asleep?* I noticed someone set new clothes on the foot of the bed. I yawned and looked through the clothes. The clothes comprised a linen button-down shirt and linen pants. I saw the note next to them, which had Glyden's handwriting: *"Don't worry, I paid for these ones."*

I smiled at the note and shook my head. I went to the bathroom and got in the shower. I realized I hadn't bathed in multiple days. After all of this traveling and figuring things out, I'd lost track of time. The cold water felt good on my skin, considering it was still hot in the room. I got out of the shower and changed into the fresh clothes. I grabbed my brush and tried to get out the knots that lingered in my hair. I hated having thick hair. There were always layers in my hair. I redid my braid down the middle and slipped on my shoes.

I opened the hotel door, which led me to squint my eyes considering the hallway light was on. I shut the door and made my way down the stairs to the main lobby area. The hotel had food every night for guests. I assumed that's where Aubrith and Glyden had gone, considering no one was in the room.

I walked into the main lobby area. The hotel staff greeted me. I kept looking around as I grabbed my plate and food. *Still no sign of them.* I sat at a table by myself as I ate meat that I didn't quite know which animal it was from. Maybe it was beef?

It was odd that they were nowhere to be found, considering we didn't know where to go in Cambodia. I kept chewing the food as I scanned the lobby. There were a lot of tourists in this hotel. They all had cameras strapped to their body somewhere. I finished my meal and put my plate in the trash. I made my way to the front desk. *Maybe they saw where Glyden and Aubrith left.*

"Hello. I'm Sasi Avias in room 404. I was wondering if you saw my friends leave the hotel?" I hesitated. The man at the desk looked at me and smiled. He nodded his head and pointed out the doors. I took that as my sign that Aubrith and Glyden had left the hotel. *Why would they leave?* I hesitantly walked outside of the safety of the hotel. I hoped they weren't doing anything stupid.

My shoes crunched in the red dirt as I walked down the strip of town. People had stands open, offering foods of some sort. Tourists were taking pictures of the locals and their food. I never understood why some people wanted to do that. I shrugged my shoulders and kept walking. I scanned the area with the merchants. Each individual stand had lights that glared at me. I squinted my eyes to get a better look at the street.

Vendors were gawking at me, asking for money. I politely told them no. The crowd of people made it feel like I was suffocating. I kept looking around until a woman in a hood bumped into me. She dropped her bag in the middle of the blocked-off road. I squatted down to help her. Her items were scattered in the street from the collision we'd had.

She quickly grabbed some of her items and shoved them in her bag. I offered the items in my hand to her. She nodded towards me. Before I could get a decent look at her face, her eyes glowed blue. I stopped in my tracks. She vanished into the crowd just as quickly as she'd collided into me. I turned to find her, but it was already too late.

I heard a familiar voice echoing behind me. I quickly turned and met with Aubrith and Glyden's face.

"Hey, it's good to see that you're awake finally," Aubrith stated. I nodded my head but looked back towards the woman, who was lost in the crowd. Glyden wrinkled his forehead.

"Who are you looking for?" Glyden asked. I shook my head.

"I have no clue. She came and hit me. I didn't even know who she was, but her eyes glowed blue," I explained to them. Glyden looked behind me but didn't appear to see anyone.

"She obviously is gone. Want to try this?" Aubrith held up a spider leg. I jumped back from him.

"Why are you eating that?" I questioned. Aubrith shrugged as he crunched down on the spider leg. Glyden had his own food, which comprised different bugs. I shuddered at their food.

"What's wrong? I thought you liked to try different

food?" Glyden guessed. I put my hand up to my mouth. I could almost taste the bile rising, imagining eating the bugs.

"Not like that. That's just disgusting." I looked away from them.

"There was snake you could eat at another stand, but we didn't want to try that. Now that looked disgusting. This is pretty good." Aubrith grinned. He put another spider leg in his mouth. I had to look away again. *That was so repulsing.* I walked with the two of them down the strip where there were several stands open.

"Thank you for the new clothes, by the way," I addressed Glyden, who looked up from his plate and nodded his head.

"We got them from a stand down there." He pointed towards the edge of the strip. I nodded my head. We kept walking until we reached this stand that sold different souvenirs.

"What are you looking at?" Aubrith questioned. He threw away his empty plate and walked back to the stand I'd stopped at.

"Isn't that a shard?" I peered into my eyes at the top shelf of the stand. Glyden peered over and began talking in Khmer.

There was a light pink shard sitting on the top shelf, glistening against the string lights. I looked towards Aubrith, who fixated on the shard as well. He gripped his backpack pads. Glyden looked towards me. I couldn't depict what he was wanting to say.

"The woman who runs this stand told me they

traded for the shard. They gave a woman six pieces of fabric for that shard. If we want it, we will have to pay more. Preferably cash," Glyden announced. Aubrith grabbed the black shard that was in the backpack and handed it to Glyden.

"Do you think we could trade for the pink one?" Aubrith asked. Before I even knew what I was doing, I snatched the black shard and started walking away from that stand. Aubrith and Glyden quickly followed. The woman of the stand lost interest and was already talking to another tourist.

"What are you doing?" Aubrith asked. He looked frustrated.

"We wouldn't get a shard that easily." Glyden was studying me before he nodded his head.

"She's right. Every shard we have, we've had to work hard for—or it's been a challenge to retrieve it." Glyden took the black shard from my hands and looked at it.

People were walking around us in the middle of the street. No one seemed to care that we were analyzing rocks. That was a good thing, at least. Aubrith kneeled in the red dirt as he searched through his backpack. He pulled out the other shards that were all connected to each other.

Glyden kneeled to get a better look at the other shards. I awkwardly looked around to make sure no one was going to come for us. Not that I could do much, anyway.

I noticed Glyden was comparing the shards to each other. He held them up so that the light from the stands would shine on the shards. They all glistened in the light, having golden flakes shimmering within. Aubrith looked closer before he brought them back down to his lap.

"Guys...did you notice this before?" he asked. I took a glance at the crowd of people that seemed to ignore us before I kneeled down with Aubrith and Glyden.

"What is it?" I questioned. Something told me it wasn't something I wanted to hear.

"The golden flakes in every shard we got. It has words." Aubrith looked up towards me and Glyden. He put the shards close together where they formed a sentence. Although the black shard looked to be the end of the sentence.

"What does it even say?" I asked. I looked towards Glyden considering he knew every language there was. He took the shards, a crease forming in his forehead.

"This is an ancient language from Lumos. Where the Goddess lives." He looked puzzled. Aubrith took the shards from him again to study them.

"So, you can't decode whatever it says?" I asked. Glyden shook his head.

"Goddesses only used the ancient language. I know every language but that one. In fact, the Goddess's Book was written in that language before someone translated it." Glyden looked stunned.

"You said the Goddess's Book was banned. Why did someone translate it if it was banned? Who would even do that?" I looked at Glyden again.

People still walked by us. We occasionally got weird looks, considering we were kneeling on the ground in a tourist area.

"There were healers. They wanted to know the ways

of the Goddess. It wasn't until a servant who was working for the Goddess fled and translated the book. No one knows who that servant was, though. They worked with the Goddess for many years. I mean, you would have to in order to learn the ancient language. The book wasn't always banished. It went everywhere until Aurelia banned it in Bolithiem, and Druda wanted their own form of the book." Glyden rubbed his eyes and sighed.

"I think this says the word 'open,' but I don't know what the other words mean," Aubrith chimed in. He smiled proudly. Glyden glanced towards him.

"How do you know that?" Glyden took the shard back and analyzed it.

"My mom used to have the book. I wasn't supposed to look through it, but she would talk with that language sometimes." Aubrith shrugged his shoulders. I fell back to sit in the street. I knew my linen pants were going to be covered in red dirt.

"Maybe it is trying to tell us something. Like a code or a clue." Glyden twisted the shard around to see if the golden flakes lined up anymore on the other side.

I kept looking at the black shard that was lying on the side next to Aubrith. I grabbed it and twisted it around to the golden flakes side. I got a pulsating headache. I closed my eyes briefly from the pain. I stared at the shard, noticing the flakes were moving around on the shard. *Maybe I was hallucinating again?* I rapidly blinked, remembering when this pain came to me back in Ireland.

"Guys, I think this is the back part of the puzzle," I

announced. I shakily handed back the shard towards Aubrith. They both looked at me, shocked.

"Well, what does it say?" Glyden calmly asked. I gulped before responding.

"It says 'by the Goddess's blood.'"

CHAPTER

THIRTY

"What does that even mean?" Aubrith questioned. They flipped the shards over again, trying to see the words. I shrugged my shoulders as I handed back the black shard to Aubrith. Glyden looked at the shards before looking back at me.

"Can you decode these ones too?" he asked. The pounding in my head didn't seem to stop. I closed my eyes briefly before trying to figure out the rest of the words.

I stared at the golden flakes, but nothing was coming to me. Aubrith slowly got up and collected the shards. He carefully placed them back in his backpack. He helped me up to my feet, and I tried to brush off the red dirt on my linen pants.

"Maybe at the hotel, you can decipher the shards there." Glyden nudged my arm. I nodded, but I didn't know how I did it the first time. I didn't even know how I was doing it now. It just came to me like it wanted me to know. I didn't learn to read anything; it just happened.

I shuffled my feet towards the hotel. I was feeling slightly weak and lightheaded. I could see Aubrith and Glyden in front of me, but they were blurry. I kept pace with them to the hotel until I couldn't see anymore. It felt like I was walking in complete darkness. I felt someone's hand on my shoulder.

"Hey, are you okay?" Aubrith whispered. I could tell that we were in the hotel lobby, but everything was pitch black. I didn't know where to go or what was going on.

"I can't see," I whispered back. Aubrith grabbed my arm. I felt Glyden grab my other arm as they led me somewhere. My feet seemed to glide on the carpet as I was being led back to the room. I carefully walked up the steps with guidance from Aubrith and Glyden. I heard Aubrith scramble for the key to the hotel room before hearing the door open. I felt like closing my eyes, even though it wouldn't have made a difference.

It was like my senses were heightened. I could feel everything in the room all at once. Just like I could sense that Aubrith was pacing back and forth and Glyden panicking.

"What do we do? It's not like we can use any powers here. I could've healed her from this madness, but we have nothing," I heard Glyden announce.

"I don't know. Does she have to sleep, or can she drink something?" Aubrith voiced.

I closed my eyes, trying to focus on something else. Although losing my sight should've scared me, it was doing the opposite to me. I felt immensely calm. I tried to focus on my breathing. In and out. In and out. That's what I used to do whenever I was nervous before a basketball game or an anxiety-ridden event. I never lost my vision in those events, but I guess there's a first time for everything.

"How did this happen? You were reading the shard, right?" I heard Glyden's voice echo in the room. I turned to where I thought his voice came from.

"I was seeing the letters rearrange. I could tell though the black shard might be the ending to whatever the words on all the shards said. I think it is a sentence. Maybe that's why the black shard wasn't connecting, considering that the shard wasn't in the right order." I could sense them both looking towards me and thinking. I laid back on the bed, inhaling the fresh scent from the room service laundry.

"So, she can't read from the shards again since her vision gets wiped. Well, that's good to know," Aubrith joked. I could sense Glyden was scowling at him.

"What if she's right? That would mean Cambodia was the last shard to get. We got it early. What does the next shard have to do with the puzzle?" Glyden shuffled his feet across the carpet. If he wasn't careful, he could've started a fire with the amount of times he paced back and forth.

In and out, I kept repeating to myself. I sat up and took off my shoes. I laid back on the bed and got under the covers.

"Sasi, we aren't done trying to think about this. You can't fall asleep," Glyden demanded. I felt the coolness of the bed encompass me. I could already feel the sleep building inside of me. I yawned again.

"I think this will be better later on," I replied. I could sense Glyden was getting annoyed and Aubrith rummaging through the backpack. I heard the shards being placed on the table in the room. Aubrith grabbed a pillow that was near me and tossed it on the floor.

"You seriously are going to let her sleep? This could mean something serious! If the Goddess's blood is involved in saving the world, don't you think we should know about this?" Glyden emphasized. I heard Aubrith lay down on the floor near where my bed was.

"She got the floor last night. She is also exhausted. We will figure nothing out tonight. If we got the last shard on accident, we can find the shard that was before this one. It isn't a big deal," I heard Aubrith sigh as he turned away from Glyden.

Glyden huffed across the room and went to the other bed in the room. He angrily pulled back the covers. He tossed his shoes towards the door in anger and got into bed. I smiled to myself because I didn't even have to see him to know that he was mad.

"We will figure it out. I need sleep," I told the both of them. I cracked open my eyes to see if my vision was getting back.

I knew the room was going to be pitch black, but at least I could make out the figures on the wall. I could tell that there was an Angkor Wat painting on the wall. I laughed to myself, knowing that my eyesight was coming back. *That didn't last that long.* I shifted in the bed so I could stare up at the ceiling.

The words from the shard kept echoing in my mind like a song that couldn't get out. It was on an endless loop. I didn't know what it meant by the Goddess's blood. It had to mean something horrible to Terra. I sighed, knowing that without the last shard, the other realm and this realm could all be over in a blink of an eye. I had to get back to the other realm and give the shards to Justorah. He would know what to do with them.

I hoped we could get back in time with all the shards. I looked up at the ceiling. *I am trying my hardest. I am confused about everything.* I wondered if the questions would ever stop coming. I didn't know what I was getting myself into.

I also wondered about my mom. She had to be connected to all of this. I didn't know how she was yet. I closed my eyes once more. I felt the exhaustion throughout my body. I felt as if the mattress itself was going to suffocate me in and never let me up. Not that I would mind sleeping for days. I knew relaxation wasn't in the cards for me yet. There was still more to be done.

I drifted off to sleep, seeing the gold flakes in my dream float away.

THIRTY-ONE

I awoke seeing Glyden and Aubrith already sitting at the table in the hotel room.

"Did you guys get any sleep?" I yawned. I stretched as I sat at the edge of the bed.

"We did. We didn't sleep all day like you, though," Aubrith acknowledged as he flipped through a newspaper.

"We've been trying to figure out where the next place is. I know that man in the leather jacket is going to be after us again if we stay in the same place," Glyden announced. I walked over to the table and noticed they'd gotten fruit from the hotel lobby. I ate a piece of pineapple, accidentally spilling some of the juice on my shirt. I rolled my eyes and grabbed a napkin to wipe the juice off my shirt. I heard Aubrith laugh to himself. I glared at him.

"What do you guys have so far?" I tried to focus back to the task at hand.

"We have nothing. All we know is that you were the

one who knew where to go this time. We took a risk coming to Cambodia, and it obviously worked out," Aubrith replied, biting into a strawberry.

I looked at their list, and it only had the list of places that we had been to.

"Seriously? This is all you have?" I took the piece of paper that Glyden was working on.

"Well, can you blame us? We don't know this realm. We only know it from you." Glyden crossed his arms. I rolled my eyes and looked at the places we have been so far.

"Toronto, England, Ireland, and Cambodia," I read the list aloud. I studied the list as I scratched my head.

"These places are so different from each other. There's no pattern. We took a chance on Cambodia for a shard, but that could've gone wrong too." I kept looking at the list.

"We knew that the reason we came here is because of your mom. We didn't know where else your mom could've had a shard placed." Aubrith shrugged his shoulders. He flipped through the newspaper again.

I nodded my head, knowing that my mom could've placed the other shard somewhere. The only problem was where. My mom had visited a lot of places before.

"I don't know where she could've gone. She has been everywhere. I could pick wrong." I put my hands over my face.

"You thought that with Cambodia too, but we got the right shard. Someone tried to lead us astray yesterday by buying a random shard. It wasn't until you noticed the golden flakes. You take the lead on this." Aubrith continued to flip through the paper. I snatched the paper away from him.

"We all need to focus here. There has to be a place where my mom was. With the three of us we can figure it out," I dictated. Aubrith laid his head on the table and let out a deep sigh.

"Fine. Brainstorm away," Aubrith said.

"My mom has been to all of these places, right?" I looked towards Glyden and Aubrith. They both nodded, wondering what I was assuming.

"England had a mythical place. Ireland was also a mythical place, a place with significance, rather." I added.

"Toronto had that tower you said that was famous," Glyden added. I nodded my head and looked towards Aubrith.

"Cambodia is famous for the Angkor Wat, and it's also a spiritual place," I added. Glyden creased his forehead, deep in thought.

"What are other places your mom has visited that are mythical or a spiritual connection?" He grabbed a writing utensil and a piece of paper, ready to write more places.

"She's been to a lot. I mean, she was in Doctors Without Borders. They go everywhere." I sighed. I kept trying to think of a place that the other shards would be.

"You said the places are mythical or very spiritual. Is there a place that comes to mind where maybe she's been or even you have been?" Aubrith propped his head up on his elbow. He looked towards me and yawned.

"I grew up in a spiritual place, I guess, but I don't

think she would go there. Few people are even from there. It's a small town. She wouldn't." I shook my head. Aubrith and Glyden kept staring at me waiting for me to say the place.

"Are you going to tell us this mysterious place?" Glyden glared. I creased my forehead and thought about the times when I was a kid. They didn't seem strange at the time, but now that I was thinking about it, maybe she did have a secret after all.

"New Mexico. It's back in the United States. I grew up there," I whispered. Glyden clapped his hands together.

"This is fantastic! Let's go there now!" He stood up and grabbed his jacket. I stood up.

"We can't just go to New Mexico. She would never put the last shard there. We don't even know if she's the one who placed the shards." I paced around this room.

"Sasi, you said it yourself. Your mom has been connected to all the shards. She has to have some input into where the shards are going. If you say this New Mexico was a place that was close to you two, it has to be the place for a shard," Aubrith explained. I shook my head.

"She wouldn't do that. We weren't in New Mexico for a long time. For all I know, she could've hidden the last shard in her apartment." I rubbed my hands over my face.

"If it was in the apartment, we would've figured that out by now. We were there in the apartment. I didn't feel any energy except for the rocks she lined the windows with." Glyden collected his items in the room.

"You say your mom wouldn't put it in New Mexico,

but you also said your mom wouldn't be a part of this. So far, everything about her has turned out to be false. I mean, you said it yourself, she wasn't in the Doctors Without Borders pictures," Aubrith pointed out.

I couldn't catch my breath. It felt like the world was ending. Aubrith grabbed my arm and gently led me back to the chair at the table.

"It has to be hard to accept that, but I don't think your mom is who she says she is," Aubrith tried to reason with me. I shook my head frantically. *She would've told me.*

"It probably wasn't a simple thing to say to you. Look, I don't know how she's connected to the other realm. But she is connected." Glyden zipped up his bag.

"I guess I've been in denial. I took a gamble on Cambodia, hoping we wouldn't find anything, but we did. Everything so far has been around her, and it's terrifying. It's terrifying to know that the person I trust most was keeping such a big secret like this from me." I felt a tear fall down my face. More came down, but I felt emotionless at the same time.

I used the sleeve of the linen shirt to wipe the tears that kept pouring out. I felt hurt. I probably know why she never mentioned to me she had some connection to the other realm, but I would've never believed her.

"We need to get out of Cambodia foremost," Glyden demanded. He threw Aubrith's backpack towards him. Aubrith grunted and shoved things within.

I nodded my head and wiped the remaining tears that were falling. I stood up and gathered my things. Glyden did one last sweep of the room before we exited the room.

It felt bittersweet to leave Cambodia, but it was the right thing to do, considering we still had someone trying to kill us. *Another question that remained unanswered.*

I hurried down the steps to the main lobby of the hotel. We headed out of the hotel easily, but we halted at the entrance.

"We don't even know where we're going," Aubrith stated.

"Yes. That's the best part of this adventure." Glyden winked towards him before walking ahead of us. I rolled my eyes and followed.

"We can't teleport, Glyden. Our powers don't work here," I reminded him. He nodded his head and turned towards me, causing him to walk backward.

"Yes. That's why we must get out of this place so we can teleport again. We can try that New Mexico place if you want," Glyden suggested. He turned back around to walk straight. His shoes kicked up red dirt as we followed behind him. I coughed slightly from all the dust that accumulated in my face.

"Why is he in such a good mood when we don't know where we're going?" I asked Aubrith.

He shrugged before responding. "I think it's because he gets to leave to a new place. Plus, we need to hurry this mission. I don't know how much longer the portal is going to hold," Aubrith admitted.

"There's a time limit on the portal being opened?" I asked. I knew we had to get the mission done fast, but if the portal was closing somehow, we really had to find the last shard.

Aubrith nodded his head towards me.

"The portal is going to stay open, but I don't want to assume the portal will be open forever. The quicker we get back, the better," Aubrith suggested. I nodded my head. He had a point. We didn't know how much longer the portal was going to be opened. I needed to get these shards to Justorah, and then I could go back to my life the way it was. Thinking about my old life, it was very dull compared to this one. Considering that I didn't know I could shoot fire balls out of my hands or push someone back with a gust of wind.

Glyden kept walking through the blazing sun. Aubrith and I were coughing more vehemently, as the hot wind would blow more dust our way. It was quite insane that we were walking on the side of the road. Tuk Tuk's were speeding by us, as their horns blared in our ears. People would often walk straight into the road too. It was amazing how no one got killed. The flow of traffic kept the same even after people would just walk in front of a scooter.

I grabbed onto the back of Glyden's shirt as Aubrith clung to mine. We formed a single line since more people started to surround us. We didn't want to get lost in the crowds.

People were on the sides of us, wanting us to buy from their stands. I kept my head down, as the heat was blistering. I was glad I was wearing linen clothes since I was sweating so much. I dragged my feet as fast as I could so we could get out of Cambodia on foot.

Glyden stumbled a little. I pulled on his shirt.

"Are you okay?" I yelled over the sounds of scooters driving by.

"I am fine. We have a little left to go," Glyden acknowledged in between his breathing. I wished Cambodia allowed powers, but there had to be something that wiped them out. I thought back to the ancient tales of the snakes that created the town. I remembered that people here also sold snakes to eat at the vendors. I shuddered at the memory.

All the red dirt kept reminding me of New Mexico even more. I knew that the dirt looked familiar, but I didn't think it would be like the one I grew up with. The more Glyden kept kicking up more dirt, the more I realized it.

I hoped that the other shard was in New Mexico. It would be horrible if it wasn't since we went all over my realm. It was still a weird combination. I didn't understand how New Mexico would make the cut when comparing it to the other places we've found the shards in.

As we kept walking, my headache seemed to come back. I kept shaking my head, hoping that I would be okay.

"How close are we until we reach a neutral area?" I asked Glyden.

"I don't know, to be honest. I keep following those signs." Glyden pointed to the signs that had Thailand border listed. I sighed, knowing that we would still be out there walking for a while.

Aubrith grabbed my shirt more intensely. I knew his legs had to be given out just like mine were. It wasn't like we got a fancy meal and left. We had sweet fruit for breakfast. There wasn't anything satisfying. I was just shocked none of us had heatstroke yet.

A man in a Tuk Tuk noticed we were walking. He pulled his Tuk Tuk across from us and talked towards Glyden. At first, Glyden didn't see him, but I nudged him. Glyden spoke to the man in Khmer. The man was pleased and motioned his head towards his Tuk Tuk. Glyden was talking back faster. I didn't know what was going on until Glyden motioned me and Aubrith to get in the Tuk Tuk.

"You are brave to be walking in such heat. That can kill you," The Tuk Tuk driver said. I smiled, knowing that he was probably right. We were all breathing heavily. Glyden wiped the sweat that was falling from his brow.

"Thank the Goddess we got a Tuk Tuk. I felt like my legs were going to give out," Aubrith announced. He motioned the small fan in the corner of the Tuk Tuk and shot it towards himself.

The cool air felt pleasant on my skin as I moved more into Aubrith's space. He positioned the fan towards both of us.

"How much is this going to cost me?" I asked Glyden, motioning towards the driver of the Tuk Tuk. Glyden had a guilty face. I sighed, knowing it would probably cost a lot more than I would spend. Though I didn't care how much I was spending, I wanted to get out of the heat. I wanted to teleport just to cool down.

It was a strange feeling. I didn't have powers for my whole life and suddenly; I felt lost without them. I was thinking to myself that with my powers, I could've cooled myself down by now. We wouldn't be needing a Tuk Tuk to get us to a border. We would've already been gone by now. I shook my head at the thoughts. I needed to focus on the now.

The traffic in the streets didn't seem to stop, either. More scooters and Tuk Tuks were flying by us. Although there were people walking in the street, there was hardly anyone going to stop when they crossed the street. They simply would just move around them in their scooters. It always fascinated me.

"So, when we get our powers back, where are we going?" Glyden asked me. I shrugged my shoulders and kept looking at the surrounding people. He sighed.

"We need to have a plan, Sasi." He glared.

"I know we do. But I am so tired. I don't know where we should go." I rubbed my face with my hands.

"If it is New Mexico, you need to lead the teleportation. I don't know what the place looks like." Glyden rubbed his neck. We neared the sign that notified us we were leaving Cambodia. The Tuk Tuk stopped as soon as we neared the border. I paid the man, and he left happily with the extra money he'd just earned. We stood on the side of the road in the middle of nowhere. Red dirt surrounded us for miles on the edges of the road.

I looked around as my hands tingled. Glyden gleefully smiled and formed a ball of water. He positioned it and shot it into his mouth. He happily drank the water that appeared.

I felt a cool sensation enter my body. This was my new normal. And I was grateful to have it. I took a deep breath as I let the magic consume me.

THIRTY-TWO

We crossed into Thailand. It was harder than I'd thought. We had to climb stairs to reach the building that was sitting above the road. Glyden used his powers to convince the border patrol in Cambodia that we had our passports and to clear us. We descended the steps on the other side and entered.

Aubrith looked around as if noticing that nothing had changed, really.

"I hate to tell you, Sasi, but that road and this area of the road look completely the same." Aubrith pointed with his hands back towards the road we'd just come from. I chuckled to myself as I looked back at the roads. Borders were really such a strange thing.

"Now that I have my powers back, where to?" Glyden asked as he stretched on the side of the road.

"It would be a gamble to go to New Mexico," I said. Aubrith readjusted the straps on his backpack. Glyden was still stretching. It was like they hadn't heard me.

"We heard you. We just don't care if this place called New Mexico would be a gamble." Glyden closed his eyes as he did a deeper stretch.

I scoffed. I forgot he could read my thoughts. The tingly feeling ran up and down my arms again. I tried to calm myself down. I grabbed onto Aubrith's hand. He looked down at our hands interlocked and smiled. I grabbed Glyden's hand and interlocked our hands together.

"Lead the way, Sasi." Glyden smiled at me. I took a deep breath, knowing that this could be a disaster or could lead us to the last shard.

"Here goes nothing." I squeezed both of their hands as I tried to envision New Mexico.

New Mexico, to me, always comprised being in a desert area. We would go to this church in Chimayo, New Mexico. It was popular. My mom would often stare at the statue of the Virgin Mary, but I always found it weird. I considered myself a Catholic, whereas she considered herself as spiritual, which is why I had crystals all over the house growing up. On certain days, she would make me wear a pendant to "protect" myself. I hadn't understood her back then. Now that my world got flipped upside down, her way of life was making more sense.

I thought about the old woman who used to watch me in the small hut. We didn't have TV, and sometimes the water wouldn't be working. My mom would say that it was a blessing that we even had water sometimes. There would be a single basketball hoop in the backyard, which was comprised of dirt. I would dribble my ball and hear the echo of the ball hitting the earth. I'd have to dribble it extra hard, considering the ball never had enough air. I remember once my ball was completely flat, and my mom had it in her room for a bit. She left the room, and the ball was filled. I knew we didn't have an air pump, but somehow it had gotten filled. Thinking back on those times, I wanted to know if she had powers too.

I shook my head at the thought. I tried to focus on getting the three of us to New Mexico. Meanwhile, we'd been standing there, having our hands linked for around thirty minutes.

I focused on the surrounding area where the hut was. It was nothing but a desert, even though there were cows in the area. That had always fascinated me, considering I didn't know where they would get water from. I kept trying to focus on what the land had made me feel. I thought about how blazing the sun would be in the summer. We would go to Santa Fe, New Mexico too, in the summer, to eat at some of our favorite restaurants. I missed that feeling of relaxing in a place and enjoying the culture instead of having to run away every time we got somewhere.

I felt the cool sensation reappear all throughout my body. I kept seeing pictures of New Mexico pass through my head. I felt Glyden's hand leave mine, as did Aubrith's. All the cool sensations around me felt suddenly hot. I thought back to New Mexico as my body hit the ground. I got the wind knocked out of me as I struggled to breathe. I looked around and realized we were somewhere entirely different.

"You really have to work on our landings," Aubrith coughed. Dirt blew around him as he kept coughing.

I looked around, trying to find Glyden, but found he'd landed next to a cactus.

"Why does my hand feel like it got stabbed?" Glyden asked aloud. I tried to hold in my laugh. His hand had several needles from the cactus on it. He lifted it, and his eyebrows shot up.

"What did you do to my hand?" he yelled. Aubrith laughed, which earned him a glare from Glyden.

I kneeled and picked the needles from his hand. He yelled in agony as each needle pierced through the skin. Blood gushed after each needle was picked.

"Should I heal my hand yet?" Glyden asked. I shook my head, still picking at some more needles.

"Wait until I get all the needles out. I'm almost done." I picked another one. Glyden screamed out in pain. I held his wrist down in the dirt to get a better angle for the last needle. Aubrith let Glyden grip onto his hand with this other hand.

"Alright, on the count of three, I'm going to pull it. One, two..." I pulled the last needle before I replied with the number three. Glyden jolted his head back into the dirt. He screamed as blood dripped down his hand.

Aubrith patted him on the back to acknowledge he'd done a good job in that situation. Glyden pulled the top of his shirt into his mouth and bit down. He hovered his other hand over the bloody one. The wounds slowly closed with his powers. Once his wounds were all fixed up, he let go of his shirt from his mouth and took a deep breath. He glared at me as he wiped off the remaining blood on his hand on his shirt. I shook my head, knowing that was the last thing he should've done. His shirt had blood spots on it open to anyone who wanted to question it.

I sat back in the dirt to look around. There were a few cars that drove by us on the two-lane highway, but they didn't stop. Glyden stood up to wipe off the dust from his pants. There was a tiny hut not that far in the distance.

"We must be near a town?" Aubrith questioned. I nodded my head.

"It should be nearby. We can at least get to a gas station to get him a fresh shirt." Glyden glared at me again.

I helped Glyden up from the ground. He brushed off the remaining dirt on his pants.

"This place is nice. Dry, but nice." Glyden looked around. I smiled and nodded my head.

"It was nice when I was growing up. I haven't been here in a long time." I looked around. I could still see the ridges in the distance in the rocks. All the small canyons and cacti that spread for miles. The road seemed to melt into the background as we kept looking ahead. There were other people walking on the road with backpacks, bypassing us.

"Where are they going?" Glyden questioned. I looked towards the group of people he was talking about.

"They're going to that church that I told you about. I think that's where the last shard is. It's a famous church, so my mom had to have put the shard there if she's behind all of this." Glyden nodded his head.

We got to a small road that dipped down. Cars were

trying to pass us on the side, even though there was hardly any room. We got into town and saw a pair of horses.

"Look at these animals." Aubrith ran over to the horses. I rushed towards him to pull him away.

"You can't go around petting random people's horses. That will get you killed, you know." He sighed and let me take him back towards where Glyden and I were. We got to the entrance of the church area.

"It's so quiet, even though there are so many people." Aubrith looked around the church grounds. We entered from the parking lot. At the entrance, there were a lot of photos of families' loved ones hanging on the fence. There were beautiful stone benches that had distinct tones of red. All the benches were facing towards an altar with different symbols created out of stone. A wooden gazebo covered the altar, providing shade in the main area. Off to the right, a river provided total serenity.

On the left were little walkways to lead to statues and offering places where artwork of Native Americans was done. Aubrith took off to go into one room. He looked so amazed by the carvings in the wood. Glyden stared at the wooden statue of the Virgin Mary.

"That's one statue my mom used to stare at." I smiled and looked at the different grooves in the wood to depict the Virgin Mary's face.

"I didn't know people in your realm worshipped the Goddess?" Glyden kept analyzing the statue.

"Oh, that's not the Goddess. It's the Virgin Mary. She's Jesus's mom. Catholicism is a little different." I tried to explain to him. He didn't really pay attention to what I was saying. Instead, he looked down at the box that lay at the statue's feet.

"What is that?" Glyden pointed towards the box.

"I think people donate money for the church so they can keep making really cool artwork here." I looked for Aubrith, who was now staring at a cross that was made out of metal roses.

I smiled and walked over to get him.

"You like this place?" I crossed my arms. I realized we must've looked weird, considering we were covered in dirt and everyone else who went to the church had nicer clothes on.

"It's very calm. It reminds me of this worship center in Jaklish. Some women from the village would go there to pray to keep their healing capabilities. My mom would go there a lot." He reached out his hand to touch one of the metal roses. He smiled to himself and glanced towards me. I realized I was staring at him. I quickly tried to cough to cover up my obvious staring. He smirked.

"We should go up to the church and try to get Glyden a fresh shirt. I know there's a gift shop there. There should also be some stands at the top of the hill so you can get food." I looked down at the ground. He walked towards Glyden. I let out a breath that I didn't even realize I was holding in.

I followed them both up the hill to the actual church itself. I told Glyden and Aubrith to go to the small store near the church. Once they walked into the store, I turned back to the church. It was an older church. It had little, fancy artwork in there, but the rustic pews made it. There were Santos all over the church—donated, of course—but it had a very New Mexican aspect to it. The floor dipped as I walked into the church. A statue of Jesus was splayed out in the front. I felt awkward being in the church. I had to save this realm from falling apart.

I noticed some people were praying silently to themselves. I made my way to the front of the church near the altar. My feet slid across the stone floor. I looked up to see all the vibrant colors displayed in the church. I smiled at all the depictions of the stories in the Bible. I turned to my left and had to duck my head to get into a tiny room.

The room was filled with pictures of random people again, all looking for some hope for their family. In the middle of the floor was a hole filled with dirt. People would often get some dirt to help them in need. I looked around the small room, trying to find some sense of energy. *Where could the shard be?* The room itself felt cold. I looked at the hole of dirt and smiled to myself. In simpler times, this would be where I had one of the better moments with my mom.

I exited the church with my shoulders slumped. I didn't know where the shard was. This was a disaster. I noticed that Aubrith and Glyden were waiting outside the church with new t-shirts. Their shirts had pictures of the church.

"Well, did you find the other shard?" Aubrith asked carefully. I shook my head. Glyden rubbed his face with his hands.

"We need to find the other shard soon. The portal could alter itself, for all we know." Glyden stood up and walked around the tiny bench that was in front of the church.

Aubrith had his pen in his hand, ready to use it in case he found the shard. He walked around as well. I followed Aubrith.

"Are you sure you felt nothing in the church?" Aubrith asked as we kept walking further away from the church. We didn't get that far until Glyden called back to us. We turned around to see Glyden frantically waving his hands.

I walked faster to Glyden, wondering why he was so animated.

"Aubrith, use that thing you used to get the shards," Glyden demanded. I looked at Glyden to figure out what he was up to. Aubrith fumbled with the pen and gave it to Glyden. I laughed at their exchange. Glyden snatched the pen out of Aubrith's hands. Glyden positioned the pen in front of a small mural with Our Lady of Guadalupe. There were candles lit near the mural, but it was a stone wall with the mural on it.

I studied the mural and noticed that one star at the bottom of the mural in Our Lady of Guadalupe was chipped. I grabbed the pen from Glyden, which earned a grunt. As Glyden and Aubrith were bickering over the pen, I carefully positioned it at the star.

The pen shook rapidly. I patted Aubrith's arm to get his attention, but he was still arguing with Glyden over who should hold the pen.

"Guys, look," I demanded. They both shifted their heads in my direction. Glyden jumped up in the air, as if knowing that the last shard could be behind the stone wall.

I kept the pen where I'd placed it at the star, but the shaking stopped. Glyden grabbed the pen from me and stabbed the star with the pen. Aubrith quickly grabbed the pen from him and tried to stab it a different way. I sighed, knowing that this was going nowhere.

I leaned against the wall, careful not to lean near a candle. I put my hand on my face, wondering what else we could do. People who were walking up the hill gave us weird looks as they walked into the chapel.

It was strange to be back at the church. The last time I was here, my mom scolded me for bringing my basketball. I laughed at the memory, which earned a strange look from Glyden. I nodded my head to let him know I was okay.

I couldn't get over why my mom had been so adamant that day she'd taken me here. I remembered setting my basketball down outside the church. After she'd done her version of a prayer, she'd pulled me away, back towards the car we had. I hadn't even had time to reach for my basketball. I looked towards the benches that were outside of the church. My basketball would've been right there, where those benches were. I sighed, knowing that my life was so different now.

I glanced towards the mural, which had been here since I was little. The only difference was they had candle holders instead of letting people place a candle all over the stone wall. *There had to be a shard here.*

I remembered the advice my basketball coach would always tell me. Not to force things and let the shot come to me. Standing here, staring at this mural, that advice felt more relevant. *Don't force things.*

An idea came to my head. I grabbed the pen from Glyden, who still had some words for Aubrith. I rolled my eyes but stood from a distance from the mural. Glyden looked at me strange. I kept backing up until my legs hit the bench where my basketball would've been all those years ago. *Let's see if you thought of this too, Mom.* I limply held the pen up towards the mural. Before Aubrith and Glyden could question me, the pen shot towards the loose star.

The pen glowed slightly as it stayed on the wall. The whole mural was glowing. In the center of where Our Lady of Guadalupe had her hands in a praying position, a golden shard popped out.

Glyden looked towards me in shock as he carefully held the shard. Aubrith grabbed the shard from him and pulled out the others from his bag. I walked back and grabbed the pen. The pen made a clicking noise, and the whole mural stopped glowing. The star pushed out the pen slightly, leaving another crack in the mural. I smiled to myself, knowing that it had to be my mom putting these shards here all along.

Aubrith looked around, noticing there weren't many people at the church area. He put the golden shard near the other shards, and it clicked into place. He grabbed the black shard from Cambodia and watched it click also into place. Once the last shard had clicked into place, a gust of wind pushed Aubrith down on the ground.

Although there wasn't anyone holding the shard, it was floating in the air. All the golden specks in all the shards were lining up to form a sentence. Aubrith quickly got to his feet and observed the floating device.

"It's still in the ancient language. I can't decipher what it's saying." Aubrith's shoulders faltered. To me, the language was in perfect English. I glanced to Aubrith and Glyden, only to realize they couldn't see what I was seeing. *They don't know what it says.* I watched as all the specs of gold kept organizing to form a perfect sentence. After it was done, it glowed.

I looked to see a full sentence connecting from one shard to the next: "*The one that dares to open, shall be met with darkness before light, by the Goddess's blood.*"

I said the words aloud, leaving Glyden and Aubrith in disbelief.

"You can read that?" Glyden asked as he looked back at the shards, now all connected, forming a perfect circle. I nodded my head. He looked at me in awe.

"What does it mean? Darkness before light? I also am still puzzled by the whole Goddess thing." Aubrith kept looking at the shards.

"I do not know. Maybe the Goddess is in danger?" I glanced towards Glyden who looked like he was panicking.

"We have to get back to the other realm, now," Glyden demanded. I creased my forehead and put the shards back into Aubrith's backpack.

"You really think the Goddess is in danger?" I asked. Glyden gulped and nodded his head slowly.

"What else could it mean? By the Goddess's blood? She has to be in danger." Glyden ran his hands through his tight curls.

"But if she was in danger, do you think Justorah knows?" I looked to Glyden and Aubrith.

"Justorah has to know, or else he wouldn't have sent us on this mission. I still don't trust that guy, but he has to know something is not right." Aubrith looked nervous.

I thought back to what the man in the leather jacket told me in Cambodia: *Something dark might happen if the portal is closed. I don't know if that's true or not, but I have to take that chance.*

The darkness before the light was what the shards said. What darkness could there possibly be? Maybe it meant the darkness from the war? Maybe the light was the portal? I shook my head and refocused on Glyden and Aubrith.

"We have to get these shards to Justorah. He will know what to do with them." They both nodded. I linked arms with them, knowing that we would have to go back to New York to go through the portal.

I took one glance towards the church. I'd had so many wonderful memories here. I wiped a tear that fell down my face unexpectantly. I knew that this could be the last time I would see this place. I swallowed down the lump that was forming in my throat. I grabbed Aubrith and Glyden's hand. I closed my eyes before I felt unsteady again.

It was time to return the shards.

CHAPTER
THIRTY-THREE

I heard sirens and cars all around me. I looked up to see the night life of New York bustling around me. I realized I was lying on a dirty sidewalk. I quickly got up to dust off my shirt. I looked around and realized that no one seemed to care that I was lying in the middle of the sidewalk. *I'm definitely in New York.*

I stretched and felt more tired than I have been. I saw Aubrith talking to someone that looked to be a security guard of some sort. I slowly walked over, but my legs felt like Jello. The security guard stopped talking to Aubrith and looked over at me.

"Really? You came to the hospital with someone who is drunk?" The guard looked towards me.

"I'm very drunk. That's why I need to go get into the hospital," I lied. Aubrith crossed his arms, looking at the guard. The guard sighed and talked into his radio. A woman came out with a wheelchair and asked me to sit in the chair. I gratefully sat down and stretched my legs.

"How much has she had to drink?" the nurse asked

Aubrith as they rolled me inside the hospital. I felt loopy, but I knew that was just the teleportation talking.

"Oh, she drank a lot," Aubrith lied to the nurse. I knew he was a terrible liar, but this was a new low for him.

The nurse moved me towards the emergency section. I tried to tell her that we needed to go the other way, but she ignored my requests. When she shut the curtain around me and Aubrith, I quickly got out of the wheelchair. My legs began to give out slightly, and I fell towards him. He caught me, but all my body weight was leaning on him.

"We have to get to the roof again for the portal," I stated. Aubrith quickly nodded his head and wrapped an arm around me so I could put my weight on him. My feet dragged as he pulled the curtain open slightly. We looked around to wait until there was an opening to the door.

I felt like I was missing something until it occurred to me that Glyden wasn't with us.

"Aubrith, do you know where Glyden is?" I looked around at other people in the emergency area. There was no sign of him.

"He ran into the hospital before the security guard could even stop him. That's why I got into an argument with that man in the first place." He let out a deep breath as he continued to let me lean on him.

My feet dragged along the tile floor. Something about hospitals always gave me a weird vibe. Maybe it was because I always had to be in them growing up because of my mom.

"Do you know where he could've gone?" I asked Aubrith as he steered me down another hallway.

"I have no clue, but I think he was trying to get to the top of the building too." Aubrith turned to get to the elevator. He pushed the button for up. We waited as we got looks from doctors who walked around.

"Sasi?" A familiar voice called out to me. I noticed it was the security guard that talks to my mom often.

"Jennifer." I nodded my head in her direction.

"Your mom. She's been looking all over for you. Let me call her." She went towards her walkie-talkie. The doors to the elevator opened. I pushed the top level and the close-door button rapidly.

"No, don't contact her," I rushed the words out to the woman. The elevator doors shut on her, leaving just me and Aubrith in the elevator.

"Why don't you want your mom involved with this? She could've helped us with the shards," Aubrith's voice echoed in the hollow elevator. I looked towards him and shook my head.

"If she was involved somehow, I don't want her to know what is happening. She should keep working her job here. I don't want to worry her." I looked down at the tile in the elevator.

It was only a few more seconds until the elevator doors opened to the top floor. We stepped out, and the brisk New York air pierced through me. I shivered imme-diately.

"Glyden?" I called out. He had to be on the roof somewhere.

Aubrith pointed to a hunched figure on the roof. We

walked over to him and noticed that Glyden was just shivering.

"Took you both long enough. Let's get back to the other realm." Glyden pointed towards a small light. The light was glowing blue, but faintly. The light flickered on and off like the source wasn't strong enough.

"Do you think it will really take us to the other realm? It doesn't look as blue as it was." I glanced back towards the light. Aubrith gulped and looked back towards Glyden.

"We need to link. With enough power, we might get a strong enough opening for us to make it to the other realm." Glyden grabbed my hand. I let go of Aubrith and tried to stand for myself. My legs were still wobbly, but I tried to focus on the light.

"Try to think of something and put all your energy towards the light, okay?" Glyden assured me. I nodded my head and closed my eyes.

"Okay, now!" Glyden demanded.

I tried to put all my energy towards the light. I opened my eyes to see that Glyden and I were glowing. A source of energy strained from both of us, creating a white glow towards the light. I could see Aubrith covering his eyes as Glyden and I kept working towards the portal.

The blue light seemed to intensify. I felt like my skin was about to rip off. I kept focusing on the portal, causing me to scream. Glyden let out a groan as we kept concentrating.

We both dropped to the ground as the blue light

surged through the air. I tried to catch my breath. Glyden helped me up to my feet.

"Are you ready?" Aubrith asked as he looked towards the light. There was more wind surrounding us now than before. Glyden grabbed my hand as the three of us made our way to the edge.

"As ready as I'll ever be." Aubrith squeezed my hand for reassurance. I felt my stomach drop looking over the edge of the building. The blue light blinded my eyes as I kept trying to look towards the portal.

"On the count of three?" Glyden nodded towards us. Aubrith and I gripped onto each other hands. Glyden squeezed my hand before he started to countdown.

"One, two, three," Glyden counted. He jumped off the ledge into the blue light taking me and Aubrith with him. I heard a scream of my name in the distance. The air hit my face at an intense speed. I flipped my body around to see a woman on the top of the edge of the building we'd just jumped from.

Mom.

THIRTY-FOUR

We landed in the red mud. I went to reach for my face and felt the cool substance on my cheek. I looked around to see the mud surrounding us. Glyden was sitting up, looking at the trees in the distance. Aubrith's backpack was soaked in the mud, slowly sinking. I quickly got up and grabbed the backpack before it sunk any further. I noticed Aubrith was face down in the mud. I tried to flip him over so he could breathe. Glyden noticed my struggle and stumbled over where I was to help push Aubrith over.

The red mud coated his face, causing Aubrith to cough up some of the mud. He wiped the mud off of his eyes and tried to blink.

"We actually did it." Aubrith sat in the mud, taking in deep breaths. Glyden patted Aubrith on the back, and I chuckled slightly.

"We're not done yet. We still have to go to Justorah," I announced as I pushed back strands of my hair. It was weird to see this place again. The first time I'd seen it, it felt like a dream. Now it just felt familiar. A sense of home.

I stood up as my feet sank into the mud. I carried Aubrith's backpack with me until I reached a better area to walk in. I looked over at Glyden. His skin was slowly being replaced with fur. Aubrith and I stood in amazement as he fully transformed back to a stag. His hooves scrunched in the mud as he walked ahead of us.

"Well, don't just stand there," Glyden grunted as he kept walking. Aubrith and I quickly moved to catch up with him.

We reached the forest area that I was once in. It was strange to be in this area, considering the last time I was running for my life. I looked towards Glyden still amazed he was back in elk form. I shrugged, grabbing a stick that was on the ground to scrape off some of the mud that was drying on my pants.

"What is this place anyway? I fell here at first, but it didn't work out so well for me." I looked at Aubrith and Glyden. Aubrith seemed to be in his own world. He was deep in thought. Glyden kept leading the way in case someone came for us. He looked happy he was back as an elk. I shook my head, knowing that I wouldn't get an answer from these two, anyway.

"Did you say something, Sasi?" Glyden stopped walking to turn to me. *Great. He can read my mind yet again.* I cleared my throat before responding.

"I was wondering what this place was called. I didn't have a chance to get to know the village the last time I came here. I was tossed over a man's shoulder." I smiled towards Glyden. He chuckled to himself.

"We are near a small village that is on the outskirts of Salcesia. Technically, we are in Bolithium." Glyden looked back at me.

I tried to keep up with all the places in this realm. I figured if Glyden and Aubrith could keep track of all the places I'd taken them, I could learn to figure this realm out.

"Aurelia probably has guards on patrol for us. That woman doesn't give up," Aubrith mumbled. I glanced towards him as we were entering the village.

"Does this bring back memories of when you were trying to kill me?" I nudged Aubrith's arm. He scowled.

"I was only doing what I thought was right. I couldn't save you and be a warrior. I had to pick one and when I couldn't save you; I had to bring you to Aurelia. I'm sorry about that but I used to work for her army sometimes because I got paid a lot." Aubrith lowered his head.

"I was joking. I know you had to do something, especially when the woman noticed me trying to take her clothes." I smiled at him so he would know that I held nothing against him. That seemed to be enough since he turned away from me to focus on the village itself.

"Aurelia usually has guards in this village patrolling for people with magic. Try nothing funny, Glyden and Sasi," Aubrith cautioned us.

Glyden snorted and kept walking through the village. I felt a sense of calmness in this realm. I wasn't on edge strangely. I didn't know if that was because I was learning I had some sort of connection here. We walked through the puddles of mud in the main area of the village.

People were gawking at us. Some were eating what looked to be chicken, but I couldn't tell. Women and children looked us up and down, scrunching up their noses.

"They have the same dirt on their face as we do. Why are we being judged so much?" I kept looking around, realizing the entire village seemed to stop talking.

"I guess they can sense we are outsiders." Aubrith dragged out his pen in case anyone would try to fight us.

"You're from this realm, though. You'd think they'd sense that." I glanced towards Glyden, who was happily chewing on a piece of grass. Aubrith looked down at his linen clothes.

"I don't exactly have the same clothing as I did, though." Aubrith gestured towards his clothes. I laughed, which got more people to look at us.

Some of the village people were sitting around a campfire. Others looked to be drying their clothing on the clothes rack. A particular one, who was glaring at us, kept sharpening his knives. I gulped and tried to stay closer to Aubrith.

"Aurelia doesn't look like she takes care of her people. I mean, do the people of this village have water?" I asked. I noticed little kids playing what looked to be soccer, but they probably called it something else in this realm.

"Aurelia is rich. Bolithium is rich. The people? Not so much. There're rumors that the queen pockets most of the money that comes in. Which leaves villages to fend for themselves." Aubrith looked towards me.

"So, basically, corruption." I looked back towards him.

"I guess, yeah. Do you have that in your realm?" Aubrith refocused his attention to the ground.

"Corruption? Yeah, we have a lot." I chuckled silently. I heard footsteps coming towards us. I spun around, only to be met with Glyden.

"The villagers told me we could keep going on this path towards the hills. We will get to Elggland faster." Glyden pointed towards the hills that were in the distance.

"Should we be traveling? It is about to be dark?" I noticed the change of the lightness in the sky. Aubrith agreed with me, but Glyden seemed to have other plans.

"We have to keep moving. We need to get these shards to Justorah as soon as possible." I sighed, knowing he was right.

℘

We left the village and entered the forest again. The noise from the bugs was deafening. I covered my ears and tried to keep a steady pace on the trail. Glyden turned to me and creased his forehead.

"Stay quiet and crouch," Glyden whispered as he lowered his head. Aubrith didn't seem to question him, so I followed what he told us. I was wondering why we had to stop walking, but the sound of the bugs was getting louder. We hid behind a tree with Glyden occasionally peeking. I didn't know what he was looking for. Glyden was nervous, so I knew it had to be something serious.

The noise stopped briefly. I slowly removed my hands from my ears and wanted to peek around the tree, but I had a feeling I shouldn't. I glanced at Aubrith who had sweat dripping from his forehead. I gulped, knowing whatever was on the other side of the tree wasn't friendly.

The noise appeared again, but it seemed further away this time. Glyden let out a breath he had been holding and shook his antlers.

"That was close," Glyden huffed between breaths.

"It was. I thought we were going to be dead." Aubrith agreed. I looked between the two of them, confused.

"What was that?" I tried to push my hair back, but I had too many flyaways.

"You don't want to know, Sasi. Think of it as a massive bug, but it has multiple legs and can eat anything." Aubrith shuddered at the thought.

"So, why did we need to be quiet?" I looked at the two of them.

"It senses vibration, and with our voice, it would've triggered to come closer to us. It would've eaten us. I'm sorry. I am powerful, but fighting off one of those beasts isn't something I would be fond of." Glyden got back on the trail and motioned us to follow him. I looked towards Aubrith, who was still panting.

We walked what felt like a few hours. I knew we were

going uphill because of the burning in my legs. I didn't notice the forest changing. In fact, it stayed the same. It was pitch black where we were. I only knew that Aubrith was ahead of me because of his light-blue linen shirt.

Glyden got down again. I knew something else had to be wrong. He was leading us so he could see the path better. Aubrith and I followed suit to crouch down and be quiet.

"Warriors from Aurelia. They're on watch," Glyden whispered to us. Aubrith gripped the pen in his hand.

I heard the metal clinking on the trail up ahead. Aubrith pulled me off the trail a bit into the foliage. The warriors seemed to have torches causing the whole pathway to be lit up now.

"We should go back to the castle, " one man suggested. I felt Aubrith tense beside me.

"There have to be some healers in this area," another man replied. I heard a sword draw from a hilt. I shuddered at the noise. I looked over at Glyden and realized that his antlers were subtly glowing. *Was he seriously going to fight these men?*

I heard the sword of the man cut through the foliage on the sides of the trail. One was getting closer to us. I held my breath for what was about to happen. I tried to think of something happy like Glyden told me to do. I felt uneasy and moved my footing back a little. I grabbed onto one of the leaves from a plant that was near us.

I felt the cool sensation course through me. I looked down at my hand on the leaf, and the leaf was glowing green, as was my hand. It was like I was draining the leaf.

"Over there!" I heard the man shout.

"Great," Aubrith sighed.

The men ran towards us, shuffling through the foliage. I concentrated on their movements towards me. I heard Glyden and Aubrith take off to go fight them up close.

Before I knew it, the warriors fell to their knees. Glyden and Aubrith looked back towards me. I got up and met them where the men dropped. The warriors' legs were wrapped in vines and twigs.

"How did you do that?" Aubrith asked, astonished. I looked towards Aubrith and shrugged.

"I focused on their legs." Glyden patted me on the back.

"You scum! You should all be banished from this kingdom," one man shouted at me. The other man spat at my feet.

I was about to say something until I saw the glimmer of a sword cut through the vines. The man charged at me wildly with his sword. I noticed the other man got free as well. Aubrith stepped in front of me and blocked the sword coming down with his pen. He held the pen on both ends. He pushed back on the sword, causing the man to stumble backward.

The man looked shocked. He regained his posture and tried to attack again. Aubrith kicked him in his knee. The man fell, gripping his kneecap. I was too busy paying attention to one man that I didn't see the other one coming towards me. Glyden thankfully shot him against another tree with a force of air.

The other man was still fighting Aubrith, who kept

dodging his strikes until one of the man's strikes hit a nearby tree. He tried to pull the sword back, but the sword was stuck in the tree. Aubrith raised his pen and stabbed the man in the chest. The man chuckled and pulled the pen out of his chest.

"Really, you think this would kill me?" the man announced to Aubrith. Suddenly, the man was spitting out blood from his mouth. He dropped to his knees and gasped for air. His entire body turned blue quickly. He looked like Jura had in Ireland. Aubrith picked up his pen again and stuffed it back in his pocket.

"Where's the other one?" Aubrith looked back towards Glyden and me. Glyden pointed to the man who was knocked unconscious from the blast.

Aubrith nodded and went back onto the trail. Glyden and I quickly followed him. We walked up the hill to finally get onto a flatter surface.

"We have to be careful. I think Links are in the area." Glyden guided us. My legs were burning from the walk up the hill. I bent over to put my hands on my knees. I felt like I couldn't breathe.

"What's wrong?" Glyden slowed his walking to stare at me. I shook my head.

"Nothing. It's just getting harder to breathe the higher we go up. I think it's the elevation." I took a deep breath. Aubrith seemed to wheeze next to me. Glyden looked at both of us.

"Do you both have issues climbing?" Glyden stood with his legs planted in the hill. Of course, he had to say something even though he is an elk and we are humans.

"We will get there, I promise." I took another deep breath. Glyden pointed with his head towards a sign that was hidden behind a shrub.

"Good, because we just entered Elggland. We need to get to Kilkley. That's where Justorah's castle is. Also, be careful, just watch out for anything." Glyden turned back around to walk again.

"I liked it better when he was in human form," I whispered to Aubrith, who laughed loudly, causing Glyden to turn around and glare at me. I subtly laughed, causing Glyden to huff and continue to hike.

We got to the mountain area, where the trees slowly disappeared. I smiled, knowing the castle was close by. After several hours we approached the fog that was condensing. Glyden nudged his head towards me. I grabbed onto his fur and reached for Aubrith's arm. We linked arms as we walked, considering the fog was getting thicker.

Glyden reminded me of the Passfinders in the area. They would morph into whatever fear you wanted them to be. I remembered the last time we were on this mountain; they allowed us to pass through to the castle. I think Justorah had them there for protection.

It was eerily quiet. Almost too quiet. I kept waiting for a Passfinder, but none approached us.

We crossed the bridge with no problem at all. The castle was still there with the stone and the moss growing on the outside.

"How did you both get in last time?" Aubrith asked. I looked towards Glyden before I spoke.

"A man in a robe came out. He had to open the gate." I looked at Aubrith. He nodded his head.

"I wonder if that will happen this time." Aubrith made his way over to one bench. He sat down and stretched out his legs. I kept hold of the backpack that was around my shoulders. I didn't realize how heavy this bag was. I felt bad that Aubrith had to carry this bag the whole time we went to get the shards. I hoped we could return the shards to Justorah, and he could save the Goddess.

A man came out in a robe again and waved us towards the corridor. I took in the torn banners and glanced down the hall with torches lighting up the hallway. The man stopped at the massive wooden door before mumbling something. All the locks from the top of the door unlocked all the way to the bottom of the door.

He motioned with his hands to go into the castle. The stark difference from the outside of the castle to the inside never failed to amaze me. There was white marble everywhere I turned.

Our feet echoed through the hallways. With every step I took, I felt like I was making a momentous decision. The castle felt cold. And not because there was marble all around, but the aura around the castle seemed...*off*.

The monk took us into the throne room. The room hadn't changed since the last time we were here. The monk shut the doors, leaving us three to stand there with two of Justorah's guards. I glanced around, realizing that the rose symbol didn't feel as pleasant to look at since the last time I was here.

I heard a man's voice before the door opened. His pointy shoes and ears gave him away. As did the bone crown that sat on his head.

"Sasi and company. It is great to see you again." Justorah smiled at us.

THIRTY-FIVE

Justorah's maroon tunic hung loose on him. He made his way to his chair as he ran up the white marble floors. The red contrast with the white gave me an off feeling.

"Where are the precious shards?" Justorah clasped his hands together as he sat on his throne. I awkwardly took the backpack off. I didn't know why my hands were shaking. *This is the right thing to do, right?* I looked back at Justorah and looked into the bag. The shards were glistening with their golden specks. I sighed and pulled out the ring of shards.

Justorah raised from his throne and gleefully hopped down the stairs. I glanced towards Aubrith, who had his fist clenched. I gulped as Justorah took the shards from me. I felt strange giving them to him. I knew that was the plan all along, but I didn't know why it felt so weird.

Justorah walked back up to his throne. He was mumbling something. He snapped his fingers to get his guards' attention. One guard had a regular box with a circle engraved. Glyden moved closer to me. I didn't know what was going to happen, but I felt like we should brace ourselves.

Justorah put the shards into the box where the circle was on the front. The box floated on its own. Justorah clapped his hands. He walked over to me.

"Thank you so much for helping me. You don't know how much I can thank you for this," he smiled. I was about to respond before he grabbed my hand and cut it with a knife. I yelped and tried to pull away. He pulled out a small flask to capture the blood that fell from my hand.

Glyden and Aubrith both tried to go towards him, but it was like they were stuck. Justorah waved his hand towards them, and they couldn't move. He smiled mischievously at me.

"You were never going to save anyone, were you?" I whispered.

"Oh, Sasi. I didn't mean to break your heart. But no. You see, I needed you. I needed you to get the shards. And I needed you to open the real portal. It's your blood that controls this whole thing." He walked back up the steps with the flask in his hand. I wanted to go after him, but my feet were stuck as well. He poured my blood over the shards. They shined brighter than they were and the circle moved.

"This is working out perfectly," Justorah clapped his hands together.

"What do you mean my blood had to be used for this?" I yelled towards him. I was frustrated that I couldn't move.

"My darling, it is your bloodline. Since you are related to Terra, I thought I might as well get her to do my dirty work. This has been easier than trying to fight in that wretched war years ago. Aubrith would know about that one, right?" Justorah looked towards Aubrith, who tried to move, but his feet were still stuck to the ground. *What did he mean I was related to Terra?*

"I swear I will kill you," Aubrith said through gritted teeth.

"Don't waste your breath on me. The war was always phase one. I knew one day my family would claim the actual power of this realm. And maybe power of the other realms who knows." Justorah looked at his nails.

"Dear, Glyden. I bet you feel foolish to know that your beloved Terra has lost." Justorah looked towards Glyden.

"I'm not so sure about that. You have always felt like your ego was small considering the Serpents have ruled for centuries." Glyden spat towards Justorah.

"They've had far too much fun over the years. It's my family's turn now. After Terra punished my family and locked them away in this little box. I knew I had to leave as her assistant. Of course, I was only her assistant to learn about the ways of the Goddess. I knew her weakness. Her weakness was her sister. It's a pity, really. That she tried to hide her sister and niece away in another realm. I knew the realm would eventually call to you. The Goddesses can only stay away for so long before they are called to their natural duty." Justorah smiled towards me. "What? Suddenly you can't talk? You had so many questions when I first met you. It was boring, really. You should've asked about the good stuff! Like how my father and mother were kept away in a box for hundreds of years in the darkness. Or how only the Goddess's blood could open the lock. Only a Goddess could find the shards."

He got closer to me and snarled.

"Only a Goddess could be so naïve to trust a man she just met." He looked at me in the eyes.

"I tried. I tried for years to get these shards. When the Goddess learned of Endy and Selene conspiring, she banished them from ever returning. Endy had to find love—ugh, gag me. Now Selene, she always was persistent. She tried to befriend your mother, you know. In that place, New Mexico. She could never find the shard. Your mother must've found out because suddenly I didn't get updates from Selene anymore. I promised her to come back to the realm. To live out her dream of being here with me when we handled the Darkness. She couldn't find the shards. Pity." Justorah now paced around the throne room. His pointy shoes clicked against the marble floor.

It was hard for me to wrap my head around that my aunt was Terra. My mom had never mentioned how we had any other family. The old woman I'd met in New Mexico was Jura this whole time? Or rather, her name was Selene in this realm. It was making more sense to me, considering when I met Jura for the first time in her hut in Ireland, she'd said she'd remembered me. She'd said she knew my mother.

Endy seemed so nice in Toronto. He didn't even

mention anything. Now that I thought back on what he said, some things were making sense:

"I mean, later on she found that person and they had a baby girl, but the point is, I found someone else. Someone who I actually could love. It was her friend Jura, and we just clicked. Now she didn't like that we were together and banished us here before I could even know what was going on. I mean, sometimes I hear from Terra, her sister, through my thoughts and she tells me what's going on in the realm."

I reflected on Endy's words. *He was in love with my mom.* I tried to make sense of it all. My mind kept racing. I looked back up at Justorah, who turned his attention to the box. He glanced back towards me and the box. The shards stopped spinning and had a blue glow around them. He grinned wildly.

He turned mumbled something towards the box before darkness flew out of the box. It went straight up into the sky, breaking through the ceiling of the castle. He turned to me with a wicked smile.

"Looks like I don't need you anymore." I saw a red glow appear in his hand. I tried to free myself from whatever spell he had on me. I braced myself, but the shot never got to me. I peered down and realized that Glyden had taken the blow for me.

"No!" I screamed. I felt a surge of energy burst through me as the spell broke for me and Aubrith . A white glow appeared from me and knocked everyone who was in the throne room to off their feet. I crouched to Glyden, who had black goo ooze from his mouth. He let out a wretched whine as he was shaking uncontrollably.

"Find... Terra," I heard him spit out. My hands were shaking.

"No, no. I have to fix you. I can make you feel better." I tried to use my energy towards the blast site in his abdomen. I shot a surge of white light towards him. Tears kept streaking my face as the entire room became blurry. I kept trying to wipe them away as they fell down my face.

"I'll be...okay... get...Terra," he said, coughing up more black goo. I screamed more.

"Why isn't this working?" I tried to put more energy into him. He looked at me in my eyes.

"I did my job. I'll be with you. Find Terra." He coughed up more black goo. I kept trying to fix the wound. I saw Aubrith crawl towards me out of the corner of my eye. He hugged me from behind and pulled me away from Glyden.

"He's gone. Let him go," Aubrith whispered repeatedly. I tried to get Aubrith off of me, but he kept his arms around me. Justorah slowly picked himself up off of the floor.

"You've gotten your powers." Justorah faced me. He spat out blood from his mouth. He had a cut on his lip.

"Guards get them!" Justorah demanded. The Darkness kept piercing into the sky. Lightning strikes were in the sky surrounding the Darkness. The sky turned black slowly from its light purple.

"Sasi, we have to go." Aubrith pulled me up from my feet, and we tried to run. A guard grabbed my arm, but I sent a fire blast from my hand that shot the man backward. He went sliding on the marble floor, leaving a streak of blood with his body. Aubrith gulped as he pulled me towards the door. More guards appeared.

I shot more blasts from my hands, causing the men to go flying. I felt so much rage and anger. I didn't care what happened.

Aubrith grabbed a sword from one of the fallen guards as he positioned himself towards another guard that was running down the corridor. He threw that sword towards the man, striking him in the chest.

"Let's move!" Aubrith shouted over the men's clanking boots on the marble floor.

We reached the door we came through before one monster from the last time appeared. Justorah had apparently lied about the monsters last time. They probably were his own creation. The beast blocked the doorway and growled at us. I positioned myself and put both of my hands together. I formed a ball of energy in my hands and shot it at the beast.

The beast evaporated into thin air. Aubrith looked at the door and realized all the locks were in place.

"We're stuck!" he shouted. I thought about the way the monk would open the door. I put my palm on the door, hearing all the locks on the other side of the door unlock, one by one. Aubrith grabbed another leftover sword as he fought to buy me time.

I pushed the doors open, feeling the cool air hit my face. The fog was more apparent than ever.

I grabbed Aubrith's arm as I led him towards the hill. More guards and beasts came after us. I kept shooting fire blasts back towards them, hitting a few of them.

Aubrith continued to fight with his sword, slicing through some guards that went towards him.

After the last beast disintegrated into black dust, I grabbed Aubrith and pulled him towards the shrub area of the mountain. I pushed him down to hide behind the shrubs.

"Wherever you are, you won't hide forever!" Justorah shouted into the night. I looked over at Aubrith, who was panting. I saw Justorah reenter the castle. He had some guards patrol the area. I looked up to the sky to see the Darkness spreading.

THIRTY-SIX

Aubrith motioned to my eyes. I touched my eyes, but I couldn't seem to get what he was saying. He whispered, "Your eyes, they're glowing blue." I sighed. I felt the most exhausted I've felt on this entire journey.

I sat down in the dirt, knowing that Aubrith and I were safe. For now. I kept replaying the events that had happened.

Glyden. He'd risked his own life for me.

I couldn't get the black goo oozing from his mouth out of my mind. Each time it played in my mind, I felt more anger.

Aubrith must've noticed. He put his hand over mine. I softened at the touch.

"I miss him too," Aubrith whispered. I nodded my head as tears fell again.

"What do we do now? Justorah has the shards." Aubrith repositioned himself to look at me.

I thought about the question for a bit. A fresh wave of

Darkness burst into the sky, causing a blast of thunder through the sky. I saw the Darkness spreading slowly. I didn't know how much longer it would take until Justorah got the power he wanted.

"We have to find Terra," I replied as I gazed up into the sky full of Darkness.

ACKNOWLEDGMENTS

I would like to thank my mother who always believed in this dream of mine. She constantly pushed me to write and made everything possible for me to have this dream. I would like to thank my grandparents for encouraging me to finish this book considering it's been years in the making. I would like to thank my best friends for looking over my book and believing in me to write this book. I couldn't have done it without your support. I would like to thank my editor, CK, for working endless hours to help get this book done. You can find him at https://www.fiverr.com/share/qdy8V5. I would like to thank my book cover designer, Cesar Pardo, for making my dream image come to life with this book. You can find him on 99 Designs. I would like to thank anyone who has come in my life to encourage me to write this book. I will never forget your endless praises to inspire me to follow this dream of mine. Last but not least, thank you to anyone who decided to open this book and escape into my world for a bit.

ABOUT THE AUTHOR

Celina Marquez is an emerging author of Young Adult Fantasy. Celina recently graduated from Regis University with a Bachelor of Science in Biology and a minor in English. Prior to graduation she studied abroad at Maynooth University in Ireland. She lives in Colorado with her dog. She enjoys traveling, experiencing new cultures, and going to concerts. She has always been passionate about writing and creating her own worlds to escape to.

To get the latest information on new books, merchandise, and behind the scenes with writing, follow Celina on her website and/or social media:

www.celinamarquez.com

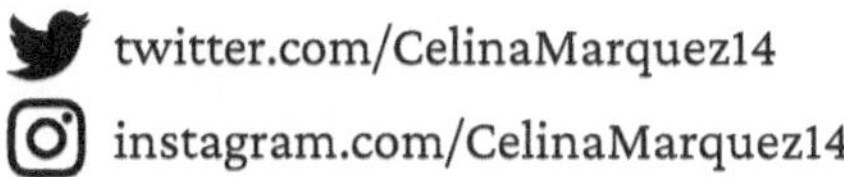

twitter.com/CelinaMarquez14

instagram.com/CelinaMarquez14